Praise for *Life F[light]*

"*Life Flight* is a heart-stopping, breath-stealing masterpiece of romantic suspense!"

Colleen Coble, *USA Today* bestselling author of *A Stranger's Game* and the Pelican Harbor series

"Romantic suspense star Eason's latest grabs you by the throat and doesn't let go; readers will have a hard time putting it down long enough to focus on real life."

Booklist

"*Life Flight* is a multilayered story filled with unexpected twists, dangerous situations, and tension. . . . Filled with suspense and romance, this thriller is an engrossing story by a talented author!"

Fresh Fiction

"I highly recommend this for those who love romantic suspense with enough twists to keep the most astute reader guessing."

Cara Putman, award-winning author of *Flight Risk* and *Lethal Intent*

Praise for *Crossfire*

"This high-octane thriller keeps up the momentum through the final page."

Publishers Weekly

"Just as intense and action packed as the first! Lynette Eason is at her best with this series!"

Write-Read-Life

"*Crossfire* is another great addition to this series by Lynette Eason—one of my favorite Christian Suspense authors. . . . A truly exceptional story."

Praise for *Critical Threat*

"Eason is a master of edge-of-your-seat inspirational romantic thrillers, combining light faith elements with twisty plots that keep readers guessing. The latest in her Extreme Measures series is one of her best."

Booklist

"Eason expertly plots the taut mystery. . . . The result is a satisfying inspirational thriller."

Publishers Weekly

COUNTDOWN

Books by Lynette Eason

COUNTDOWN

LYNETTE EASON

Revell

a division of Baker Publishing Group
Grand Rapids, Michigan

© 2023 by Lynette Eason

Published by Revell
a division of Baker Publishing Group
Grand Rapids, Michigan
www.revellbooks.com

Printed in the United States of America

Library of Congress Cataloging-in-Publication Data
Names: Eason, Lynette, author.
Title: Countdown / Lynette Eason.
Description: Grand Rapids, Michigan : Revell, a division of Baker Publishing
    Group, [2023] | Series: Extreme Measures ; 4
Identifiers: LCCN 2022054647 | ISBN 9780800737368 (paperback) | ISBN
    9780800743123 (casebound) | ISBN 9781493441297 (ebook)
Classification: LCC PS3605.A79 C68 2023 | DDC 813/.6—dc23
LC record available at https://lccn.loc.gov/2022054647

Baker Publishing Group publications use paper produced from sustainable forestry practices and post-consumer waste whenever possible.

23 24 25 26 27 28 29   7 6 5 4 3 2 1

■ ■ ■ ■

Dedicated to Susan Gibson Snodgrass,
who was a huge supporter of my novels—and of all Christian Fiction.
From serving on the launch team to sharing social media posts
to writing messages of encouragement, I say thank you.
You will be so very much missed in the community.
Enjoy your rest in the Savior's arms and read all the stories!
Until we meet again . . .

■ ■ ■ ■

So do not fear, for I am with you;
  do not be dismayed, for I am your God.
I will strengthen you and help you;
  I will uphold you with my righteous right hand.

Isaiah 41:10

CHAPTER
ONE

SUNDAY MORNING
MID-JANUARY
BULL MOUNTAIN, EAST OF ASHEVILLE, NC

Flight paramedic Raina Price looked out the window of the chopper and pointed. "There! Two of them as reported."

Penny Satterfield piloted the aircraft with an expert touch, aiming them toward the two stranded hikers on the side of Bull Mountain. Raina grabbed the binoculars and held them to her eyes. "One is on her back. I see blood on her head. The other one is moving and appears unhurt. She's waving at us and looking pretty frantic."

"There's no place to set this bird down," Penny said, her low voice coming over the headset.

No, there wasn't. Not even for Penny, who could land pretty much anywhere. "Looks like it's a day to go rappelling," Raina said.

"Looks like," Holly McKittrick, the nurse practitioner, echoed.

Raina didn't particularly enjoy hurling herself out of the

chopper—not like some who actually hoped for it. But she was skilled at it, and if it saved someone's life, then . . . okay.

She worked quickly, efficiently, strapping herself into the gear. She'd go down, assess the situation, and radio her findings.

After fastening the medical bag to her belt, she clipped the rope to the other hook and nodded to Holly. "I'm ready. You?"

"Ready."

Holly would lower the basket and, if necessary, follow it down. Other emergency personnel lined the edge of the cliff, but no one had been able to get down to them.

"A little closer, Penny."

"Getting there."

Raina slid the door open, shuddering at the blast of cold air followed by a face full of snowflakes. She looked back at Holly, who had the stretcher ready to winch down. "Okay, here we go."

"Let me know if I need to come down too."

"I will. Stay tuned."

She stepped out of the chopper and began her descent. With precision, Penny moved her right to the ledge that jutted from the cliff. Less than a minute later, Raina was next to the girls, while Penny continued to hover close, but not so close the wind from the blade interfered with the work.

"Help her," the nearest teen pleaded, pointing. "She hit her head."

The gash had stopped bleeding, but she'd taken a hard hit. "What about you?" Raina asked. "Are you hurt?"

"No. I climbed down." She pointed to the rope behind her—the one still tied to her waist. "Sadie tripped and fell, then rolled over the side of the mountain." A sob ripped from her. "I thought she was dead."

"She's not, hon." Not yet anyway. *Please, God, don't let this child die.* "Sadie, huh?"

"Yeah. I'm Carly."

"Hang in there, Carly, we're going to get you both out of here, okay?"

But Sadie's head wound was concerning. A gust of wind cut through her winter clothing, and Raina grimaced, shoving aside the cold and focusing on the patient.

"When I saw how bad she was hurt," Carly said, "I was too scared to move her. I . . . I didn't know what to do, but I have my dad's SAT phone, so I called for help."

"You did exactly the right thing." She lifted Sadie's lids to check her eyes. Concussion. "All right, Carly, you're doing great. Where are your parents? Have you called them yet?"

"Yes. They're completely freaked out. I called them after I called you guys."

Raina could understand freaked out. If this was her child—

She cleared her throat. While she talked and gathered information, Raina triaged the unconscious girl, speaking into the headset to those on the other end. Blood pressure, pulse, breathing status. ". . . And uneven pupils indicative of a concussion. The gash on the side of her head is going to need stitches." She moved down, her gaze landing on the bone protruding from the leg. "Broken right tibia." Raina ran her hands over the girl's body as gently as she could, searching for more injuries. A low moan escaped Sadie when Raina's hands grazed her ribs. She unzipped the light windbreaker and lifted the girl's shirt. The bluish area under the skin alarmed her. "We've got some internal bleeding, maybe some broken ribs." She listened to the girl's lungs once more. "Breath sounds are still good, so no lung punctured." Yet. She got the cervical collar on, then moved down to stabilize the broken leg.

More chopper blades beat the air. Farther away, but close enough to capture her attention. She took a moment to shoot a glance in the direction of the noise. "Great," she muttered under her breath. A news chopper. *Ignore it and focus.* It was all she could do.

That, and keep her head down.

"Hey!"

Raina's head jerked up at the shout that came from above. So much for keeping her head down, but at least her back was to the news chopper.

A man leaned over the side of the cliff. "I'm Larry Owens with the fire department. If I throw this line down, can you send up the uninjured girl?"

"Sure can! And I need someone to come down here and help me get Sadie in the chopper basket." Holly could do it—would do it if necessary— but she absolutely hated to rappel down.

"As soon as she's up, I'll come down."

"Perfect."

"No." Carly clutched Raina's arm. "I want to go with Sadie."

"You're both going to the hospital. They'll let you see her when you get there, but we need to focus on Sadie right now, all right?"

Carly bit her lip, then nodded. "Yeah. Okay."

In less than two minutes, she had Carly in the harness and Larry was pulling her toward the top.

"Send down the basket," Raina told Penny.

"On the way."

And so was the firefighter named Larry. Working together, they got Sadie into the basket. "She's ready," Raina said, "take her up." Raina watched her lift gently off the ground and head for the belly of the chopper. She turned to Larry. "Thank you."

"Anytime. See you around." He signaled his readiness to return to the top, and his team moved into action.

"Ready," Raina said into her mic. She noted the location of the news crew still hovering in the sky and positioned herself accordingly, never more thankful for the helmet and other gear covering most of her face. The line pulled her up off the ledge and she started her ascent.

The line lurched and Raina gasped, fingers clutching the rope. "Penny? What was that?"

"No idea."

The line jerked again and Raina dropped twenty feet before it stopped. "Penny! Holly!"

"Something's wrong with the winch," Penny said, her voice low and controlled. "Hang tight." A pause. "No pun intended."

Raina almost laughed but couldn't quite get the sound through her tight throat. "Don't let me fall."

"You're not falling. Just hold on a sec."

After what felt like a lifetime later, Penny's voice came through the headset. "Bringing you up."

Raina held tight as she started moving upward once more. She decided not to look down while steeling herself for another abrupt stop. Thankfully, that didn't happen, and soon, Raina was back in the chopper, kneeling next to Sadie.

Holly looked up from the still unconscious girl. "You good?"

"I will be when my heart rate gets back to normal. Then again, I'm here, so we'll count that as a win."

Holly nodded. "Definitely. All right, Penny, take us to base."

■ ■ ■ ■

US Marshal Vincent Covelli sat on the couch that belonged to his best friend's fiancée, Julianna Jameson. The big-screen television mounted on the wall across from him held a fraction of his attention. Mostly, he was interested in the dark-haired woman chatting with Holly McKittrick, Penny Satterfield, and Grace Billingsley.

Raina Price. Beautiful, but . . . haunted, distant, seemingly unreachable. For some reason, those facts didn't stop him from being drawn to her. Her sage-green eyes with the hint of yellow had captivated him from the moment he'd met her about a year ago when he'd been invited to watch a football game at this very house. It was Julianna's, who was getting ready to marry

Vince's best friend, Clay Fox, in three weeks. Vince smiled. He was happy for his friends. Clay and Julianna had been through so much. They deserved their happily ever after.

He couldn't help wonder if he'd ever find his own. Not that he was looking.

Much.

Again, his gaze settled on Raina.

Okay, he might be looking *now*.

"Hey, Raina, what did they say was wrong with the winch on the chopper?" Penny asked. "Have you heard? I haven't checked."

"Mm, yeah. That it needed to be replaced, but thanks to all the safety measures, I was never in any danger of it coming disconnected."

Penny snorted. "Well, I suppose that's good to know."

"It is." Vince noted Raina's absent agreement and rapt attention on the television. It was halftime and the station was doing a special report on Olympic hopefuls.

A young boy identified as Michael Harrison, age thirteen as of yesterday, according to the banner at the bottom of the screen, stood on a snow-covered mountain in Colorado's Arapahoe Basin, snowboard in hand. Raina moved closer to the television, no doubt trying to hear over the chatter. But it was the fact that her face was two shades whiter than normal that made him frown. She snagged the remote from the mantel and turned on the captions.

"How does it feel to be the youngest person ever to win a national competition in the US? Not only in halfpipe, but also slopestyle?" the reporter asked. She held the mic out to the boy while the words continued to pop up on the screen as they spoke.

"It feels amazing."

"Will we see you at the Olympics in four years?"

Michael laughed. "I hope so."

"What about this year—will you be there, to watch the competition?"

"Not the competition," Michael said, "my future teammates."

The reporter turned and the camera zoomed out to include a woman. "Mrs. Harrison, has this always been a dream of Michael's?"

"'Always' is pretty accurate. The dream started when he was about four years old and watched the snowboarders that year on the Olympics. He pointed at the television and said, 'I want to do that.' My husband went out the next day and bought him a snowboard and signed him up for lessons. He took to it right away, and it finally got to the point that we had to make some decisions about what to do. Four years ago, we moved from the Burbank area of California to Colorado, and snowboarding has been our life ever since." She gave her son a warm smile. "I wouldn't trade a minute of it."

The reporter nodded to the button Mrs. Harrison was wearing. "I see you're pro-adoption. Is there a story there?"

"Of course." The woman shot a look filled with intense love at her son. "I'm not able to have biological children, so my husband and I went through the adoption process. We took Michael home the day he was born, and he was legally ours shortly thereafter. We're so grateful to Michael's birth mother for giving us the chance to be his parents." A sheen of tears glimmered in her eyes and the camera zoomed in to catch the expression.

"Aw, Mom, stop." Michael rolled his eyes but grinned at her, and she ruffled his hair before he could duck.

The reporter stepped back. "All right, Michael, it's time. We've got a clip that showcases your talent here. This is the run that earned you enough points to qualify you for the Olympics. If only you were old enough. You ready?"

"Yes, ma'am."

The screen cut to the video of Michael's run culminating with the Triple Cork 1800 and thunderous applause of those watching. The sound faded and the camera returned to the reporter. "Thank you so much for being here with us, Michael. We wish you all the best and look forward to watching you compete in a few years. This is Camille Johnson with *News-Break*. Thank you for joining us. I know we're all excited to see if young Michael Harrison can bring home the gold in the next Olympics."

The station cut to another site where an Olympic hopeful was in the middle of an ice-skating rink, but Raina's eyes had shifted away from the TV to the far wall, still holding a frozen expression. Then she blinked, cleared her throat, and excused herself to slip into the kitchen.

Vince waited a good sixty seconds, then followed. Her back was to the door, arms braced against the kitchen counter, head down, gulping deep breaths. Her phone lay face up in front of her, a number programmed. "Raina?"

She squeaked and jumped back, the blazing fear in her eyes cutting him to the core. He stood still and waited for her to realize he posed no danger.

Finally, she shuddered, then sighed.

"You okay?" he asked, knowing the question was a dumb one, but asking it anyway.

"Yes. Fine. Sorry. You just startled me."

"You seemed pretty upset in there."

"Hm."

"Anything I can help with?"

"No . . , I . . ." She looked like she might say something else, then, "No. Thank you."

He nodded. "Because I'd be more than happy to help you out. If you needed it."

She shook her head, then tilted it to stare at the ceiling. "I'm okay. That kid on the news, Michael Harrison, just reminded me of someone I used to know." She lowered her gaze to meet his. Her green eyes had shuttered and gave nothing away. "Seeing him brought back a lot of bad memories."

"The kid did?"

"Yeah."

He waited, but she bit her lip and looked away. "Okay," he said after several seconds of silence. "I'll leave you alone then." He turned to go, hurt she wouldn't confide in him and frustrated because he'd done nothing but try to reach her, to show his interest. To let her know she could trust him. That he cared. At times, he thought she felt the same, but he honestly didn't know. Maybe she just wasn't into him. And while the thought made him sad, it was what it was. He'd move on. And yet he found himself unable to leave. He turned back, catching her gaze.

CHAPTER
TWO

Raina didn't look away from Vince. She wanted to tell him. Wanted to spill every last detail to the man who was looking at her with the very expressive dark brown eyes. Eyes that held hope she'd confide in him and let him help, but that wasn't the way she did things.

Because the last time someone wanted to help her, that someone had died. And once Vince found out exactly how much baggage she had in her past, he'd move on. So, she bit her lip.

Vince started to say something, but footsteps heading their way snapped his mouth shut.

"Hey," Grace said from the door. "Everything okay in here?"

Raina forced a smile. "Everything is good. We were just chatting. Are we ready for the s'mores yet?"

Grace pursed her lips, obviously not buying the explanation. "Yes, ma'am. The firepit is lit and everything is on the table outside."

"Then I'm first," she said with a relieved sigh that Grace allowed the change of subject. She nodded to Vince, then gave her friend a wink before stepping around her and heading for the french doors that led to the patio.

Their footsteps fell in behind her. She made it to the patio with the smile still on her face, but she couldn't help wondering how long she could maintain it. She'd give it thirty more minutes, and if the man she'd called while in the kitchen hadn't called her back, she'd have to try again.

Because if the man who called himself Kevin Anderson—a man she'd sworn she could defend herself against, if he ever dared come near her again—was still out there, she needed to find him and put her past to rest for good.

One way or another.

She settled into the chair Vince had pulled out for her, his kindness cramping her heart and making her wish for things she couldn't have. She'd shut him out and he was still being nice. Still making the effort to let her know he was interested and there for her without being weird or creepy while doing it. And that said more about his character than anything else.

The truth was, she liked him. A lot. And she'd give almost anything to let him lead them into a relationship. But . . .

Raina gripped her hands together. There was a huge "but" hanging over her head. She pictured the young teen who looked way too much like the man who'd almost killed her. A man who would go after that child if he thought the boy was his. And the person who might be able to help warn the child's family that they could be in danger wasn't answering his phone.

The whole situation had stirred up feelings and emotions she'd buried for so many years, and now she was on overload, unsure which emotion to deal with first.

"You okay?" Vince asked.

She jerked and cleared her throat. "I'm okay. For the moment."

He nodded and slid the marshmallow he'd just toasted onto a graham cracker, then smooshed it with a piece of chocolate. He handed it to her. "Think this will help?"

"S'mores? Always." She shot him a small smile, and a flash of something deep and sweet glinted back at her before he dropped his gaze and snagged another marshmallow.

She bit into the sweetness and let the taste coat her tongue. Unfortunately, she was too distracted to enjoy the treat and set the uneaten portion on the small plate next to her. She could feel Vince's eyes on her but refused to look at him. He wanted to help. And frankly, she wanted to let him.

But fear held her back.

Flashes from her past were coming fast and furious, keeping her silent. Afraid. Locking her words in her throat. Finally, she glanced at Vince while he talked with the others. He was a good man. A kind man. A man who would do battle for her if she'd let him. A man she often pictured by her side when she thought about the future. However, before she could do anything, let *him* do anything, she had to make sure that her past had no path into her present.

But if what she'd seen tonight held any truth, her past might very well be steamrolling right into her present.

Which meant she had to keep Vince at arm's length.

For his own safety.

■ ■ ■ ■

Monday, just after lunch, Vince found himself sitting at his desk, computer open, case file in front of him—and his mind on Raina Price. Every minute he had time to stop and think, he thought about her. And the fact that he was falling for a woman who wouldn't talk to him. Wouldn't trust him enough to confide in him no matter how much she might want to. And it was obvious she wanted to, because he'd been watching her closely. So closely. And yet, she continued to stiff-arm him.

He should have his head examined. Then again, she'd let him make her a s'more. The thought didn't help much. As much as she loved s'mores, she probably would have taken the sweet treats from just about anyone.

But she'd sat in the chair he'd pulled out for her and he didn't think it was just because she was polite. She'd acted like she wanted to talk but couldn't find the words.

Was he a fool to grasp onto the hope that produced?

Probably.

"Yo, Vince. You ready to go?"

He snapped his gaze to his partner, Charlie Maxwell. A former linebacker, Charlie never had gotten out of the habit of a daily workout, and he carried his muscle well. He stood with a nod. "Ready."

They were taking a shift at the hotel, guarding a witness with a hefty hit on his head.

The FBI had somehow convinced a top member of the Russian mafia to turn on his boss with stolen evidence and a verbal testimony. The trial was next week, and Vince and Charlie were part of the team tasked with making sure the man lived to testify.

So far so good, but there'd been rumblings that there was going to be an attempt on the man's life. As a result, they were moving him every twelve hours, and Vince was about ready to take the guy home with him and lock him in his basement.

Which would be an undeserved vacation for the dude, but at least Vince would know, one, where the guy was, and two, exactly how secure the place would be. Vince never said much about his home's security, but he did take it seriously and had no doubt he could protect Pavel Fedorov just as well—or more likely, better—than he could locked up in some hotel room.

But the powers that be would never go for it and he didn't blame them. He didn't want the guy in his home anyway.

"I'll drive," Charlie said.

Vince had already grabbed everything he needed and was heading for the elevator.

Thirty minutes later, Charlie pulled into the hotel parking lot. When they got to the top-floor suite, the two marshals on duty nodded toward the other room.

"All's quiet for now. But be ready to roll." They were always ready with a plan B, but right now Vince felt like they'd already reached plan Z, and if something didn't change soon, there was no plan double A.

"'Bout time you two got here," Fedorov said, coming out of his bedroom and into the main living area. "I'm starving and those jerks said I had to wait for you two before I could order."

If the man had gotten out of bed at a reasonable time, he could have had his food by now, Vince thought.

The twelve-hundred-square-foot area was set up more like an apartment than a hotel room. And wasn't nearly large enough when Fedorov entered the space.

"We're here," Vince said. "I'll order for you now." Vince didn't care for a lot of the people he protected but made sure he kept his dislike covered with a layer of professionalism. That included Fedorov.

The man grunted and rolled his eyes, thrusting a piece of paper at Vince. "Here's what I want. Say it just like I wrote it. I don't want it messed up."

Vince snatched the phone. The other two marshals left, and Charlie checked the windows, the exits, the balcony. Vince hated room service. It was too dicey, but at the end of the order, he said, "Don't send it up. I'll be down to get it shortly."

Fedorov scowled at him. "That's going to take forever."

"Do you want to eat or not?" he snapped.

The man rolled his eyes and turned away. Vince clarified the order, then hung up. "Said to give them fifteen minutes, but they'd call when it was ready."

Fedorov nodded and Vince paced the room. He wasn't usually so itchy, but this case had him scratching and pacing. And rechecking the windows. Going down to get the food was an extra precaution. If he got it directly from the kitchen, it would change hands only one time, which made it less likely for anyone to get to it.

Fifteen minutes later, when the phone rang, he jumped. Charlie glanced at him, a question in his blue eyes.

Vince waved him off. "I'm fine. I'll be right back." He answered the phone, confirmed the order, checked his weapon, reholstered it, then slipped out the door. Once in the hallway, he paused and tapped out a text to Raina.

> I'm thinking about you today. A lot. Are you okay?

He walked to the elevator and stepped inside when the doors opened. A glance at his screen showed she'd read the text, but no three little dots appeared to indicate her responding. Maybe she was just busy and would respond later when she had a moment. He needed to quit assuming the worst. The problem was, he'd never been so insecure about asking a woman out. He almost smiled. His sister would say he deserved every insecure moment that came his way, that he needed to be taken down a notch or two. The smile slid away. What was it about Raina that tugged at him so hard? If the woman wasn't interested, then she wasn't interested, right?

Grabbing the food from the kitchen interrupted his internal debate only for a few minutes and then he was back on the elevator and heading up.

So . . . fine. Move on.

But he couldn't and that very fact was driving him nuts. He had to figure out why, then maybe he'd be able to let it go. Let Raina go and quit chasing her. He tucked the phone into the clip on his belt and wondered what would happen if she actually let him catch her?

The mental picture of his heart shattering into a million pieces was not exactly encouraging.

■ ■ ■ ■

MONDAY AFTERNOON
LOS ANGELES

Simon Baldridge pinched the bridge of his nose, huffed a sigh, then closed the spreadsheet on his screen. No matter how many times he went over the numbers, they weren't going to change. Real estate could be a tricky business, and in the beginning, when he'd first gotten involved in developing, he could seem to do no wrong. His fortune had accumulated quickly, and soon he and his wife had been living the good life. He'd never expected that to come crashing down, so he'd lived well and spent more than he brought in. Now he was in danger of losing everything.

Thankfully, the recent sale of the Burbank property would keep him afloat for a couple more months. Maybe three if he was careful.

Susanna, one of the cleaning ladies with the service he used, stepped out of the bathroom, the lemon scent of whatever she'd sprayed coming with her. She tossed him a slight smile, even though her forehead wrinkled. "All done in there, Mr. Baldridge. So sorry to have to clean while you're here."

"It's okay, I had a change of plans."

"Thank you, sir, have a good day."

"Thank you, Susanna. You have a good one too."

She slipped out of the office. His mind returned to his financial situation, and he closed his eyes, wishing he could just go to sleep and forget everything. But the reality was, if something didn't happen to turn things around, he was going to have to say goodbye to Susanna and start cleaning his own bathrooms.

He snorted. Like that was going to happen. He had a plan. A good plan. He just had to make sure it played out.

A knock on the door pried his eyes open to see Christopher, his eldest son, just inside the entrance. Simon forced a smile. "Ah, there he is. The future governor of California and, hopefully, future brother-in-law to Daph—" The ominous expression on Christopher's face stopped him. "What?"

"We may have a problem." Christopher walked toward the desk and perched on the edge of the chair across from his dad. He placed both elbows on his thighs and clasped his hands between his knees.

"Of course we do." Couldn't anything just go how it was supposed to? "Does this have to do with the Granger case?" Christopher was in day two of negotiations to keep Senator Granger from going to prison. The senator had hired Christopher's firm when he was charged with embezzling government funds. "You have a few more gray hairs than you did yesterday."

Christopher rolled his eyes. "Funny. No, nothing to do with that."

Simon lifted the picture of his deceased wife from his desk. "I guess it's a good thing your mother isn't here to have to deal with all of this. I still can't believe she left me."

"She died, Dad. It wasn't exactly her choice to leave."

Simon replaced the photo. "She always said the only way she'd ever leave me was if she died." He drew in a shuddering breath. He still missed that woman every day of his life. "Okay, back to what you were saying. What's this problem?"

His son nodded to the television in the corner where the football game was playing. "Were you watching the game from the other night?"

"Yeah, but then halftime came on." He waved a hand. "I had work to do, so I muted it and just let it play instead of running it forward. Don't tell me who wins. I want to watch it."

"Forget the game."

"What? Why?"

Christopher picked up the remote from the desk, aimed it at the television. Found the halftime show and turned up the volume.

Simon cut his eyes at his son. "What's this all about?"

"Just watch."

Simon watched. "Interviews for Olympic hopefuls and those who've already qualified?"

"Yes. Keep watching."

As soon as the boy came on the screen, his heart plummeted. And the more he watched, the tighter his lungs got. "You've got to be kidding me," he whispered.

"Nope. And anyone who sees this is going to wonder the same thing that's going through your head right now. What went through my head when I saw it yesterday."

"Yesterday? And you didn't call me?"

Christopher's nostrils flared. "No, Leslie and I had a long talk about it."

"What's Leslie got to do with this?"

His son's eyes narrowed, and Simon thought he might have been working hard not to roll them. "She's my wife, Dad. We talk."

"And what did you decide?"

"To bring it to you and see if you knew anything about this."

"Of course I don't. Who is he?"

"Michael Harrison. Thirteen—and one of the best snowboarders on the planet."

Simon gaped, then snapped his mouth shut. "I don't believe it."

Christopher nodded. "I didn't either. At first. I've watched it about twenty times on different speeds and each time just confirms my suspicions. That kid has to be Keith's son."

Keith. Simon's younger son. The one who he'd never understood, but the one they all protected and the one who would save the family. "Has he seen this?"

"If he has, he hasn't said anything to me."

"Can we keep him from finding out? I don't need him distracted right now." Simon's gaze drifted back to the screen that was paused with Michael's wide innocent eyes smiling and looking back at him. Along with the prominent birthmark he couldn't deny.

But mainly those eyes. Keith's eyes. Christopher's eyes. His own eyes. Shock waves rippled through him.

He turned and looked at Christopher. The son he'd always been able to count on. The one he loved the most. "Tell Leslie to stay quiet and do whatever it takes to keep Keith from finding out about this."

Christopher nodded and rose. "Good. I'm glad we're on the same page."

"What page would that be?" Keith asked from the doorway. His eyes landed on the television screen and widened a second before Christopher managed to hit the power button. "What's going on? That looked like me when I was that age. Who's that kid?"

Simon released a heavy sigh. "Nothing's going on. Just discussing your future."

"Really? Seems like I should be a part of that discussion. Turn that back on. I want another look at the boy you had up there."

"Keith—"

Keith's eyes narrowed. "What are you hiding from me? You might as well tell me. You know I'll find out."

"How long are you home for?" Simon asked.

"What does that have to do with anything?" Keith worked as a creative director for a national hotel chain. Simon wasn't sure of everything the young man was responsible for, but apparently he was very good at his job and it paid well enough to let him lead a very comfortable lifestyle—in addition to the family money, of course. Or what was left of it.

Simon exchanged a look with Christopher and heaved a sigh. "Come in and sit down. We have some planning to do."

CHAPTER
THREE

Monday afternoon, Raina walked across the parking lot to the hospital gym, even while the hairs on the back of her neck stood up. She paused at the double glass doors and looked back, unable to prevent the shiver that skimmed up her spine.

Someone was watching her.

She'd felt it before. Not every day and not often, but enough times over the past couple of months that the thought of running was never very far from her mind.

Seeing nothing that should cause her alarm, she yanked open the door and stepped into the gym.

"Hey, Raina."

"Hey, Terry." She passed him her member card. He swiped it and returned it to her with a little salute. Terry manned the front desk like the drill sergeant he'd been before retiring from the Army.

"Have a good workout."

"Thanks." She hurried to the locker room to stash her duffel bag, then tucked her phone into her side pocket and walked out to find the free weights.

Whenever she had a day off, she enjoyed a good workout. So when RJ, her favorite trainer, was available, they ran through a series of self-defense moves that had become second nature for her over the past ten years. She'd done them over and over and over. Determined to never be anyone's punching bag ever again.

She shoved aside the memories that tried to invade her thoughts when she unintentionally lowered her defenses—or something battered them.

And that child on television had knocked her off her axis. He looked way too much like the man who'd put her in the hospital for that to be a coincidence. Kevin Anderson was the stuff of nightmares. At least *her* nightmares. And if she noticed the very strong resemblance, it was highly possible *he* noticed if he saw the clip. Which all meant that the boy's family had to be warned. So, she'd made a phone call to the one person who had the connections to help. It had been long enough that contacting him was a minor risk. But she'd called six times and she still hadn't heard from him.

She was half afraid she was going to have to hop on an airplane or get Penny to fly her across the country to find him.

With a muffled groan, she eased into her routine, her eyes scanning the other patrons. Many were familiar faces. Two were not. She watched them with her peripheral vision until she decided they weren't a threat. Yet.

She sighed and pushed through fifteen more reps, curling the twenty-pound weight, hating that her paranoia had returned full force. Not that some of her watchfulness wasn't valid, but . . .

"Raina?"

She flinched, almost dropping her weights, and turned, hoping RJ hadn't noticed the reaction. She forced a smile. *Relax.* "Hey, glad you made it."

His eyes narrowed. "You okay? You look stressed."

She raised a brow. "You do know what I do for a living, right?"

He laughed. "Right. Wanna put those weights down and do some hand to hand?"

"Sure."

For the next thirty minutes, they sparred, with him getting in way more hits than he usually would. He finally dropped his hands. "What's going on with you?"

Raina swiped the back of her arm across her sweaty forehead. "I'm distracted," she finally admitted.

"No kidding."

She checked her phone. Still no call from the one person who might be able to find the boy's family and warn them.

And the text from Vince glared at her. Why hadn't she answered him? He was just being kind.

And she was not.

"Give me a second, okay?" she asked.

"Sure." RJ screwed the cap off his water bottle and swigged. Frustrated with herself, Raina tapped out,

> Sorry for the delay in responding. I'm okay. I'm at the gym. Hope you're having a good day.

Too vague? Too distant? Should she be more personal? *Quit overthinking it!*

Before she could change her mind, she hit Send even while a sense of urgency tugged at her. "I'm sorry," she told RJ. "I need to cut this short. I've got some things I need to take care of, and postponing it isn't working well for my mental health."

His raised brow said he was curious, but he just nodded. "Text me when you want to go again?"

"Yeah. Thanks."

Raina showered and changed in record time, then raced out of the gym. If her friend wasn't going to call her back, she had to find the boy's family and warn them. But . . . how?

Sitting in the car, she tapped a second message to Vince.

Can you talk?

Three seconds later her phone rang. "Hi."

"Hey, what's up?" His deep voice rumbled in her ear, and she blinked at the emotion that raced through her.

She cleared her throat and focused. "Are you busy?"

"Never too busy for you."

She thought she heard a door shut. "If I'm interrupting—"

"You're not. I'm just babysitting, but Charlie can cover for a few minutes. What's going on?"

"I . . . was wondering if you'd . . ." She stopped, her heart chugging.

"I don't know why you find it so hard to ask for what you need, but you can trust me, Raina. Just ask."

She huffed a breath and let his words wash over her.

Just ask. He had no idea how hard that was, but protecting the boy trumped her fears. What if she didn't ask and something happened to him? "Fine. I want you to find Michael Harrison's family and warn them that he might be in danger."

"What? How do you know that?"

She sighed. "You know how I said the boy reminded me of someone from my past?"

"Yeah."

"That guy was . . . abusive. A narcissist. He went by the name Kevin Anderson, and if he sees that footage and thinks Michael is his—which they did say he was adopted, so . . . But anyway, Kevin won't stop until he has him—and that would end very badly for all involved."

"You don't think you may be jumping the gun here? I mean, that's a big leap, isn't it? Just because the child is adopted doesn't make him the child of the man you knew."

"They look exactly alike, Vince." She paused. "He has the same birthmark. The one on his chin. Kevin used to rub it when he was thinking—or angry." She paused. "Most birthmarks aren't inherited, but some are. I think the one on Michael's chin was inherited from his birth father."

Vince went quiet.

"Anyone who saw that footage—*national news footage*—and knows Kevin will bring it to his attention. It's unmistakable. I'm telling you that child is Kevin's son, and Kevin is a monster who will hurt him and his family." Her fingers tightened around the phone at the thought of her attacker going after the boy. "And the one person who might be able to help me find them is ghosting me. Which is why I'm calling you." More silence. "And that sounded really bad. Like you're second choice. It's not like that, I promise. I just thought that this other guy could—"

"Hey, it's okay. I'm not feeling slighted. I'm just thinking."

"Oh. Okay. Good." A pause. "Thinking what?"

"Well, for one, what makes you think Kevin doesn't know about him? Just because he's adopted doesn't mean his biological father doesn't know of his existence."

Raina closed her eyes and pulled in a deep breath. "That's a valid point. However, I *know* Kevin, and if he knew he had a child, he would not let another family raise him. He used to talk about having kids and being a father and . . ." She pressed fingers to her eyes, thinking. "Trust me. He doesn't know about Michael. Or didn't before that broadcast."

"Okay." He fell silent and Raina waited.

And waited.

"Vince?"

"Just thinking again. But I'll think out loud so you can follow along. We know his name and who his parents are, so it probably won't be hard to find them. I can contact the station that did the interview and get the information."

"Exactly. If you can do it, so can Kevin. Or whatever his name is." She paused. "I don't know this guy's real name, Vince, but I *know* him. I *know* that he's obsessive, possessive, and violent.

If he thinks that kid is his—and he will—he'll go after him. And he won't let anyone stand in his way."

■ ■ ■ ■

Vince caught the quiet desperation behind her words. "Hold on a sec." He glanced at Charlie, who was busy tapping on his laptop and ignoring Vince, but he still wanted a bit of privacy so he stood and walked out onto the balcony, staying in the shadows and keeping his back against the brick. She was truly scared that the man from her past would see the broadcast and make the connection. Even while his heart was dipping into his toes, Vince had no trouble believing her—or believing that the situation was dire. The only thing he could be glad about was that he'd just learned more about Raina in five minutes than he'd been able to pull from her in over a year. At the same time, he had to shut down flashes from his past. Memories of another woman in an abusive situation. Only she hadn't escaped.

His phone buzzed and he glanced at the screen. A text from his mother.

Are you coming to dinner this week?

"Vince?"

Raina. He pressed the phone back to his ear. "I'm here. You're sure Kevin Anderson isn't his real name?"

"It's not." Another sigh and the sound of a car door shutting. "I'm scared for Michael and his family, Vince."

Vince rubbed a hand over his eyes. "All right." If she said he'd go after the kid, he would, and Vince couldn't take the chance that he wouldn't. "I'll find him."

"Thank you."

"Do you have a picture of Kevin?"

"No. He never allowed them."

And that spoke volumes right there. He frowned. There was something in her voice. "What are you thinking?"

"I . . . Just a feeling we don't have a lot of time. The guy I knew—Kevin—was very into snowboarding. He loved it. I think that part of him is real. If there was something about it on television or in the paper or whatever, he was all over it. If he hasn't seen the footage of the interview for himself, like I said before, someone will bring it to his attention."

"I'm on it, I promise."

"I hate to ask, but . . . thank you."

He paused, not wanting to bring up the next thing but knew he had to. "You know what this means, right?"

"No. What?"

"If you think this guy Kevin is going to be looking for Michael—should he know about him—and he finds out the family was warned about him by an anonymous party, it might not take much for him to find out where the tip came from. I mean, there might be several people who know his true nature—family, the women in his past, the child's mother, et cetera. But if he decides to find out who the tipster is, it wouldn't be impossible for him to track this back to you—or at least turn his focus back to you."

"I know. I've thought of that, but the truth is, I'm not sure his focus ever left me. He just didn't know how to find me."

"Raina?" Another voice came through the line. He thought it was Holly.

Raina's voice faded for a minute, then came back to him. "I've got to go in about three minutes. There's a wreck on the interstate with multiple injuries."

"I thought you were off today."

"I'm the backup. Guess they need backup. One last thing though, in regard to Kevin, I've also thought that I can't be his only victim. If he did what he did to me, it's highly likely he did it to someone else."

"Yeah, someone who had his child."

"Right." She blew out a shaky breath. "I tried to find him so he could be stopped, Vince, I did. The leads just went nowhere." The unshed tears in her low voice nearly shredded his heart.

"Hey, don't focus on that," he said. "You did what you had to do to survive. But there may come a time when things get dicey. You could very well come face-to-face with him at some point."

"I've thought of that too." She cleared her throat. "But . . . what am I supposed to do? Just hope that Kevin doesn't find out? Take that risk and simply assume the child will be safe?"

Vince shook his head. No, that would never be an option for her. "Of course not."

"Okay, I'm not panicking over this for nothing. I think there's serious urgency here to warn this family, but maybe thinking Kevin can somehow connect this to me is a paranoid stretch. I mean, he has no clue where I am or if I'm even still alive."

"You sound sure."

"I am. About that." She fell silent and he could almost picture her chewing on her lip. "I mean, if he knew where I was, he'd be here." Another pause. "And even if there was a chance it was possible, even if there's something I'm not thinking of, I still have to risk it and warn these people he's out there."

"Then let's warn them and find him. We'll deal with any fallout after."

"That was basically my plan—at least until I could come up with a better one. I've really got to go. I need to be on the chopper in about thirty seconds."

She was always thinking ahead. "Okay then. Meet you tonight for dinner? We might need to strategize."

"I thought you were babysitting."

"Just for another few hours."

"Okay then, where do you want to meet?"

"The Bad Burger Barn?"

"One of my favorites."

He knew that. It was why he'd chosen it.

"We're in the air in one!" The voice sounded distant and he could hear Raina running.

"Six o'clock?" he asked.

"Depending on how long this takes, I'll be there." The roar of churning chopper blades split the air. "If not, you know why."

"Be safe."

"Will do my best. See you in a few hours. Bye."

She hung up and Vince did the same, blowing out a low breath. He walked back into the living area and secured the balcony doors.

Charlie looked up from his laptop. "Everything okay?"

With their charge in the shower, Vince let himself relax for a fraction of a second. "Yeah. Maybe." He paused. "I don't know, to be honest." He tapped a reply to his mother's text.

I'm not sure. I'll have to let you know.

"This have anything to do with the flight paramedic?" Charlie asked.

"Raina."

"Mm-hmm. Raina."

"It does."

His partner studied him with narrowed eyes. "This is the first woman you've been interested in since we became partners."

Vince shrugged. "She's not like any woman I've ever met before."

"How so?"

"I don't even know where to begin."

"It's going to sound cliché, but . . ."

"The beginning?"

"Yeah."

It seemed like a good time to check the doors and windows again while he figured out what he was going to say. Once that was done—much too quickly—he leaned against the wall near the bedroom door, listening to the shower. The guy did like long ones. How many showers a day did one person need? Maybe it was a symbolic thing. Like he felt the need to try and wash off the filth of the life he'd chosen. Who knew? At least if he was in the shower, he was easy to keep up with and no one had to talk to him.

Charlie waited patiently.

Finally, Vince sighed. "You know the history. I met Raina the same week I started with the marshals. She's a friend of a friend. Anyway, I just noticed right away she had depth . . . and mystery." And a deep pain that emerged in her eyes when she thought no one was looking. Just like his sister.

"Ah," Charlie said, pointing an index finger at Vince, "and there it is. You have a mystery to solve. Once you do that, the real question is . . . will you still be interested?"

Vince chuckled. "I have a feeling Raina is kind of like an onion. The more you peel, the more layers you find. In other words, I'm not sure the mystery is solvable." And surprisingly, he was okay with that.

Charlie raised a brow at him. "Let's just hope she doesn't make you cry."

"Aw, stop it. I'm just saying I find her interesting and . . . courageous." He shrugged. "I don't know. I like her. Yeah." And the shower was still running. He frowned. "I'm going to check on our guy. He takes long showers, but this is going on longer than usual."

Charlie nodded. "I was thinking the same thing."

Vince twisted the knob and found it unlocked. He pushed open the bedroom door and stepped inside. The room was neat as a pin. Clothes folded, bed made. "Fedorov?" No answer, but the shower was still running, so maybe the man just couldn't hear him. Vince went to the bathroom door and rapped on it. "Fedorov! You okay?"

When there was still no answer, Vince looked at Charlie and tried the bathroom knob. The door swung inward. Fedorov lay on the floor, towel wrapped around his waist, his upper body still wet and his face a pasty gray.

Vince dropped beside the man. "Call an ambulance!"

Charlie was already dialing while Vince checked his pulse and started CPR. "Don't you dare die on us, Fedorov, you hear me? Don't you die!"

CHAPTER
FOUR

Raina could see the smoke from the wreck, illuminated by the streetlights, before the scene came into view. "Oh boy," she whispered into the headset. "This is a bad one."

"Drunk driver," Holly said, clenching her fingers into fists.

The familiar wave of rage washed over Raina, and just like every other occasion with a wreck caused by a DUI, she shoved it down. She'd take care of any victims, her father's face on each one. Her goal, to make sure no one lost a mom or a dad—and that the driver lived to face the consequences. She watched the ground grow closer. Emergency vehicles clogged the area and the first responders worked together like a well-oiled machine. "Gonna be a tight fit, Pen. Only place I see is between that fire truck and the two police cars."

"I've got it." And she did.

Within minutes, Raina was on the ground racing toward the paramedics—Greg and Tracey—working on a young woman. She had a tourniquet on the upper part of her thigh and blood soaked her lower leg. "Hey, guys, who goes with us?"

Greg looked up. "Not sure, but this one's going to lose the leg if she doesn't get into surgery ASAP."

She nodded. "Got it."

An ambulance pulled to a stop and two more paramedics bolted out of the front. Another woman in a white coat followed. "I've got her," the woman said. "I'm a surgeon and have what I need to take care of this."

Raina raised a brow at Greg, who shrugged.

"Over here!" A police officer Raina recognized as Jean waved at them. The doctor took over the patient, and Holly darted toward the car wedged under a city bus.

"According to witnesses," Jean Tagget said, "that's the driver who caused this mess."

Raina nodded, swallowed hard, and followed after Holly.

The drunk driver who'd killed her father hadn't lived to face the consequences of his deed. Her jaw tightened. But this guy would if she could help it. She tamped down her emotions once more and curled her fingers around the medical box. Jean and Griff Jett were the two officers on the scene. "What do we have?"

Holly knelt next to the man behind the wheel, who blinked up at her while blood ran down the side of his face. "Sir?" she said. "Can you talk to me? Tell me what hurts besides the head?"

"He just woke up," Jean said to Raina. "He's under arrest, but we didn't want to move him until someone could figure out how to get him out of the car alive. According to the plate, this is Felix Hamilton."

Raina nodded and walked around to the other side of the vehicle. "Is he the one you called the chopper for?" The Honda Civic's front end was crushed. If his vehicle had gone any farther under the bus, he would have been decapitated. She shuddered.

"Yup. Got a piece of broken steering wheel jammed in his thigh. Firefighters need to cut him out of there but, like us, didn't want to do anything until they were sure you were on hand to get him airborne and to the hospital before he bleeds out."

"Well, we're here now," Raina said.

The guy was coming around a little more. She worked fast to get his vitals, then looked at Holly, who frowned. "That leg looks bad," Raina said, keeping her voice low. "Let's knock him back out and get him out of here. He doesn't need to know how close he is to—" She bit her tongue on the rest of the words when she realized his eyes were on her. Unfocused, hazy green eyes. The same green eyes as the smiling little girl in the picture taped to his dash. The woman next to her looked radiantly happy and held a toddler on her left hip. He had a wife and kids. Wow. She felt sorry for them. Maybe they'd be better off if he—

No. She refused to think those kinds of thoughts. Ever. She'd worked many DUIs and managed to keep her emotions out of it. This one was no different.

"Meds are in," Holly said.

The man's eyes closed once again and his head lolled to his right shoulder.

Raina backed up to let the firefighters in.

"Okay," Holly said, "here's the plan." She outlined how she and Raina would be ready with a lifesaving plan of action once the steering wheel was removed from the leg.

"No," Raina said. "Wait."

Holly's eyes collided with hers. "What?"

"Leave it in. I think it's acting as a plug, so you need to bind it to him and cut the area around it, leaving that part in his leg." Raina checked the man's heart rate and breathing once more. "Pulse is fast." She looked at Holly. "We need two large bore IVs in the ACs, and 1000 ml of normal saline administered."

Holly nodded. "And we'll push TXA and two units of blood."

The TXA should be enough to stop the bleeding. "Please let it be enough," Raina whispered. Hopefully, the blood flowing in would counteract the blood that was getting ready to flow out. Because no matter how careful they were, he was going to bleed.

Once everything was ready, Holly looked behind her. "All right. I'm moving out of the way. Raina's got him for now." Then she pulled a tarp over the unconscious man, and Raina and the firefighters went to work. Raina monitored his vitals, watching for bleeding while she did her best to tune out the sound of the saw.

And then he was free, a firefighter's gloved hand holding tight to the part of the steering wheel still attached to the leg. "All right, let's move!"

At the firefighter's shout, Raina passed the IV and other items to Holly, who followed the victim as he was lifted ever so gently out of the vehicle. Raina started to back out of the car when the picture on the dash seemed to call to her. She hesitated and grabbed it, then scrambled out to beeline for the chopper.

Only her attention was snagged by a man on the fringe of the onlookers. She had no idea what made her stop and try to get a good look, but she did, only to see him turn and walk away.

"Raina?"

Holly's prompt sent her scurrying for the chopper, where she put the man out of her mind and focused on helping Holly keep the patient from dying. Because she had a few words for him when he woke up. But until then . . .

She glanced at the clock and was glad to see she might actually make it to dinner with Vince on time.

CHAPTER
FIVE

Raina's phone rang just as she pulled into the Bad Burger Barn's parking lot and relief flooded her when she looked at the number. She tapped the screen. "It's about time. What took you so long?" She bit her lip at the silence that greeted her words. "Sorry. Something's happened and I—I just really needed you to call me."

"I'm only doing so to tell you not to call me again," the low voice said.

"There's a child in danger," she snapped. "And you have the connections to find him and warn his parents. His *adoptive* parents."

"*We're both* in danger now that you've called this number. I guarantee you, he's still monitoring it somehow, some way. Just like everyone in connection with your stepfather. I'm packing up a few things and disappearing. I suggest you do the same. Leave wherever you are and run. If you don't, he'll be coming for you."

She closed her eyes, trying to find patience for the man she'd once turned to for help. "It's a chance I had to take. Now listen—"

43

"No, you listen. He sends me a reminder every year that he's still watching me. Just waiting for me to make contact with you. I'm out of here until this blows over."

"Sends you what?"

A gasp whispered through the line. "I've got to go. Don't call me again."

Click.

"Trent! Trent Carter, don't you hang up on me! Please!" She was yelling at a disconnected phone. With a groan, she tossed the device into the passenger seat and dropped her forehead to the steering wheel, taking deep breaths. She let two minutes pass, then picked up the phone and dialed Trent's number once more.

It went straight to voice mail.

She looked up his personal cell phone number. A number she'd only kept in case of an emergency with no plans to ever use it. But if ever there was an emergency—

She dialed it. Voice mail. "Trent, please, if you won't talk to me, call the family. Warn them. Run if you must, but let them know. Please. And be safe. I'm sorry for contacting you. Please know I had no choice," she finished with a whisper and hung up. She hated the situation. Hated it with everything in her, but like she said, she had no choice. She had to do whatever she could to make sure Michael Harrison and his family were safe. "God, protect us all, please."

Trent's comment that they were both in danger now that she'd called him swirled in her mind. Did Kevin really send him something? Send him what?

After all this time, Kevin really and truly hadn't given up finding her. She curled her fingers around the steering wheel and let that sobering fact settle deep into her mind.

So . . . now what?

■ ■ ■ ■

With his heart pounding in his throat, Trent Carter snapped his briefcase shut and set it on the desk. He studied the security monitor once more. All looked still. Normal. No shadows, no masked figures slipping into the building. His pulse slowed a fraction. He was panicking over nothing, his paranoia pushing him to be careless.

He shouldn't have called her. No, *she* shouldn't have called *him*. She'd promised to never contact him again no matter the reason. He'd done his part, kept his promise, and up until now, she'd done the same.

And now she'd possibly ruined it all.

Or maybe not. Maybe enough time had passed.

Maybe—

The floor creaked just outside his office door and Trent froze. "Who's there?"

Silence. Trent darted toward the open door with every intention of shutting and locking it. He was halfway there when a man rounded the doorjamb and lifted his arm. Trent only had time to glimpse the ski mask, dark eyes peering through the rounded holes—and the gun with the suppressor attached to the end.

So . . . it didn't matter how many phone calls she'd made. It was only the first one that had mattered. He held up a hand. "Please—"

A low pop reached him a millisecond before the bullet hit him in the center of his forehead.

■ ■ ■ ■

MONDAY EVENING

Simon entered the formal dining room. He always ate dinner around seven in the evening. A habit ingrained in him by his mother, who always waited for his father to get home from work because she wanted the family to eat together. He'd done the same thing with his boys growing up, and they still usually found their way to the table three or four times a week. Especially Christopher and Leslie since they lived there. Keith had his own place, but Simon wasn't sure why, since the man spent more nights in his old bedroom than his apartment.

"Sorry I'm late," Simon said to those already there. "Had a phone call that went long." A phone call that would hopefully pad his sorry bank account a little more. He helped himself to the buffet-style dinner, then took his plate to the table. He sat at the head, of course, while the others seated themselves accordingly.

To his right was Christopher and Christopher's wife, Leslie. They had no children yet, thanks to Christopher's desire to establish himself as the youngest governor in California. But . . . soon, they planned to start trying. A pregnant wife was good campaign strategy. Simon couldn't say he disagreed.

To Simon's left was the bane of his existence. One that he loved simply because he was his son. Keith had so many issues, it was a wonder he'd managed to keep his nose clean and everything out of the media.

But he had, and with much effort and a lot of money, the boy's reputation was still spotless. His good looks and charming personality—when he chose to use it—made him popular with everyone who crossed his path. Which was why Daphne Valentine, heiress to the Valentine fortune, sat next to Keith.

Somehow his wayward son had charmed the woman, who was obviously smitten with him. Keith had set his sights on Daphne at Simon's order and had succeeded in his quest to win her heart in a fairly short amount of time. Thankfully, the boy was on the right path at the moment, and Simon intended to make sure he stayed there. Because while Daphne was incredibly intelligent, when it came to emotions and love, she appeared blinded by Keith's good looks and utter devotion. If Simon hadn't been well aware that his son was only devoted to himself, he might be fooled as well—which was why he didn't stand in judgment of her inability to see beneath Keith's surface.

He swallowed a bite of dry roast and grimaced. Why was it impossible to get a good cook? He tossed his napkin on the table and noted everyone staring at him. "What?"

Christopher cleared his throat. "Leslie just asked if she could get you anything, since the roast doesn't seem to be to your liking."

"Oh." He cast a glance at his daughter-in-law. He liked her. And for whatever reason, she seemed to like him. Not in a "sucking up" kind of way, but in a way that a daughter looks up to a father. He didn't understand it, but he was touched by it. She and Christopher had been married for only two years, but she'd definitely grown on him. Maybe because they were a lot alike. "Ah, no. Thank you. The ham and vegetables will be just fine."

"What was your phone call about?" Keith asked.

Simon bit off his retort and pasted a pleasant expression on his face. "Just some real estate business. Nothing pressing." He turned to Daphne. "How is your father doing? I heard he was under the weather last week."

The woman smiled, revealing a deep dimple in her left cheek and a row of orthodontically straight white teeth. Her dark eyes glistened with life. And kindness. For a moment, the sting of an unfamiliar emotion settled on him—could that be guilt? He shoved it away to focus on her answer.

". . . just fine now. He's on medication for A-fib and he'd not taken it for a day or so." She shook her head. "The man needs a keeper. My mother was always the one who made sure he took his medication, but . . ." Simon captured the flash of pain in her gaze. Daphne's mother had passed away three years ago after a short battle with cancer. Daphne drew in a breath and smiled again. "Well, it looks like I'll be handling that from now on. Thank you for asking."

Simon studied her for a moment. She really was a lovely woman. Much better than his son deserved. "He's a lucky father to have a daughter like you."

She shot him a small smile, and he turned his attention to his eldest son. "I'm assuming you had a busy day?"

Christopher's gaze met his. "Still waiting to hear from a potential donor, but yes, very busy and, hopefully, successful."

"Good. Good." He tried the cinnamon pastry and found it dry. "Who cooked this anyway?"

"Gary did," Leslie said.

"Tell him he's fired. I'm tired of paying for this kind of food. A cook should know how to cook."

Leslie smiled at him. "You're so right. I'll take care of it."

"Please." Having Leslie run the household was one of the benefits of her and Christopher living under the same roof. Granted, it was a very large roof and they could go days without seeing one another if they so chose, but she was a good woman, a doting daughter-in-law, and would make a wonderful governor's wife.

Simon's hands tightened around his silverware, and he could only hope everything would turn out like he'd planned.

Because if not . . .

He shuddered. It didn't bear thinking about. Everything had to go as planned. Period.

After dinner, Simon motioned for his sons to join him in his office. Once behind the closed door, he looked at Keith. "Who's the mother of the child?"

"What are you talking about?"

"I did a little digging. Michael Harrison was adopted by that family the day he was born. He's obviously your kid, so who's the mother?"

Keith's eyes narrowed. "I don't know."

Simon studied his son. It bothered him he could never tell when the boy was lying. Of course, he wasn't a boy now, and some days, he wished he could kick his son to the curb. But when did a father stop protecting his child? Especially when the future of the family rested on the young man's shoulders. "Then figure it out. We have to assume that she's seen the footage, the news coverage and the kid. She knows what you look like, so it doesn't take a genius to assume she'll put it together too. If that's the case, she may reenter the picture somehow."

"Why does it matter?" Keith asked. He appeared nonchalant about the idea, but Simon could tell Keith was thinking, calculating, trying to figure out how he could make this benefit him in some way.

For a man who was so smart about some things, he sure was stupid about others. "So we can have a plan in place just in case," he answered evenly. "I want to know who she is, Keith, so think hard and figure it out."

"Why don't you? You're the one with all of the resources."

Christopher huffed a sigh that was borderline growl. "Keith—"

Keith held up a hand to stop Christopher's low warning. "Both of you. Stop. I know who the mother is, but she's been out of the picture for so long that it's not worth bringing up." He rubbed a hand over the birthmark on his chin, and Simon noted the familiar gesture. He did the same thing when he was thinking hard. "What an interesting twist of fate."

"Keith . . ." Christopher's sharp word connected the brothers' eyes.

Simon noted the look. "What is it?" Both men blinked and looked away. "What are you not telling me?"

"Nothing," Keith said, "but if that's my kid, I'm going to find him." He slammed a fist into his palm. "I can't believe she'd do this to me."

Christopher's hand shot out and he grabbed his brother's throat to shove him against the wall with a thud. Simon cut off a gasp but didn't interfere. Christopher's nostrils flared. "Now, you listen to me you spoiled, self-serving brat. I've cleaned up your messes for years and I'm done with that. It's time for you to grow up and do your part to save this family and all we are. You leave that kid alone. And you leave that woman alone. It's all in the past and that's where they need to stay, you understand me?"

"But—" Keith seemed as stunned at the uncharacteristic outburst as Simon was.

"No buts, little brother. You keep your focus. You play your part and marry Daphne. Then you get your hands on all that money that's going to bail us out of our financial issues and then, and only then, can you even think about that boy. Now, get Daphne to marry you. The sooner the better. And keep your head down and out of the news. I'm being asked about my sibling and other family members. So far, I've managed to deflect the questions, and no one's unearthed any pictures that could be troublesome, but you need to stay under the radar. Got it?"

Keith's cold eyes never left Christopher's face, but he didn't lift a hand to defend himself either. It was like he didn't have to because he knew something no one else did. And for the first time, a tug of fear pulled at Simon. Did he even know Keith at all? And what had Christopher meant about cleaning up his brother's messes and Keith needing to keep his head down? He had a feeling he didn't want to know and wasn't about to ask.

Finally, Keith gently removed Christopher's hand from his throat and nodded. "I got it. You're right. All that matters is doing whatever it takes to save the family."

Christopher stepped back and straightened his shirt, then took a deep breath. "Good." He patted Keith's arm. "Sorry about that. I just kind of lost it there for a minute."

Keith nodded, but his gaze was on Simon's. "I understand." Then he moved his focus to Christopher. "And you're right. You've been there for me since we were kids and I appreciate that." A pause. "But, know this. I'll find out if he's my son one way or another. And"—his eyes narrowed, cold, hard chips of tundra—"don't ever put your hands on me again."

CHAPTER
SIX

Raina glanced at the clock and realized she'd been sitting there shaking for ten minutes. She tightened her fingers around the wheel until her knuckles glowed white. "Stop it." She spoke the words aloud, then released the wheel to slam her fists onto it. "Stop it! He will not do this to me." Her heart hammered in her chest and her blood flowed with fresh fury.

Pulling in two more deep breaths, she waited until the shaking eased, then opened the car and stepped out, only to stop when she noticed Vincent standing a few feet away, hands shoved into the front pockets of his khakis, watching her, eyes concerned, lips frowning. She suppressed a groan and walked over to join him. "Hi."

"Hi," he said. "You all right?"

"Not really." It had gone against everything in her to ask someone to do something for her. To ask for help or anything else. But when it came to a child's life, she simply had no choice.

If she didn't ask, if she let Kevin continue to control her actions, then she would have no life. And that simply could not happen. She cleared her throat. "Any word from your marshal friends?"

"The Colorado marshal's office is going to work with local law enforcement and have someone move them to protective custody."

"So they know?"

"Yes. And are taking big-time precautions."

Raina almost didn't know how to handle the massive surge of relief flowing through her. All her frantic efforts to get ahold of Trent were for nothing. And the risk . . . She stifled a groan. She'd taken a huge risk by breaking her promise. And she hadn't needed to. "You did that? For real?"

"For real, Raina."

She threw her arms around his waist and squeezed. "Oh, Vince, thank you," she whispered, even while relief mixed with regret. She shouldn't have asked him. She shouldn't have involved him, but the boy—Michael—he was so young and so vulnerable. She couldn't just walk away if she could do something to protect him. *Please don't let anything happen to Vince because I asked him to help.*

He hugged her back. "Of course."

She couldn't help but notice how amazing it felt to have Vince's arms around her. And the fact that she could be all right staying there for another couple of hours or so.

She cleared her throat and stepped back.

The family was safe from Kevin. That was all that mattered. But even as she thought that, a shiver danced up her spine and she shot a glance back over her shoulder. The sun was long gone below the horizon and the evening breeze blew like a frosty breath across the back of her neck. Trent's paranoia had triggered her own.

A shudder rippled through her. A hand landed on her bicep, and she jumped, a gasp slipping from her. She met Vince's concerned gaze.

"Raina?"

She shook her head. "I know. I know. I'll admit I'm jumpy."

"No kidding." He led her into the restaurant and then to a table in the back.

"It's stupid," she murmured. "I don't *think* there's any way for him to find me or even suspect I had anything to do with the family's disappearance. Should he even be looking. But my paranoia is at an all-time high."

"Well, it seems like that would be a natural response. I mean, just from what little you've told me . . ."

The waiter approached and Raina left the unfinished sentence unanswered.

Once they'd ordered, she pressed her palms to her eyes. "I just can't help feeling like the other shoe is going to fall and it's going to hit me in the head. Hard."

Vince nodded, and she fell silent, wondering if she should just spill the whole thing. But while her brain formed the words, her mouth wouldn't say them.

"You work tomorrow?" he asked after several minutes of quiet.

"Yes."

He nodded. "Well, this is just my opinion, of course, which you're welcome to ignore, but I think you should fill in Penny and Holly about the fact that something from your past may have caught up with you and they need to help you watch your back."

Raina bit her lip, wanting to shoot down the idea. Instead, she hesitated. "I'll think about it."

"They'll ask questions, but I doubt they'll push the issue if you make it clear you don't want to go into details."

That was true. "Just like you're not pushing?"

"I only want you to tell me what you want to tell me." He paused. "No, that's not true. I want you to trust me. To tell me everything so that I know how to help you best."

". . . *how to help you best.*" The words echoed as she studied him. *Tell him.* A flash from her past flickered through her mind and she closed her eyes for a moment. When she opened them, he was studying her. "I'll consider talking to them." But they'd want to help too.

Another brief flash from her past sent shudders up her spine. *Tell him.*

The food arrived, and while Raina knew she needed to eat, her stomach wouldn't unknot. She picked up a french fry, dipped it in ketchup, then put it back on her plate. "Okay," she said, "fine."

Vince paused, his burger held in his left hand while he sipped tea from the glass in his right. He lowered his drink. "Okay fine, what?"

"I'll talk to Holly and Penny." He raised a brow and she shrugged. "You're right. They're my friends. Although, just for the record, not telling them everything has nothing to do with not trusting them." Not completely anyway.

"Okay." But his gaze lingered on hers as though he were mentally trying to pull the information from her. "What does it have to do with?"

She opened her mouth, searched for the words, found none, and clamped her lips together.

"Right," he said. "Trust."

She tried not to grimace at his words. "Okay, yes," she said, "but not in the way you're thinking."

"So what is it? Why do you feel you can't trust us?"

She flinched at his soft question, laced with something that sounded a lot like hurt. "I do trust you—and them."

"Then what?"

"Vince, I know you want me to talk to you more. Tell you about my past, and the truth is, I want to. At least part of me wants to. It's just . . ." She chugged her water. Could telling him really put him in danger? Maybe. Or maybe, it was because once he knew everything, he'd think differently of her.

"Raina?"

She blinked. "Never mind. I'm sorry." She couldn't do it. She was too tied to her past. And she hated it. Tears clogged her throat and she swallowed hard to get rid of the tightness.

His hand covered hers and she stilled even as she met his gaze. "Don't apologize. It's okay. I promise. You're right. I'll stop pushing. You can tell me if and when you're ready."

And that seemed to be the signal to stop talking and finish eating, but she wasn't hungry anymore. Raina got a to-go box. She'd eat the burger for breakfast.

Vince's phone rang and he snagged it to look at the screen. "I've got to take this. You mind?"

"Of course not."

He slapped the device to his ear. "How is he?"

Raina tried the dessert she'd ordered, thinking something sweet might help loosen the knot in her belly, but she kept circling back to the whole trust thing. She'd been honest when she said keeping the others in the dark wasn't a lack of trust. Not that they'd betray her confidence or anything like that.

It was an overabundance of fear. Fear that if she told them or Vince everything, they'd insist on *doing* something with the full intention of *helping*. Which led to the fear of what would happen if she let them.

Or she'd be judged and found guilty. Then again, maybe it wasn't an either-or situation. Her friends loved her. They'd want to help—or feel *obligated* to help—but would they still feel the same about her if she came clean?

The thoughts tumbled over one another faster than the speed of light, and she wanted to scream. To stop them.

She knew that little taunting voice was a lie, but it was one she found herself unable to push away.

However . . . this was a whole different scenario.

Vince was trained law enforcement. Maybe if she told him—and gave him an even clearer picture of what Kevin was capable of—he actually *could* help. After all, he'd managed to get the Harrison family taken care of and he was still in one piece.

Tell him.

She really wanted to ignore that insistent little voice.

■　■　■　■

"Uh-huh," Vince said. "Yeah. Okay. Thanks for the update." He hung up, his gaze on the far wall, while he processed the fact that his protectee was going to be all right. *Thank you, Lord.*

"Everything okay?" she asked.

He pulled in a deep breath and met her gaze. "I think so. Our witness had an incident today and almost died on the bathroom floor, but we got him help in record time and he's going to make it."

"Oh, Vince, I'm so sorry." She reached across the table to grip his fingers. "Here I am going on and on about me, and I didn't even ask you about your day and I'm sor—"

His grip tightened around hers. "Raina, shhh. It's okay. Really. We think we know what happened. It appears that he had an allergic reaction to the food he ordered. Apparently, he has an allergy to shellfish and didn't bother to tell them. There was some cross contamination and . . . there you go."

"Oh man."

"When I was in the bathroom trying to figure out what happened, I noticed the EpiPen on the counter. I grabbed it and jabbed." He shrugged. "He's doing better."

"I'm so glad."

"I am too. I can't express how glad." He really was. He didn't care for the guy, but he didn't want him dead. For more than one reason. Having the man die at all would not be good, but freak accident or not, having him die on his watch would have been so very bad any way one looked at it. And—as much as he hated to admit it—he did have some compassion for the man. His history was not one designed to produce an upstanding citizen. Some people could rise above that, of course, but Fedorov hadn't been able to.

Raina looked at her box, picked up her fork, then put it down again.

"Okay, I know I said I'd wait until you're ready, but I think you're ready even if you don't want to admit it. Talk to me, Raina," he finally said. "You're going to explode if you don't." He raised a brow, silently inviting her to do as he'd urged.

She eyed him. "You're right. I am."

"Then talk."

Raina sighed, then looked down. "In case you haven't picked up on it, I have kind of a . . . weird past," she said, her voice low, her words slow and drawn out. "A painful one. I don't like to talk about it. With anyone. Usually."

"I've noticed. I get it." How could he convince her that he was a safe place to unload? Why did she find it so hard to let down her walls and just trust him?

Because you're not trustworthy?

The little voice in his head taunted him, and he wanted to bat it away like an annoying fly, but it continued to buzz with persistence.

A soft groan escaped her. "No, you don't." Her hand clenched, then relaxed, only to fist once more on the table.

He refused to ask her again. At least not out loud. *Trust me, so I can fix it.* He flinched at the involuntary thought.

"It's just not that simple."

"Okay then."

To give her credit, she did sound like she was in agony over the whole thing.

Minutes ticked past while she studied her hands, obviously thinking. "Why does it matter so much to you?" she asked softly. "I mean, I know we're friends, but this seems to be something . . . more."

Because it was. "I don't want anything to happen to you, and if you don't let someone help you, then it's possible something will happen. I just want to make sure nothing happens."

She blinked at him. "That was cryptic."

"My sister's husband killed her."

Her mouth formed a small O and he nodded. "She wouldn't let me help her and she died, so if I'm a little pushy . . ."

"That's why."

"Yeah."

"That's terrible."

"Yes, it was. It is."

"When?"

"Six years ago. And she and I had a similar conversation to the one you and I are having. So, I think I'm having a few PTSD moments."

She swallowed hard. "I see."

"Do you?"

"Yes." She studied him, her gaze so compassionate that it almost did him in. "You've been a very good friend to me, Vince. Thank you."

He blinked. "Uh . . . you're welcome." He'd been a good *friend*. That was kind of a kick in the pants. A *friend*. Better than those she'd known most of her life?

"Which means I need to be the same to you," she said. "I need to give you a heads-up, because forewarned is forearmed, right?"

Even though he was slightly confused, he kept that to himself. Then the rest of her words processed. "What do I need to be forewarned about?"

She bit her lip and looked away. "I'm ashamed to admit it, but I have this *fear*—a fear I've lived with for so long—an irrational fear maybe, but a fear nonetheless—"

"What fear, Raina? I really want to know." He wanted to know *her*. And everything about her.

"A fear that if I let anyone help me, do anything *for* me, something bad will happen to that person."

The words were so low he had to lean forward to catch them. "What happened to someone who tried to help you?"

"Not just someone, multiple someones. But one was . . . she died. Was murdered actually."

"Oh my— What? How?"

"I was coming home from a stint in the hospital, and our housekeeper, Mrs. Atwater, went to the house because she wanted to make my favorite cake. When I got home, I found her. Dead on the kitchen floor."

He stared at her for a flicker of a second, letting the words penetrate. "Oh no," he finally whispered. "Oh, Raina . . . that's . . . I have no words."

He wasn't sure what it was in his response that finally broke through and convinced her, but she pushed the box aside and linked her fingers. Before she opened her mouth, he could tell she'd decided to talk to him. "I don't need any words. I just . . . I was involved with the guy I told you about," she said.

"Kevin."

"Right. In the beginning, he was amazing. Kind, attentive, catered to my every whim. I'm ashamed to say that it only took him a month to talk me into giving up on the idea of college and moving in with him."

Vincent stayed still, unsure what to say or where she was going with the story. He just knew he didn't want to do anything that would close her back up.

"In a nutshell, shortly after that, I was under his control— and I mean that literally. Mentally, emotionally, and finally, physically. To the point that I landed in the hospital the day I told him I was moving back home with my parents, that being with him wasn't healthy for me."

Every muscle in his body clenched.

"He beat me to the point that I almost died. I had a number of broken bones, a ruptured spleen. Things like that."

"Things like *that*? That's horrible." Horrible didn't begin to describe it. He had to make the effort to keep his hands from curling into fists and push aside the desire to give the coward a taste of his own medicine.

"At some point after I'd passed out, he left, probably thinking I was dead. But I woke up and somehow got to my phone and called 911. That part's kind of fuzzy and got fuzzier after the next week or so. Anyway, two months later, after healing and a stint in rehab for physical and occupational therapy, I was cleared to go home."

"And Kevin never made contact in all that time you were in the hospital and rehab?"

"When I was close to getting released. Not with me, but with others. And no one could seem to find him." She rubbed her eyes. "Right now I'm more worried about the future than the past. Michael looks enough like him to the point that he could be that man's son. And I've been thinking . . ."

"About?"

"What if we can catch him? Catch Kevin?" And she could finally put the past to rest and never worry that it was two steps behind her.

He studied her. "Let me guess. You want someone to keep an eye on the Harrison family and see if he shows up?"

"It was a thought." She pinched the bridge of her nose. "They're not going to agree to stay hidden forever, and as soon as they pop out of hiding, he's going to show up. I can almost guarantee it."

He pursed his lips, then sighed. "I don't know, Raina, it sounds—"

"Farfetched? Crazy? I'm aware." She jabbed the air with her finger while fire flashed in her eyes. "I've built a good life, Vince, but I'm trapped. I can't go home without the fear that even after all these years, he's still got someone watching my parents' home. That if I show up or call or whatever, he'll know." She drew in a shaky breath. "I've thought about him over and over, trying to figure out what I know that couldn't be a lie."

"What did you come up with?"

"He's got a lot of money, he's charming and fun when he wants to be and can make you think *you're* the crazy one. He's a control freak. He loves power. He hates to lose. He's most likely a sociopath. A narcissist. And, whether I want to admit it or not, he's *always* there in the back of my mind." Her fingers twisted together and she leaned forward. "I'm tired of always having to look over my shoulder. I've stayed hidden for a long time for a lot of reasons, but I think it's time to be proactive and get my life back." She looked at him. "I just have to figure out how to make that happen." Without putting anyone else in danger.

"You can't do this alone."

She swallowed. "I have to."

He sighed and leaned back in his chair. "How do you plan to do that?"

"I don't know."

"Exactly. I have resources you don't."

"I can't ask you for help. Okay, any more help. You've done the biggest thing, and that's making sure that Michael is safe. I just—"

"You're not asking. I'm offering."

"I . . . I . . . no." She pressed her palms to her eyes, her inner struggle a tangible thing.

He reached across the table and snagged her hands, grateful she didn't pull away. "Nothing's going to happen to me if you let me help."

Her hands fisted in his grasp. "You don't know that."

Vince studied her. "Okay, that's true. I don't. But I do know that if something happens to me, it won't be because I chose to help you. God's in control of all that. Not you."

■ ■ ■ ■

Raina blinked at the matter-of-fact statement, letting his words sink in while she processed. Heat climbed into her cheeks. And maybe that was the problem. She didn't want God to be in control, because God seemed to fail her at just about every turn. And she couldn't trust that God would keep Vince safe. Or that she could trust her judgment when it came to trusting another man. But something kept her turning to God even when she didn't want to. Why was that? Because he kept chasing after her to do so. He hadn't given up on her like she'd given up on him? Feeling body-slammed by the thoughts, she nevertheless kept her face neutral and chose her response carefully. "I know," she said. "Mentally. Unfortunately, my heart seems to believe something else."

"Well, we both know the heart can be deceitful, don't we?"

"Yes," she said, "yes, we do know that." Raina couldn't believe she was spilling all her secrets to Vincent Covelli. Okay, maybe not *all* of them, but close enough. But she didn't *do* that. *Ever.*

Just walk away. Go get in your car and end this conversation now.

But . . . for some reason, she didn't want to do what came naturally. Easily. Instinctively.

Not tonight.

Not with Vince.

And maybe not even with God. She'd have to think about that one a bit more.

She huffed a short laugh. "I must be more shook than I thought. I haven't even told my best friends about that time in my life."

His eyes widened slightly. "Oh. Really?"

"Yes. Really." She tried to decipher the look on his face and settled for stunned.

He cleared his throat. "I'm . . . uh . . . honored you'd share with me."

Raina forced herself not to fidget. "You sharing about your sister helped. I'm so sorry you went through that, but it makes me feel like you really do understand."

"I do."

They fell silent for a moment. Then she looked at him. "I'm asking you for help, aren't I? In a non-asking way."

His lips curved into a sweet smile. One that she wouldn't mind kissing off his face. The heat that had faded was back and climbed into her cheeks again. *No, no, no, no, no.* She would *not* go there. After the number Kevin had done on her, she'd sworn off anything related to relationships and men. And yet, there was something about Vince that—

"How do you know Kevin Anderson isn't his real name?" he finally asked.

Raina cleared her throat and pulled her thoughts back on track. "Because my stepfather—and the private investigator he hired—tried to track him down and came up empty. The man I called Sunday night from Julianna's kitchen is friends with my stepfather and the PI he used." She waved a hand. "I couldn't find the PI's number, so I called Trent to see if he could help. He called me while I was sitting in the parking lot and told me not to call him again."

"Why?"

"He thinks Kevin is still somehow monitoring his calls." And this is where she'd like to quit talking, but . . . "It's a little confusing on the timeline, but shortly before I was going to be released from the hospital, Kevin sent little mementos to several people in my life. Pictures of their loved ones with threats that if anyone helped keep me from him, they'd die."

Vince frowned and leaned forward. "It's blowing my mind that no one's ever tracked this guy down."

"I know, but he never showed up himself. At least not that we could ever catch. If he was there, he was in the shadows. But it was like, while he knew he couldn't be with me without finding himself arrested, he didn't want anyone else to be with me either."

"That's not unusual. He was trying to scare people into cutting you out of their lives, which would give you no one to turn to but him."

"Yes. Exactly." Raina pressed fingers to her temples. "My stepfather and mother were almost run off the road on the way to pick me up from the rehab center to take me home. Before that, three of my father's best friends all received the threats or had terrible things happen. Trent's wife was kidnapped, killed, and dumped in a ditch with a note pinned to her shirt saying to have nothing to do with me or next time it would be their daughter." She shuddered. "Their daughter was four at the time, and I babysat for them fairly often. She'd be almost eighteen now." She shook her head. "Everyone I ever mentioned in conversation, everyone he knew I was close to, he found and terrorized. Only, I didn't find out about all of it until my parents came to pick me up at the rehab center. My stepfather had private security on my room at the hospital, then the rehab center."

His eyes narrowed, looking thoughtful. "How long were you with him?"

"About eight months." Eight months of his brainwashing, then the realization of what was happening, the confrontation—and the beating that put her in the hospital.

Her mind flipped back to Trent.

It's too risky, one voice whispered. *He said not to call again. But he sounded so frightened and you really should ask Vince to check on him*, the other countered.

"Raina?"

She drew in a deep breath. "Vince . . . this is between you and me. I may share with the others one day, but for now, I don't see any reason to." Mostly because she hated talking about that time in her life and being reminded how gullible and . . . blind . . . she'd been. She refused to call herself stupid. She wasn't stupid. She'd been deceived but had finally caught on and done something about it. She'd fought back and gotten out alive. That was more than some victims could claim.

Vince rubbed a hand over his lips and nodded. "All right. Of course. That's your call. I just can't help wondering why the fake name. I mean, obviously, he wanted to keep his identity from everyone, but *why*. If you knew that, it might be possible to track him down."

His words pierced her. "Trust me, we all wondered that too. The only thing I—and everyone else—could come up with was that he had a criminal record or another family somewhere. He said he was in pharmaceutical sales and he *did* travel a lot, so it's very possible he was deceiving someone else just like me."

"Yeah. Another family was my first thought. I'm assuming they ran his prints."

She nodded. "Of course. He wasn't in the system, though, which ruled out the criminal past along with other things like certain occupations."

"Or he just hadn't been caught."

"Or that." She rubbed her eyes, then dropped her hand to her lap. "I worked with a sketch artist, but again, nothing came from that. I should have known something was weird when he refused to take pictures. He claimed it was because he was self-conscious about his looks, that when he was a kid, someone had posted a picture of him in the boys' bathroom at school for everyone to make fun of. He said he'd never let anyone take a picture of him again." She shrugged. "That story may very well be true, but obviously he had other reasons for not wanting his likeness anywhere." And she'd been so head over heels, she'd believed him. Had felt sorry for him. Her hands fisted on a wave of regret at the way she'd ignored her own instincts. "I'm not that person anymore," she whispered.

"What?"

She shuddered and looked up. "Nothing. The PI showed me

picture after picture of numerous Kevin Andersons, and none of them were him. He didn't actually work at the pharmaceutical company he claimed to be employed with—surprise, surprise—and everything else the investigator tried led to a dead end. The man finally admitted defeat." She took a deep breath. "At that point, I almost didn't care. I was happy to be alive. I was glad Kevin—or whoever he was—was gone. I just wanted to forget him and get on with my life."

Vince's eyes narrowed. "But?"

It was scary how good he was getting at reading her. "But," she said, "then I walked in the day I came home from rehab to find a bouquet of black roses on my parents' table with a note that said, 'You'll always be mine' and . . ." How she hated revisiting that moment in her life.

"And?"

"And that's when we found Mrs. Atwater, our housekeeper, dead on my parents' kitchen floor."

"Again, Raina . . . I'm so sorry."

"I . . . can't even . . ." She stopped and grappled with the surge of emotions that she'd kept buried for so long. "I know it was him who killed her, but there was no proof, no evidence left behind, nothing. At least none that led to him. Anyway, Kevin got in the house somehow. We're not even sure how. The cameras never picked up on him. Nevertheless, he did. But Mrs. Atwater wasn't supposed to be there, and we think she surprised him. She lived around the corner in a house my stepfather built for her and her husband, so she usually walked to work, but she'd driven that day. Maybe because it was cold, maybe she just didn't feel like walking while carrying a cake. Who knows?"

"So, he should have seen the car and known someone was there."

"Exactly. And he didn't care. Anyway, my stepfather told me everything that had happened with his friends and, of course, what I learned about mine when I was discharged, but after

66

Mrs. Atwater and the attempt to run my parents off the road earlier that day and then the other incidents my stepfather's friends reported . . ." She shrugged. "I told them I had to leave. That I *was* leaving and they couldn't stop me. When they realized there was no talking me out of it, my stepfather called in a few favors, and I left that night after the cops were finished with me." She met his gaze. "My stepfather had a US Marshal friend who helped me out." And that was one of the last times she'd accepted help from anyone.

He straightened. "Who?"

"John Tate."

He shook his head. "I don't know him, but being on opposite sides of the country, that's not surprising."

"Well, John was a pilot as well. He picked me up at my parents' home, took me to an airfield, and flew me to Arizona, where he gave me the paperwork for three different identities—just in case I had to run again. I landed in the care of some very kind people, and I stayed with them while I went to paramedic school, then got a job. I worked a lot, but one day, I . . . felt watched. This happened several times, but each time, I could never spot anything . . . or anyone . . . out of the ordinary. Until . . ."

"Until?"

"One day I looked up and saw someone who looked like he might be Kevin. It terrified me. I didn't think twice. I left in the middle of my shift, went to the nearest ATM, and pulled out the max amount of money allowed out of all of my accounts. I had four *in-case-of-emergency* accounts. Using my second identity, I then got on one bus after another, changing routes, buying and dumping phones, getting strangers to buy my tickets, and more. Five days later, I landed in Asheville, North Carolina, on Penny's doorstep. I simply told her I was trying to stay ahead of a stalker, needed a change of scenery, and she got me a job at the hospital. I was too scared to work as a paramedic because I'd talked to Kevin about wanting to do that, so I worked in housekeeping. Then I decided to take a chance, contacted John, and he got all my paperwork transferred to my new name. When the paramedic position came available, Dr. K already knew who I was and hired me to work on the chopper. My rappelling experience put me slightly ahead of the competition."

"Where'd you get the rappelling experience?"

"My stepdad loved to hike and go rappelling. He taught me."

"He sounds like a good man."

"He is." Sadness flickered deep in her soul. She'd stuffed those memories away because they were just too painful to visit. It made her miss her parents almost more than she could bear.

"Penny and the others didn't ask about the name change?"

"They did. But once I told them about the stalker and decided changing my name was the best way to start over, they were good with that. We haven't talked about it since, and that's the way I prefer it. Thankfully, they respect that."

"And this Kevin guy doesn't know about Penny and the others?"

She laughed. A hard sound that held no humor. "No. I was too ashamed to tell him how I met them—which worked in my favor, obviously." Vince knew they'd all met in juvie, so she had no qualms about sharing that bit.

"Why don't you let me see if I can find him without involving the Harrisons first?"

She hesitated. "You think you could when so many others failed? I mean, this is still an ongoing thing. If I could tell authorities where Kevin is, they'd arrest him." But then there would be facing him once that happened.

CHAPTER
SEVEN

"Wow. Thanks. I *am* a US Marshal, remember? I know how to find people. I mean, I obviously can't make any guarantees, but, yes. Maybe."

She straightened her shoulders and lifted her chin. "It's been almost fourteen years. I'm a very different person than I was back then." Saying the words out loud seemed to help her somehow. Give her strength. She met his gaze once more. "I *think* I could handle you finding him. I just . . ."

"Don't want to?"

A small smile curved her full lips. "More like don't want to have to find out if I can."

"You can," he said, his voice low and soft. "I have complete faith in that."

She went silent, then sighed. "Well, that makes one of us." She peered out the window. "I'm sure you've heard the story about when we landed the chopper on the mountain with Darius Rabor on the loose."

"The serial killer? Yeah, I heard."

"When we finally got away, we had to leave Penny behind." She shuddered. "But Holt was there and they managed to get away safely." She waved a hand. "You know the details. When they finally made it back to base, the media was waiting on them."

"Because of Penny's mother, right?"

"Well, not so much because of Penny's mother, but mostly because we had a terrible supervisor who thought he could use the fact that Penny's mother was Geneva Queen to provide a distraction from his incompetence—while getting the hospital in front of the public in a good light."

"Geneva Queen. The famous actress, known to every person in America," he murmured. "It still blows me away that she's Penny's mother."

"You're not the only one. Anyway, Penny was so mad, she risked her job to call that supervisor out and he was let go." She turned and shot him a small smile. "I had been terrified for her and Holt. We all had. And there she was, safe, fighting mad, and willing to accept the consequences for doing the right thing. And you know what I did?"

He frowned, confused. "No. What?"

"I hid. I was subtle about it, but I made sure I wasn't in the line of sight of the cameras. Because with Geneva Queen around, you can better believe there are going to be cameras and a national news report. I couldn't take a chance . . ."

"Of course you couldn't. You did the right thing."

"Then why do I still cringe when I think about it?" She scrubbed a hand over her face. "Penny didn't run," she whispered. "She faced down a serial killer, her mother, and the possibility of losing her job—without seeming to flinch."

"She flinched."

Raina sighed. "I know, but that's true courage. Facing what you want to run from." She glanced up at him. "I want to be courageous like that."

"I'd say you're already there."

"Ha. I wish." She shook her head. "I'm terrified of everything, Vince, I'm just very good at hiding it." She swallowed and Vince reached out to grasp her fingers. Raina met his gaze. "I've made up my mind, though. I'm not hiding anymore. I'm scared, but I'm not hiding and I'm not running."

He'd almost prefer she hide. "Raina, let me just be clear here. If you don't let me help you, I'm not going to be much good to anyone."

"What? Why?"

"Because I'll be too worried about you!"

She groaned, then looked at him with a frown. "You're not above using guilt trips, I see."

"It's not a guilt trip, Raina. It's just fact." He sighed. "Look, I don't want to come across like I'm pushing myself on you or forcing you to let me help, however, I'm here if you need—or want—it." He paused.

"Thank you. I think."

"How about we compromise. Let me start by doing something that's related to my job. Let me try to find Kevin." He was going to try anyway, but really wanted her on board with this.

"Ugh!" She dropped her head to study her hands. Finally, she looked up and nodded. "Okay, you win, but if you can't do it using your resources, then I plan to use myself as bait."

Vince blinked. "I'm sorry, what? I thought you said you were going to use yourself as bait. But that's crazy, so I must have heard wrong." Her gaze didn't waver, so he shook his head. "No way. I don't think we need to resort to that yet."

"We?"

"Yes." He narrowed his eyes at her. "You just agreed to let me help. You're not doing anything alone, remember?"

She raised a brow and a flash of anger glinted at him before she snuffed it, but her nostrils flared and he realized he'd messed up—especially in light of what she'd just shared with him about her controlling and abusive ex. "Look," he said, hoping to backtrack. "You're a big girl and can do what you want, obviously. It's not my place to say what you can and can't do. I misspoke."

"Yes, you did, but I get where it's coming from." She took a sip of water. "It's okay, really. I'm not the person I was fourteen years ago, and I can stand up to you if I need to. Don't start walking on eggshells with me."

She sounded like she meant it. He'd have to trust she did. "Okay, I won't. I've never been very good at that anyway. So, here's me not walking on eggshells. The whole using-yourself-as-bait thing does have me concerned and I can't just walk away from that. Not if you really mean it."

"I know you can't. And I'm sorry." She raked a hand over her head. "It might not look like it, but I really am smart enough to know that it's a dumb idea. I'm just . . . desperate."

"I know that feeling. So desperate you don't know which way to turn." Boy, did he. "But don't let that feeling make you do something you regret."

"You sound like you speak from experience. Your sister?"

He shrugged. "Yes. And I'll share more of that story with you someday, but for now, I want you to promise you won't do anything without running it past me first." Vince kept his eyes locked on hers, willing her to make the promise. "Please, Raina."

"Okay, yes. Fine. I promise. I don't know what setting myself up for bait even looks like at the moment, so it's a promise I can make." She pressed her lips together, then rubbed her eyes, smearing her mascara under her bottom lashes.

He smiled, dipped his napkin in his water, and grasped her chin with his left hand.

"I rubbed the mascara wrong, didn't I?"

"Yep." He cleaned it up for her but didn't let go of her chin. Still looking into her eyes, he decided to go for it. "I care about you, Raina."

Her eyes widened, then softened. "I . . . uh . . . thank you." She shifted in her seat. "I think I'm ready to go. You?"

He studied her again, trying to read her, and got nothing. "Sure." So, that was that. He'd laid his heart on the line and she was running in spite of her vow not to. A different kind of running, true, but running all the same. He'd let her for now.

Once they'd settled the bill, he stood and guided her toward the door, wishing he could read her mind, but she was as closed off as Fort Knox and he didn't have the key to get in.

■ ■ ■ ■

Once she was through the door, Raina stopped on the steps of the restaurant, the hair on the back of her neck lifting while goose bumps pebbled her skin. From Vince's declaration or something more?

"Raina?"

She blinked and shuddered. "Sorry, I guess I'm spooked." But she couldn't help probing the darkness beyond the edge of the poorly lit parking lot. She rubbed her arms and noted Vincent's narrowed eyes. He stepped closer to her, and she was tempted to let him. Instead, she slipped around him and lifted her head. "It's nothing, I'm sure." She hated the slight shake in her voice.

His hand landed on her arm while he continued to study the area she'd been watching. "Don't discount your instincts. They're there for a reason."

Old feelings, fears, and insecurities washed over Raina, and she stood there, still focused on the area in the distance. Beyond the parking lot was the four-lane street. Nowhere for someone to hide really. She started walking.

"Where are you going?" Vince caught up with her.

"I don't know, but I'm not going to be afraid."

"That's well and good, but don't be . . ." He stopped.

"Don't be what?" She kept walking. "Stupid?" Raina picked up her pace and so did Vince.

"I wasn't going to use that word. I'd never use that word

with you. But . . . is there a good synonym that doesn't sound so . . . mean?"

"No. But don't worry, I don't plan on doing anything synonymous with stupid."

"Thank you." A sigh reached her. "If you truly think someone's watching you, you can't go after them unprepared."

"I'm prepared," Raina said, her voice soft, her eyes searching the faces of the people on the sidewalk and those in the cars on the street. Then she saw someone pause, look right at her, then dip into the alley across the street. "There."

"Where?"

"Follow me. And for the record, I've been in preparation mode for more than a decade." She didn't have a timetable, she didn't have a target. But she'd known this moment, this season, would arrive at some point. And she'd been determined to be ready.

"I see."

Did he? She wasn't so sure. She reached the crosswalk and waited for the cars to pass, then hurried across, aiming herself at the alley.

Vince fell silent but stayed on her heels.

She darted into the alley shared by two restaurants and hurried down the length of the buildings, only to come to a stop. They could go left or right, but a chain-link fence kept them from going straight ahead. A gust of wind sent the odor from the large trash bin wafting their way, and Raina held her breath while she spotted Vince's right hand hovering near his weapon.

He held up his left hand. "Listen."

She stood still.

Faint footsteps on the other side of the fence reached her, and her gaze met Vince's. "You think he was watching us?"

"I don't know, but the fact that he stopped to look right at you, then hopped a fence to get away kind of makes me wonder."

"Same here."

"Was it him? Kevin?"

She hesitated, then shrugged. "I don't know." Another pause. "Which is weird because his face is engraved in my memory. Right down to the last detail, such as the very faint scar on the left side of his nose."

"Well, it's dark, and the guy we followed was dressed in baggy clothes, wearing a hat . . ." He lifted a shoulder. "Even I couldn't describe him to a sketch artist if I had to. And it might not have been him."

"It might not have." But if it was, he probably expected an easy target.

She never wanted to see his face again but was *prepared* to deal with him if it should happen.

"Come on," Vince said, "let's get you home."

"Yeah." They walked together back to the restaurant where she got in her car, tapped a text to Penny, who was still at base, and asked about their drunk driver's condition.

He's still in surgery.

> Wife and kids there?

No sign of them.

> Okay, thanks.

She noted Vince waiting and flashed her lights to let him know she was ready, then pulled out of the parking lot, with him following right behind her. She was more touched than she wanted to be at the care he was taking of her. Watching over her. Helping her.

Oh please, God, don't let anything happen to him. I understand what he's saying about you being in charge of what happens, but that doesn't stop me from being anxious about it. Which I know is something you and I probably need to address.

75

She paused in the prayer. *I want to trust you, God, I do. I'm sorry it's so hard for me. I'm trying. So . . . help me. Please.*

■ ■ ■ ■

Simon's phone rang and he rose from the couch to take the call in the sunroom. "Well?"

"I got what you wanted."

"And?"

"There are advantages of having access to a private plane."

"Agreed." He'd planned on selling the plane as soon as possible—even had an interested buyer—but he needed the plane and the pilot for the moment if he was going to have his man going back and forth across the country. Hopefully, everything would be wrapped up before the buyer wanted to do the test flight next week. "You flew there, then what?"

"I went to the kid's home. They're not there. Looks like they're either just gone for the night or a few days. Everything looks normal, though. Neat, tidy, and waiting for them to come back."

"You got in the house?"

"Yeah. Found some stray hairs in what looked like the kid's bathroom, so I bagged them and sent them to be tested."

"Excellent."

"But get this. I talked to one of the neighbors. Told them I was a real estate agent and asked them some questions pertaining to real estate that got them comfortable."

"Are you going somewhere with this?"

"Don't be rude. I wouldn't tell you if I didn't have a point."

Simon drew in a deep breath and pressed his fingers to his eyes. "Right. Sorry."

"That's better. Anyway, I asked them if they knew when their neighbor would be home and that I had an interested buyer for their home. Of course they had to point out that the house wasn't for sale, but anyway, long story short, I found out that the little family of three took off like stealth ninjas and never said where they were going or when they'd be back."

Simon raised a brow. "Okay."

"Here's what I think. I think the mother saw the same footage you saw and warned the family that Keith might come looking for their kid."

A cold feeling settled in the pit of his stomach. "I see. And you think they ran because of that?"

"I don't think it's a stretch."

No. No, it wasn't. "Did you find out who the mother is?"

"Now, that's another story. Went from Colorado to a lawyer's office in Burbank. Old-fashioned kind of dude. Kept a lot of his files in a huge cabinet on the wall."

"Do you think I really care?"

"Come on, Simon. We've already had the chat about being rude. If you want to hear this, let me tell it my way."

Drawing on every ounce of what little patience he had, Simon gritted his teeth. "Please, continue."

"That's better. Anyway, I found the name of the woman."

"Is she anyone who might be a problem?"

"It doesn't look like it. Her name's—"

"I don't want to know what her name is. I just want you to know." He had no use for anyone his son may have dated in the past. Not even the *possible* biological mother of his *possible* only grandchild. "Assuming the child is Keith's—and I won't admit he is until the results come back—but, just assuming . . . I wonder why she didn't tell Keith about the baby. Surely, she had to know she could get a fortune out of him."

"You're sure she didn't tell him?"

He flashed back to his son's reaction at seeing the boy on the television. "Positive."

"It could be she didn't want him to know about the child because . . . well, because."

"Because Keith is Keith and she knew it? Yes. Possibly.

Which would fit with her warning them that he might come after the boy." And she wasn't wrong. Keith wanted his son. He could see it all over his face. Simon hesitated once more, then pursed his lips and blew out a soft puff of air. "The fact remains, she could potentially cause a lot of problems for my family. In fact, while she might not know it just yet, she could devastate us in so many ways." Mostly financial, but almost even worse, she could destroy his family name if she was able to finger Keith as someone who hurt her in the past. And Simon had no doubt Keith had done something to her. After all, she'd been pregnant and not told Keith about the baby. And she'd put the child up for adoption, then dropped off the radar of life. "I'm not sure I want that kind of threat hanging over my head."

"Don't get ahead of yourself just yet. We've got the DNA. Let's see what happens from here on out. If we need to do some cleanup, we will."

"Right. Right." He nodded. "Yes. I agree. Let's hold off on any further action until the results come back." He scrubbed a hand down the side of his face. "But keep an eye on her. Make sure you know what's happening and what she's doing. And like you said, if we need to do some cleanup, we can make that happen."

"You're sure you don't want to know more about her?"

"I'm sure." In this instance, the less he knew, the better. Depending on what had to be done. "As long as she doesn't appear to be looking for trouble, leave her be."

"Got it."

Simon hung up, his mind spinning with everything. And he couldn't help wondering if he was doing the right thing by doing nothing. He turned to head back into the den and found Leslie standing in the open door.

She met his gaze. "Sorry. I didn't mean to interrupt."

"Not at all. Something I can help you with?"

She held up a gold pen. "You left this on the end table. I didn't want you to wonder where it was if you went looking for it."

He took it from her with a smile. "Thanks." He never went anywhere without the pen, given to him by his late wife on their last anniversary before her death. Tucking the pen into his shirt pocket, he followed her back into the den.

"Everything okay?" she asked him.

"Yes, hon. Everything is fine."

"Good." She kissed his cheek and walked out of the room.

He'd been blessed with an amazing daughter-in-law. Simon sighed and let the smile fall from his lips. Everything was definitely *not* fine. But it would be. Soon. And if there was anything he had to say about it, he would be blessed with two amazing daughters-in-law. The newest one with enough money to bail him out of his current financial mess and keep his family's name out of the gutter.

CHAPTER
EIGHT

Once Raina was parked in her spot in the garage, Vince pulled into her drive with every intention of following her inside to make sure her home was clear. If she'd let him. Thankfully, she didn't lower the garage door before she climbed out of her vehicle and turned to face him. "I'm fine. I promise."

"Can I clear your house?"

"Seriously?"

"Seriously."

She studied him for a moment, seemed about to refuse the offer, then nodded. "Okay. Sure." She walked back into the garage, and Vince followed her, relieved she hadn't put up a fuss about him doing so.

"We'll go in through this door," he said. "I'll clear the house, and then go out the front door. At which point—"

"I'll set the alarm."

"Good."

She pressed the button on the wall and waited until the door was down, then she walked inside while Vince shut the door behind him. He paused a moment, breathing in the scent of lavender and something else that was uniquely Raina. A cross between vanilla and—

"Essential oils?" he asked.

"Yep. Love them."

He did too now. "You'll have to give me the name of what you use so I can get some."

She raised a brow. "Seriously?"

"Absolutely."

Her lips curled in a small smile. "I'll text the names to you."

"Thanks. All right, closet to the left." He gestured. "May I?"

"Of course."

He opened it, then shut it. Raina let him pass her and the washer and dryer and step into the kitchen.

"Nice kitchen," he said.

"Thanks. It's one of the reasons I rented the place." The kitchen led into the den she'd set up with two couches and a large-screen television mounted over the fireplace. The place was cozy and warm. He hadn't expected that for some reason.

Vince held a hand out to her. "Stay here, okay?"

"Vince, no one is in here."

"And I'll feel better once I've proven that. I just need to do the two bedrooms and the bath and we'll be good, all right?"

She planted both hands on her hips but nodded. "Okay."

It didn't take him long to make his rounds through the other rooms and come back into the den area. "All clear."

"Thank you."

"I wouldn't have been able to sleep tonight if I'd not done that," he said, "so thanks for letting me."

She smiled. "Well, I appreciate it. Now, go home and get some rest."

"I'm going. Set the alarm?"

She walked him to the front door. "Setting it."

He slipped out onto the porch, turned, and looked into her green eyes. "Call me if you need me?"

"I . . . will."

"You're making progress."

She laughed. "I'm trying. Good night, Vince."

"Night."

He shut the door behind him and waited until he heard the faint beeps of the alarm being set, then started toward his car.

Then paused.

Raina's story had struck more than an emotional chord with him, it had rung a few memory cells. And now that he had a few minutes—because he wasn't comfortable with leaving just yet—he pulled his cell phone from his pocket and dialed Holt's number.

"Satterfield."

"Holt."

"Hey, Vince, what's up?"

"I have a question for you about a case I remember you talking about."

"Sure. Shoot."

Vince rubbed his head, trying to get his thoughts in order. Should have done that before he dialed the number. "All right," he finally said. "About four years ago, there was a young woman who was found beaten to death in her apartment. I only remember it because it was the second woman found in a similar manner even though their deaths were six months apart. And then you found yet another woman, same MO. All in different cities. You wondered if you had a serial killer."

"Yeah," Holt said, "of course I remember those cases. Then the deaths stopped and that was that."

"But you never found who did it, right?"

"Right. All three families thought it might have been a boyfriend, but they'd never met the guy and had never seen a picture of him. The names they gave us were different and seemed to be bogus. Local detectives chased it for a while, consulted with us, then eventually, the cases rolled to the cold case department—and then one more came to light about two months ago."

"Really?"

"Someone finally entered the case details into VICAP, and it pinged as a match to the other three. Three years ago, a woman was beaten to death, but the boyfriend disappeared without a trace. No pictures on social media, no friends remember meeting him, nothing. Exactly the same as the other three. And because they were in three different states, we got pulled in."

An ominous shudder rippled through Vince. "Would you mind sharing everything you have on those cases? They sound an awful lot like a case that I was just told about. I'll fill you in a little later once I have all the details."

"Sure. I'll send them on. Let me know if you find anything. I'd love to catch this guy if he's still out there."

"Will do. Thanks." Vince hung up and did a walk around Raina's home. All looked peaceful and calm from his perspective, so he climbed in his truck, keeping his gaze on the home. Lights shone around the plantation shutters and a glow came from the master bedroom at the far end of the house. He cranked the truck and shot one last look at the house. "Keep her safe, Lord, please?"

■ ■ ■ ■

Raina locked the door to the garage she and Vince had entered. Normally, she left it unlocked, but after the incident with the man outside the restaurant, she'd feel better with it secured. With that done, she snagged her laptop from the kitchen counter, walked into the den, and aimed the remote at the television.

Settled on the couch, she opened the laptop and did a search for Kevin Anderson, then clicked images. And, of course, got nothing. She huffed a sigh, leaned her head back against the cushion, and closed her eyes.

And heard a noise.

She froze, opened her eyes, and listened. Then closed the laptop and rose. Grace's story about the intruder who'd broken into her house and tried to kill her flipped through her mind. But . . . no. It wasn't possible. Vince had cleared her home and she'd set the alarm. No one was in her house.

And yet . . .

She grabbed the heavy crystal vase from the end table and walked toward the kitchen. Peered inside. Empty. The house was older and not the popular open floor plan, but Raina had never felt like she needed that. She liked her cozy rooms, although right now, she'd give anything to be able to see into every square inch of her home.

Still, the closet just inside the entrance from her garage was cracked. And she had a mental picture of Vince closing it after checking it.

A slight scuff sounded from the hall.

She snagged her phone, fumbled it, and it landed with a thud on the hardwood floor. She ran to the front door, twisted the lock, even while she glanced down the hallway to see a dark figure step out of her bedroom. A scream escaped her, but she yanked on the doorknob and jerked the door open just as a hard hand landed on her right wrist.

While the home alarm warning went off, instinct—and years of practice—kicked in. She spun and jammed the palm of her left hand at the man's nose. It was just a graze, as her aim was off, but he cried out and stumbled back, releasing her arm. She tumbled out the door and onto the front porch, then down the steps. The man lunged after her.

Her left ankle twisted beneath her and she went down hard. As he reached for her, she rolled, wanting to scream but not willing to waste the breath.

"Raina! Hey! Get away from her!"

Her attacker paused for a brief second. Long enough for her to kick out and land a heel on his shin. He yelped and staggered backward. Then spun and raced down the street toward the subdivision's exit.

"Vince!" She had no idea why he was still there, but she was grateful.

"Are you okay?"

"Yes!"

As soon as he had her confirmation, he raced after the guy.

"Vince! No!" No, no, no, no. What if—

She rolled to her feet. Her ankle twinged but held her weight, and she bolted after Vince and the intruder. By the time she rounded the corner, Vince was stopped between two fences, his head swiveling, phone pressed to his ear.

"Where'd he go?" she asked.

"I don't know. Probably found an open garage or front door. I keep waiting for someone to come out of their house or—" He directed his attention back to his phone. "Yeah, I'm here. Sorry." After providing the address, he tucked the phone into his pocket and ran a hand down his face. "They're sending units to search, and I'm going to stand right here in case he shows his face."

"Well, if he does, it'll have a mask on it." Or he'd take it off to keep from attracting attention?

"How did he get in? I cleared the place, you had the alarm on."

She sucked in a breath and blew it out slowly. "That's an easy answer. He was already in there when you cleared the place."

"But that's not possible. Your house isn't that big. Where could he have been hiding?"

She shook her head, her mind spinning, adrenaline crashing. "The same way he got into my parents' house in California."

"What do you mean?"

"He must have already been in the garage when I pulled in." She shrugged. "I don't normally keep the kitchen door locked because I always have my garage closed, but it wasn't until after you cleared the house and left that I locked it."

"So, he came in the back as I was leaving out the front."

"And slipped into that closet just inside the door. I noticed it was cracked, but didn't—" She blew out a shuddering breath. "He managed to get into my bedroom without me noticing." The mental image of him coming out and down the hall sent a shaft of nausea through her. She shivered, turned on her good heel, and headed back to her house just in time to see the first cruiser pulling to a stop at the curb.

Vince stayed on her heels, and for the next hour, they gave their statements while the officers examined her house. All in all, it was over before she could blink, and now she sat on her couch trying to wrap her head around everything.

After seeing the officers out, Vince sat next to her and took her hand.

"I was scared," she said, her voice low.

"I would have been too. Anyone would have been."

"But I handled him. Up to a point anyway." She looked at him. "I don't know what I would have done if you hadn't been here."

"Like you said, you handled him."

But would she have been able to get away in the end? She wasn't sure. "Not that I'm not grateful, but why *were* you here? I thought you'd left."

"I almost did, then I decided to take a look around outside your house, look for any vulnerable issues. I really didn't see anything or anyone, so I got in my truck. Even cranked it. But then couldn't leave you. Not after that weirdness at the restaurant. Just as I cut the engine off and settled in for the night, you came slamming out of the front door with the Hulk not far behind."

She shuddered. "He *was* a big guy, wasn't he?"

"Very."

"It wasn't Kevin."

"You're sure?"

"Yes. Kevin is about six feet tall, but he's lean. That guy was bulked with muscle like he works out on a daily basis and has a little help staying that way." She paused. "Not that Kevin couldn't have developed different habits since I last saw him, but as much as he claimed to hate the gym—" She sighed and rubbed her head. "Unless that was a lie too. I don't know."

"It's most likely he stuck to the truth as much as possible in order not to trip over his lies. So, it's very possible he loved snowboarding and hated the gym. And if you say the intruder wasn't Kevin, then trust that instinct."

"I quit trusting my instincts a long time ago," she muttered, thinking about how she questioned and second-guessed every decision. Kevin had done that to her. And she'd let him.

She lifted her chin. "I need to put him in the rearview mirror, Vince. I have to. No more running, no more looking over my shoulder and being paranoid that he's going to be there when I turn around. I want him out of my thoughts, my life, my . . . whatever. I want him gone."

"Then let's do whatever we have to do to make that happen."

■ ■ ■ ■

TUESDAY MORNING

Seated at his desk at the office, Vince shook himself, realizing he'd been staring at his computer with his fingers resting on the keyboard, but he couldn't get the incident with the intruder in Raina's house out of his head. When he asked her to let him help her, she'd flinched.

Then nodded.

An agonizing, slow nod, as though she had to battle to make her head move. But it had definitely been a nod. So . . . progress. Now, he was doing more than just looking for Kevin. He was going to make sure he kept her safe. He'd made a few notes on how best to do that, and right now, he was waiting for Holt to send him everything related to Raina's case.

In the meantime, she'd gone in to work in spite of his desire that she not. Then again, being at the base and surrounded by coworkers was probably one of the safest places she could be.

So, first things first.

He glanced at the clock while he sipped his second cup of coffee for the morning. He had time to run a little errand before heading out to the hospital to babysit Fedorov.

Twenty minutes later, he pulled into the alley where the man they'd been after had disappeared. Vince exited his vehicle and walked up to the fence. He climbed over it and landed with a thud on the other side into the overgrown weeds, grass, and bushes. He didn't really expect to find anything but couldn't help wondering where their "fugitive" had emerged. Broken branches and other debris gave evidence that the man from last night had pushed through. So Vince did the same, and following the path—although *path* was definitely an exaggeration—he came out behind one of the other buildings. The only way back onto the street was via another side alley. He took it, scanning the area. And stopped when his eyes landed on a camera attached to the corner of the end building. A liquor store. An idea formed and he hurried inside the shop.

"Help you?" The guy behind the counter was in his late sixties, with a full silver beard, a shiny bald head, and kind eyes.

Vince approached with his hands at his side and a smile on his face. "Yeah, I hope so." There was only one other person in the store, so Vince leaned in. "Last night, there was a guy who may have been stalking a friend of mine. We chased him into the back alley a couple of doors down, but he vaulted over the fence and came out around the corner of this place."

The man raised a brow. "No kidding."

"I came back to kind of scope things out and noticed your camera on that side. I was wondering if—"

"I'd show you the footage?"

"Please."

"You being straight with me?"

"Would it help if I showed you my badge?" He wasn't here on official business and didn't want to come across like he was.

"You a cop?"

"US Marshal, but honestly, the guy I'm looking for isn't a fugitive. At least not one I'm officially after. It's possible it's not even who I think it is." He shrugged. "I won't know until I can see the footage."

More hesitation on the man's part. The bell over the door signaled someone entering, and Vince glanced at the mirror over the counter to see two guys who looked well under the age of legal. He turned and eyed them. They stopped. Looked at him, then each other, then bolted back outside.

The man at the register chuckled. "I guess you are law enforcement." He glanced toward the back. "Hey, Simone!"

Seconds later, a young woman with purple hair poked her head out of the back room. "What you need, Crank?"

"Come watch the register. I need to check something on the computer."

"Sure." She approached, eyeing Vince, who remained silent.

"And let me know if Dumb and Dumber come back in."

She groaned. "Seriously? When are they going to figure out they're not getting anything from here?"

"They're regulars?" Vince asked.

Crank nodded. "They hang out on the corner at The Game Room a lot after school." The Game Room was a popular spot for families, but most especially teens after school. "Dumb is the mayor's nephew and Dumber's dad is a cop. Those boys come in here thinking I'm going to break down and sell them alcohol." He shook his head. "It's getting ridiculous."

"You talk to their parents?"

"I did."

Vince raised a brow and followed the man into the office. "And?"

"And nothing. If those parents said anything to the boys, it didn't have any effect." He waved a hand. "I just keep chasing them off. Figure they'll get tired of it and go somewhere else. I do worry that they'll come in and steal something when I'm not here, but"—he shrugged—"nothing much I can do about that." He smirked. "But they're just one reason why I have great security and working cameras. What time would you say this happened?"

"Around 7:30 last night."

His fingers flew over the keyboard and Vince glanced at his watch, then texted Charlie that he might be slightly late, but was working on something.

Charlie
Got you covered, man. No problem.

"Okay," Crank said, "I think I've got what you need. Take a look."

Vince stepped forward and peered at the screen. The footage played, and it didn't take long to see the man he and Raina had chased come into view. And the one behind him. Just a shadow, but he was there. Interesting. He focused on the first one. "Yeah, that's him." Vince watched, looking for a good angle. "Come on, come on, show me your face."

Finally, as the guy rounded the corner, he looked up and Vince got a profile of him. "There. Can you give me a printout of that?"

"Sure can." In seconds, the printer whirred and Crank handed him the picture. "It's not great, but I think that's the best one you're going to get."

"I agree. Any way to see who the guy is behind him? I don't know that he's important, but I'd like to see him if I could."

Crank narrowed his eyes. "Possibly." He clicked a few more keys and zoomed in on the shadow that turned into a man. A blurry one, but enough that if Vince saw him on the street, he'd recognize him.

"You want a picture of him too?"

"Nah, I got the one I needed." He met the man's eyes. "Thank you for your help."

Crank shrugged. "I can read people pretty well. You came across legit."

"I'm legit, I promise. Just trying to keep someone safe."

"I hope you can."

Vince tucked the picture into his pocket, thanked the man again, then headed for his vehicle. Once he was connected to his Bluetooth, he snapped a picture of the hard copy, then sent the digital picture to Amanda Wright. She was part of TOG, the Technical Operations Group that handled a lot of the tech stuff for him and Charlie. He called her right after the picture went through.

"Wright here."

"Hey, Amanda, I just sent you a picture. Can you see if you can get a hit with the facial recognition software?"

"Sure. What case is this related to?"

"I'm not sure it's an official case yet, but if I'm right, then this guy is a possible serial killer."

"Whoa. All righty then. I'm on it. I'll let you know if anything pops."

"Thanks." By the time he hung up, he had reached the exit for the hospital. The same hospital where Raina worked. He might have to make a side trip to base to check on her. Not that he would *call* it checking on her, as she would probably balk at the idea she *needed* checking on, but . . . he'd figure out a reason to go by there.

When he made his way to Fedorov's room, he found Charlie just outside the door talking on the phone. At Vince's approach, the man said his goodbyes and hung up. "They're getting ready to release Fedorov. I just made arrangements for an escort. Should be here within an hour."

"Good. How is he?"

"Fine. Bet he won't make that mistake again."

"I'm just glad he had the EpiPen in plain sight."

Charlie shook his head. "How did that *life-threatening* allergy slip through the cracks in his profile? We're always supposed to know that stuff."

"I don't know, but I'm sure it will be a topic at the next training meeting."

So much for going to see Raina. He shut down his disappointment and focused on doing his job. At least until his phone buzzed ten minutes later. "Hello?"

"Yeah, hey, this is Amanda. I think I have an ID on that guy for you."

"That was fast. Who is he?"

"His name is Freddy Harper. He's a private investigator out of California."

CHAPTER
NINE

Tuesday morning, before her shift, Raina found herself at the hospital gym, hoping that by going through all her self-defense moves, she'd emerge in a better frame of mind with her confidence restored. Someone had managed to get into her house and most likely would have killed her if Vince hadn't been there. The thought still sent shudders rippling through her. After a shower and a power bar, she checked her phone and headed to base.

Raina pushed through the door to find Penny on the floor, rag in hand.

"Hey," Penny said, looking up.

"Hey. What in the world are you doing down there?"

"I spilled syrup. We're going to be cleaning that up for the next two weeks."

"Ugh."

Penny sighed and stood. "No kidding. How are you this morning?"

"I'm . . . okay. I think."

Penny's expression immediately morphed into concern. "What is it?"

She filled her friend in on the events of the previous evening, and Penny's eyes widened with each word. "Raina! Why are you here at work? You should be at home, taking it easy."

"You know as well as I do that staying home isn't an option. All I'd do is pace and think. And create scenarios in my head that would have me more wigged out than I already am."

Penny shook her head. "I guess."

"So . . . I'm going to go over the checklist and—"

"Already did that. Dr. K just called and said the ER needs all hands on deck. An eighteen-wheeler went head-to-head with a passenger bus about ten minutes ago, and while there are no reported fatalities, the ER is getting ready to be overrun. You're on the trauma unit."

"Got it." Raina stashed her stuff in her locker and headed for the ER.

For the next hour, she worked nonstop, but in spite of her busyness, she noticed that the workout hadn't done much for her concentration level. She kept revisiting the intruder last night, trying to remember every last detail. Which was not a good thing when patients were counting on her to focus.

Hours later, when some of the urgency died down, she had a moment to grab a much-needed break. Her protein bar had long since worn off and she was starving. She headed for base and the refrigerator, craving something healthy and filling. Chopped chicken salad, a side of fruit, crackers, and a small bowl of strawberry ice cream were on the menu.

Holly followed her into the kitchen. "Hey."

Raina shut the refrigerator, balancing the items she'd just pulled out. "Hey." Holly grabbed the bowl of chicken salad from the top of the stack and set it on the counter. Once Raina emptied her hands, she turned to the woman. "Slow day today. Well, not the ER obviously, but here."

"I can't believe you just said that."

"I'm not superstitious." Mention how slow it was and it was bound to get busy.

"I'm not either," Holly said, "but the correlation between those words and our workload can be downright freaky."

She wasn't wrong. "Okay, I take it back."

"Too late." Holly hesitated and Raina frowned at her.

"What is it?"

Holly smirked. "Just waiting for the alarm to sound."

"Oh stop, what's going on?"

"That's my question for you. Discounting what happened last night, I mean. Penny told me about it and also assured me you were okay."

"I am." At least for now.

"So?"

Raina quirked an eyebrow at her friend. "So what?"

"You and Vince? In the kitchen the other night for a long time? Then when you came out, you were both frowning, and while he couldn't take his eyes off of you, you wouldn't look at him? What's the scoop?"

Raina gaped. "Seriously? Are you looking to join Grace at the Bureau as a behavioral analyst?"

"No. Those were actually Grace's observations. I was just trying them out on you."

Raina didn't know whether to laugh or walk away. She chose to roll her eyes. "I have no idea what you're talking about."

"She said you'd avoid talking about it."

"Ugh!" Raina barely refrained from stomping her foot. "You two are the worst. Talking about me behind my back." Holly simply watched her and Raina sighed. "Okay, I know you weren't being mean about it and that you're concerned. Rest assured, I also know I've been acting weird." She shrugged. "But I'm not ready to talk about it yet. At least not until I have more to go on."

"More to go on?"

Raina bit her lip and Holly nodded. "Okay, no talking about it. But Vince knows?"

"He knows . . . some."

"Then as long as someone's got your back, that's all that matters." A flash of hurt flickered in Holly's gaze before she turned away. Raina dropped her chin to her chest. Why was she doing this to one of her best friends? Someone she could trust with anything? She'd known Vince for only a little over a year and she'd spilled most of her life story to him in the span of a thirty-minute conversation. Well . . . not *everything*, but more than she would have ever thought possible. "Holly, wait. Stop." She'd promised to talk to her friends about this even if she hadn't talked to Vince.

Holly turned.

"I have a past that I'm not really proud of," Raina said, her voice low.

Holly wrinkled her nose. "Most of us do."

"I know, but for some reason it's easier to listen to others share than it is to be the one sharing."

"Raina, we know your past. You were in juvie with Penny, Grace, and Julianna. We also know how you, like them, overcame so much to be the wonderful, amazing person you are today. What is it you're so ashamed of?"

Raina opened her mouth to respond, then snapped it shut, holding back her knee-jerk response.

Time to come clean.

"Raina?"

Raina pressed a hand to her temple, the sudden stress-induced pounding there making her wince. "What am I so ashamed of?"

"Yes."

"Hey, guys," Penny said, bounding through the door, "what are we doing for—" She stopped, her gray eyes taking in the scene. "Oookay . . . ," she drew the word out, "what's going on here?"

Holly stayed still, letting Raina handle the interruption. Raina wasn't sure whether to thank her or not. Finally, she tossed her hands up. "Okay, you two, it's time we had a talk."

She motioned to the conference room where she could shut the door and make sure no one else in base overheard.

Once she had her two curious and concerned friends behind the locked door, Raina clasped her hands together and faced them. "So, when I showed up here with a different name and begging for a job, you guys didn't ask a lot of questions. Well, I didn't know you, Holly, so you wouldn't have known any different, but"—she drew in a deep breath—"Penny, you welcomed me right in, no questions asked."

"You said you had a stalker and that's why you changed your name." Penny frowned. "I had no reason to believe otherwise."

"I know. And it was true. I never lied. I just . . . didn't tell you the whole story."

"And you don't have to now if you don't want to." Penny reached out and squeezed Raina's hand.

"Yes, she does," Holly said. "I want to know."

Penny scowled. "No, she doesn't. As long as it doesn't directly affect us, it's not necessary."

Holly's mournful sigh was almost enough to make Raina smile. Almost. The woman was more curious than a cat, but as much as it would kill her, she wouldn't press it if Raina was serious.

"It doesn't directly affect you," Raina said, "but . . . you're my friends and, in answer to Holly's question, what I'm so ashamed of is the fact that I haven't trusted you like you've trusted me. And I'm sorry for that."

Penny frowned. "What do you mean?"

"I mean . . . there are things in my past that I've never told you, and I'm ashamed that I hid those things from people who've trusted me and shared with me. I'm ashamed that I didn't return that trust." A tear slipped down her cheek and Penny gasped.

"Raina, my friend, oh, honey, it's okay." Penny wrapped her arms around Raina's shoulders, and Holly joined her, the two women squeezing until she couldn't breathe.

When they finally released her, Raina stepped back. "It's just really hard for me to let people in, because every time I do, someone winds up getting hurt." Or dead. She pushed that thought away, honestly confused about what she should say and how much she should share. But the truth was, her past was just that. In the past. She could start trusting again. Sharing and letting people see the real her. Couldn't she?

Holly met her gaze with tears shimmering in her own eyes. "I didn't mean to be pushy, Raina. You never have to talk about or say anything you don't want to. Your past is yours. Not mine. So keep it to yourself and I promise never to say another word about it."

Raina nearly choked on the emotion swelling in her throat. She drew in a ragged breath. "Okay, let me pull myself together, then I'll share with you what I shared with Vince." She glanced at the clock. She'd have to be quick. "I'm going to fix lunch while I talk because my break is almost over." She glanced at them. "You want some too?"

"Absolutely."

Thirty minutes later, she was done and so was her break. Penny and Holly expressed their complete support, and most of Raina's guilt was put to rest.

Most of it.

But not all.

■ ■ ■ ■

Armed with a background report on Freddy Harper—which wasn't anything hair raising, but still interesting—Vince left Charlie and hospital security guarding Fedorov and went to find Raina. He located her in the emergency room, but she was involved with a patient, so he waited and simply watched her work. And while he watched her, he watched her back, scanning the people in the ER, patients and staff both. They were busy—and it looked like they were short a few workers. If Raina had to take off in the chopper, the ER would be hurting.

But for now, they worked. Tirelessly. From crying babies, to screaming toddlers, to wilting parents. And then there were the car accident victims, one gunshot wound, and the heart attack.

Raina finally stopped to grab her drink from the counter and chug the contents. When she lowered the cup, her eyes landed on his and she smiled. Then tilted her head and walked over to him. "Hey. Everything okay?"

"Yeah, just waiting on you to catch a break."

"I had one a few hours ago." She glanced at the iPad she held. "But I can take another short one." She waved to one of the other nurses. "I'm taking a little break. I'll be back in about ten minutes."

The man nodded and Raina led Vince into a private room just outside the doors of the ER. She turned to him and blinked. Then rubbed her eyes and yawned. "I'm sorry. For some reason, I'm more tired than I should be." She cleared her throat.

"You were going ninety miles an hour in there. I would have fallen over by now."

"Oh stop." She yawned again and coughed.

"You getting sick?"

"No, I just n-need something to drink. I left my c-cup out there, but . . ." She walked to the water cooler in the corner and swayed.

"Hey, Raina. You okay?"

"I . . . I'm n-not sure." She turned and wobbled. Her arm shot out to brace herself against the wall. "I don't feel . . . right . . . Vince . . ."

"You're slurring your words." He gripped her forearms and lowered her into the nearest chair.

"I . . . I . . ." She sucked in hard—or tried to. Her gaze met his, panic swirling in the depths. "Vince . . . can't . . . breathe

. . . help . . . think drug . . ." Her eyes rolled up in her head and she was out.

Vince didn't waste time by hollering at her to stay awake. He gently eased her to the floor, then bolted out of the room in search of a doctor. "Hey! Hey! I need some help in here!" A doctor spun and every eye in the place turned toward him. "Got a woman who can't breathe! Possibly drugged!" The vision of her swigging the drink just before she led him to the private room played in his head.

Two hospital personnel bolted after him. No doubt flashing his badge helped get the immediate response. He led them to her, then stood back while they dropped to the floor next to her.

Vince raked both hands through his hair.

The nearest doctor turned to him. "What did she take?"

"I don't know, but she was slurring her words and her balance was off right before she passed out. I'll be right back." He raced out of the room and headed for the ER.

"Vince?"

Penny's voice spun his head to the left.

"What's going on?" She hurried toward him while he never broke his stride.

"I think someone drugged Raina."

"What!"

"Get me a glove and a paper bag?" he said as he spied Raina's cup still sitting on the counter where she'd left it and rushed toward it.

With questions burning in her eyes, Penny handed him the items he'd requested. He donned the glove, then used a pen to hook the handle and slide the cup into the bag. "Tape?"

A wide-eyed nurse pushed a roll to him.

Once he'd taped and labeled the bag, he tossed the glove into the trash and bolted back toward the room where he'd left Raina in the hands of those who would help her. "Please, God, let her be okay."

Penny stayed on his heels, and together they arrived just as Raina was being transferred from the floor to a bed.

"Gayle, how is she?" Penny asked the dark-haired woman hooking an IV to a rolling pole.

"Respiration is depressed. Oxygen seems to be helping. We don't know what she took, but we sent blood to be analyzed ASAP. Should know something—" Her phone pinged and she glanced at it. "GHB. It's GHB."

The doctor nodded. "Let's get some diclofenac in her." He grasped the rail of the gurney. "Out of the way, people. Head to room 5."

Penny touched his arm. "I'm going to let Dr. Kirkpatrick know what's going on. He'll have to call in another paramedic to take Raina's place. If she wakes up before I get back, reassure her that everything is taken care of. She'll worry."

"Sure. Of course." He fell into step behind the gurney while Penny took off for the elevator. He gripped the evidence bag, his mind already churning through the next steps to take to find out who'd drugged her. He tapped a speed-dial number that went to his buddy Clay, hoping the guy would answer. As a school resource officer, he wasn't always available, but he had contacts in the department and Vince wanted the best on this.

"Vince, what's up?" Clay answered halfway through the second ring.

"Someone drugged Raina. This is a police matter. I know you have resources with the local police department that I don't have. Do you have a contact here in Asheville that you could ask to come over to Mission downtown campus?"

"Wait. What? Drugged Raina?"

"I'll explain later. Right now, doctors are working on her to make sure she keeps breathing and minimize the effects of the drug. I need cops to get security footage and track this person down."

"Okay. Right. Wow. I'll call Gabrielle Perez. She's a detective buddy of mine."

"Great. I'll be looking for her." He hung up and stalked to room 5, where he stopped just outside and leaned against the wall to text Charlie an update. Once that was done, he called his supervisor and asked for someone to take his spot ASAP, since he was going to be busy giving his statement and making sure Raina was taken care of. The man granted it.

And then Vince bowed his head and prayed.

After what felt like a lifetime, but was only fifteen minutes later according to the clock on his phone, the doctor emerged.

"How is she?" Vince asked.

"Stable. Breathing better. Hopefully, in an hour or so, she'll wake up."

"Thanks."

The doctor walked toward the nurses' station, and Vince caught sight of Penny and Holly heading his way.

"Is she okay?" Holly asked.

"Yeah. Or she will be."

Penny rubbed the worry lines creasing her forehead. "How in the world did she get dosed with GHB?"

He held up the cup. "I think in this. She was drinking out of it earlier."

"She always has a cup of water going," Penny said. "Keeps it on the counter at the workstation. Anyone could get access to it if they really wanted to."

"And apparently someone did."

Holly frowned. "But why? Who would do such a thing? Especially to Raina."

"No idea," Penny said. "But I'd give anything to see the security footage."

Vince nodded. "Already ahead of you. As soon as I'm sure Raina's going to be all right, I'm going to ask to watch it."

"I'll stay here," Holly said. "Go watch it."

"You're sure?"

"Of course."

Penny backed toward the elevator. "I'll head back to base. Holly, keep your phone close and text me if there's any change or she wakes up, please?"

"Yes. For sure. And if we get a call, I'll come running."

Penny left and Vince checked in on Raina to find her still unconscious. He squeezed her hand. "I'm going to figure out who did this to you, Raina. Hang in there. I'll be right back."

Vince made his way down to the security office where he located one of the officers sitting in front of the computer, playing the footage for a woman with a badge on her belt. "Gabrielle Perez?" he asked.

"Vince Covelli?"

"That's me." He shook her outstretched hand. "I owe Clay for asking you to come."

"Happy to do it." She nodded to the television screen. "Getting ready to see what we can see."

"All right, let's take a look." The officer clicked a key, and the footage rewound to the moment Raina arrived in the ER and set her cup on the counter next to one of the computer stations. "There's nothing for a while, then this. Watch that person right there." He tapped the screen with his index finger, and Vince narrowed his eyes.

"I can't make the person out."

"I can't either. The footage isn't that bad, but with the scrubs and the white coat, the surgical cap and mask . . ." He shrugged. "I can't even tell if it's male or female."

"What about the badge clipped to his lapel?" Gabrielle asked. "Any way to get the name he used?"

"No, but one of the housekeepers reported her badge missing at 10:02 this morning."

"Right."

"They voided it so that it wouldn't work, of course, but clipped to a coat, it still looks legit."

"And someone would most likely hold the door if he asked," Vince muttered.

"And here," the guard said, pointing at the screen, "is where he puts something in her drink. The desk is empty, no one watching. He takes a syringe from his pocket, snags the drink, and empties the contents into the straw."

Vince scowled. "And puts the drink back without anyone really noticing what he's doing."

"It's busy and everyone is running like crazy to keep up. No one's going to look twice at someone dressed like they belong."

"But he doesn't," Vince said, "and I want to know why he targeted Raina." He paused. "Can you follow his movements through the hospital? Find out where he comes out and possibly takes off his mask?" He glanced at the detective, who watched him with a smile. "Sorry. I guess I should shut up and let you do this?"

"Naw, you're doing fine. If I have a question, I'll ask it."

A knock on the door interrupted them, and two uniformed officers stepped inside at the guard's invitation. "We got a report of a woman who was drugged?"

Vince introduced himself and Gabrielle, then explained he was there when Raina passed out. "Not just drugged. This could have killed her."

Gabrielle laid a hand on his arm and gave the officers a nod. "I don't want to step on any toes, but this is going to get passed up the line. My partner is on his way. You guys good with that?"

The officers exchanged a glance and a shrug. "Sure thing," the nearest one said. They left and Vince rubbed a hand over his eyes.

"You'll want to talk to her when she wakes up," he said, "but in the meantime, there's footage of the person who drugged her."

"Yeah," the guard said, "and now I've got his face. At least I think it's him. There were a couple of places I lost track of him, but he's got the scrubs on, the hat on." He sighed. "I don't know."

Vince looked at the screen. The man had pulled off his mask as soon as he'd exited the hospital. "That's the PI, Freddy Harper, from California." He blinked and leaned forward. "Wait a minute. Who walked out right behind him? He looks familiar."

Gabrielle raised a brow. "Let's run facial rec and see if we can ID him. Where do you know him from?"

"The last piece of security footage I saw Freddy Harper in. That's good enough for me. Let's bring Harper in for questioning."

CHAPTER
TEN

Raina drew in a deep breath and opened her eyes. She found a blurry Vince looking down at her and registered the fact that his left hand held her right. She blinked. Blinked again to finally bring him into focus. "Vince? What's going on?"

Was she slurring her words? And why did she feel like she was reliving a time in her life she never wanted to revisit? Hungover and trying to remember what she'd done. But that was all in the past. She didn't do that anymore, so why—?

"Hey," Vince said, "are you awake this time?"

"What?"

"You've been trying to wake up for the past thirty minutes but kept dozing back off."

She scrambled for a memory to latch on to but came up empty. She swallowed her panic. Vince was here. She was okay. "What happened?"

"Someone drugged you."

Raina digested the words, then pushed past the ripples of shock. "I'm sorry. Did you say drugged me? Why? Who?" She pulled from his grasp and shoved up onto her hands, ignoring the lingering weakness. Vince gripped her biceps and helped her, straightening the pillow behind her. His musky scent wafted around her and she inhaled. "You smell good."

He stilled, then met her gaze. "And you're still drugged so I'm going to forget you noticed."

"You always smell good." Had she really said that out loud? Twice? She giggled.

He laughed. "I'm glad you think so."

"Did you get some essential oils?"

"Not yet."

"Well, you don't need them. Whatever you use is just fine. Come closer."

He did so, his eyes tender, filled with emotion she wanted to explore and run from all at the same time. She breathed in, thankful to be able to do so. Her eyes fluttered shut.

"You going back to sleep?" he asked.

"No." With her eyes still closed, she shook her head and her eyes opened, her still blurry gaze met his, and her hand lifted to touch his cheek. "I like you, Vince," she whispered.

"Ah, Raina, I like you too." He cleared his throat and pulled back a fraction. She frowned in protest. "We will have to revisit this whole situation at a later time—for now, I'm just glad you're okay. What's the last thing you remember?"

"Um . . . talking to you, I think. In the private room off the ER. I . . . felt funny. I remember that."

"Okay, good. Yeah, that was right before you passed out, so you're not missing much." He sat in the chair next to the bed and Raina wished he would come back.

Closer.

So she could get another whiff, maybe even kiss the cheek she'd caressed. "I'm losing it," she whispered.

"Losing what?"

"My mind." She waved a hand. "Hopefully, this will wear off soon. Did anything happen while I was unconscious?"

"Yeah. I think I know who drugged your drink. I just don't know why. The cops are looking for him."

He knew? "Who?"

"A private investigator out of California. His name is Freddy Harper. You ever heard of him?"

"No." But California? A shudder rippled through her. "He's found me, hasn't he? Kevin's hired a PI to find me and now he knows where I am and he's going to finish—"

Vince was by her side, sitting on the bed and holding her hands before she could blink. "He's not going to finish anything."

Raina drew in a shaky breath. "Right. You're right. He's not. But . . ."

"But?"

"But why would a PI drug me or try to kill me? PIs don't usually do that kind of thing, do they?"

"Depends on the PI, I guess—and who they're working for. Just like anyone, there are some who can be bought." His hands squeezed hers and she drew strength from his comfort. "Once the cops track the guy down, they'll find out what's going on. Attempted murder is pretty serious business."

"Attempted murder. Wow."

"I'll admit I'm confused about how he found you. If it was him. I mean you've stayed under the radar for a long time. Years. Then all of a sudden, he's got someone coming after you?"

She rubbed her forehead. "I called that friend in California. Trent Carter. The one I thought might be able to help find the family. Before you jumped in to help. It's possible they were monitoring his phone and traced my number back here."

"Why would they be monitoring his phone?"

"Because he's a friend of my stepfather's—a very good friend. But I thought calling his business line might be some-what . . . safe. But I'm worried about him, to be honest. I really hope he's safe. He sounded so scared when he called."

"And you used your personal cell phone?"

"I did." She pressed a hand to her eyes. "I should have gotten a burner. I know better, but that would have taken time. Time I didn't want to waste, so I risked it." She knew she shouldn't have, but that child . . . *Please protect him, Lord.* "I messed up. For the first time in almost fourteen years, I acted on impulse."

"Panic?"

"Impulse driven by panic, I guess, and it was an unnecessary risk. You were the one who found the family and warned them off." She closed her eyes and wished she could go back in time to make different decisions. But she couldn't. She'd just have to figure out how to live with the current circumstances. Emphasis on *live*.

A knock on the door interrupted them, and Penny and Holly stepped inside. Julianna followed. "Surprise," she said, her voice low and serious.

"Jules!" Raina held her arms out and her friend stepped closer to hug her with a gentle squeeze.

When she leaned back, Julianna shook her head. "You, my friend, had a close call from what I hear."

"I know. I'm grateful it happened in a hospital and that Vince was right there to get help."

Julianna turned to Vince. "And?"

"And they're looking for the guy," he said. "A PI out of California did the deed."

She drew in a deep breath and nodded before turning back to Raina. "Any idea who you've made so mad?"

"That's the million-dollar question, isn't it?"

Her phone rang and she snagged it from the end table where someone had been so thoughtful to put it. She frowned at the strange number. "Hello?"

A throat cleared. "Hello, Brianne."

She froze at the sound of the voice—and the name—she hadn't heard in a little over thirteen years and the breath whooshed from her lungs. "Dad? What are you doing calling me? How'd you get this number?"

Penny, Holly, Julianna, and Vince all looked at her, then one another. One by one they started to slip out of the room, and while she was grateful for the privacy, she didn't want to be alone. As Vince passed her bed, she wanted to grab his hand, but couldn't bring herself to do it. She'd handled things solo for so long, the thought of asking him to do more than he already had made her queasy.

"Brianne? Are you there?"

"I . . . yes . . . I am. I . . . ." And there went her voice. Plugged up and cut off with tears that she refused to shed.

"I don't want to talk too long. This is one of those burner phones that supposedly can't be traced, but these days who knows? But I need to let you know that Trent . . . Trent is . . . ."

"What? What about Trent?" She forced the hoarse words out, dread curling in her stomach, a bad feeling that she knew what was coming.

"He was found dead, Brianne. Murdered. Shot in the head. It happened yesterday."

She gasped. A low, wheezing sound she couldn't stop. "No, please, God, no."

"I'm sorry, but his office was ransacked, his computer stolen. He was mostly working from home but went into the office a couple of days a week. That's why he . . . wasn't found right away. I don't know if Kevin was behind it or not, but it's very possible they could have found something in his office—or he could have told them something before they killed him. I'm just worried he may be coming after you, hon, so I had to call you as soon as I heard."

"Oh Dad," she whispered. "What do I do?"

"Come home." His instant answer wrapped warmth around her like nothing else had in a very long time. "Let us protect you."

If only she could. "No," she whispered. "I can't. Not while he's still out there. Watching. Listening. If he killed Trent, then we both know the minute I turned up, you would all be in more danger than ever."

He sighed. "I know that tone. I'll never convince you. So, you have to run again."

"What about you and Mom?" She'd give anything to talk to her mother, just for a few seconds.

"She's fine. Missing you. We've increased security and have personal protection officers—bodyguards—with us twenty-four-seven. I'm just worried about you."

"I've been so careful for so long." She'd gotten slack, fallen into a comfort zone. And royally messed up everything that had been pounded into her head by the US Marshal who'd helped her go into hiding.

"You've done well, Brianne. Your mom and I are so proud of you. Now, I've got to get rid of this phone. Be careful. We love and miss you. One day we'll get to see each other again."

"Wait . . ."

But he was gone.

She lowered the phone and dropped her face into her hands. The panic threatened to send her straight over the edge into hyperventilating, but she pulled on the years of learned coping mechanisms and managed to head it off. However, stopping the tears was impossible.

A moment later, the door opened, and she ducked her head, swallowing hard. When she finally looked up, Vince stood there.

"You okay?" he asked, the frown on his face announcing his concern.

No. No, she was definitely not okay. "Um, yeah. I just . . ." What could she say? If she started talking about it, she'd blubber all over him and she really didn't want that.

"That was your dad on the phone?" he asked.

"It was."

"What did he want?"

Do not cry. Do not cry. She took a deep breath. "To tell me a man that we both knew once upon a time was murdered."

His eyes widened. "Sorry, what?"

"The guy I called Sunday night. Trent. This is no coincidence, Vince. He's dead because I called him."

"Aw, Raina, that's not your fault."

"I tried to ask for help and . . ." The tears pushed to come again and she shoved them back. "But God's in control, right?"

"Absolutely."

"This was bound to happen at some point, wasn't it?"

"Probably. Not only is God in control, his timing is perfect. He's got a reason for letting all of this happen now."

It was a comforting thought, but the guilt about calling Trent still cut at her. "My dad thinks I should run because the guy's murderer is probably coming after me next. Only I think *next* has already arrived." She bit her lip. "I know I've hesitated in asking for help, but this is too important to let my fears get in the way. So, while I know you're working to find Kevin, I need you to work harder."

He sat beside her on the bed and took her hand. "Thank you," he said, his voice low.

She raised a brow at the odd tone. "What? I mean, you're welcome, but why do you sound like . . . that?"

He cleared his throat. "I just appreciate you letting me help. For trusting me enough to ask. That's all."

"That's not all. What?"

"I'll tell you a little later, but for now, I have a picture I'd like to show you."

"All right." She frowned, wondering what had him so on edge. He tapped the screen of his phone, then turned it around so she could see it. "What am I looking fo—" She gasped. "Where did you get this?"

"From a new friend. His name is Crank. But that's not what's important. You recognize the guy behind us?"

"I do. That's John Tate, the US Marshal who helped me get out of California and gave me the new identities. Why is he on that security footage?"

"That's a really good question, because he was at the hospital too." He showed her the man who walked out of the hospital exit shortly after Freddy Harper.

Raina stared at him. "I must be more affected by the drugs than I thought, because I'm not tracking why John would be following the man responsible for drugging my drink and almost killing me."

"I don't know either, but I'd sure like to ask him and find out."

■ ■ ■ ■

Vince paced from one end of Raina's small den to the other. He'd brought her home from the hospital and called Holt on the way, to update him and let him know that he'd be staying close to Raina. He hoped he wasn't being presumptuous, but there was no way he was leaving her alone. Not that she *had* to be alone. He wasn't completely discounting the fact that she had friends who would be more than happy to stay with her if she asked.

Only he knew her well enough by now that she wouldn't ask and her friends wouldn't push.

Much.

But he *would*, because he believed it was in her best interests for him to do so. He'd just have to do it without her realizing what he was doing.

He dialed the number for his supervisor, James Godfrey, grateful when the man answered on the second ring. "I know it's late, but I have someone I need you to find."

"Sure. Who?"

"US Marshal John Tate. He's most likely assigned in or around the Burbank, California, area, but I've seen him in two different security videos following a guy I think tried to kill a friend of mine."

"Whoa."

"Yeah."

"And he didn't intervene?"

Vince hesitated. "To give him the benefit of the doubt, I'm not sure he could have. The first time, there would have been no reason to, as no attack occurred. The second, he may not have had any idea what the guy was doing."

"All right. Let me see what I can find out and get back to you."

"Thanks, James."

As soon as he hung up, the guilt hit him. The thought of keeping things from Raina made him want to squirm, indicating that it might not be the best plan, but for now, he had to roll with it.

"Hey," she said from behind him.

He turned and couldn't help but laugh.

"What?" She planted her hands on her hips. "You think my pj's are funny?"

"Hysterical. You like reliving your childhood?"

"Wonder Woman was my hero when I was a kid," she said. "I wanted to be her when I grew up. You can imagine my disappointment when I discovered I couldn't even visit Themyscira."

He blinked. "Themy-what?"

"Are you kidding me? The all-woman island paradise, of course. And when I found out Wonder Woman was molded from clay and not even a real person . . . well, that about did me in."

"And yet you wear the pajamas?"

She shrugged. "Yeah. They were a Christmas present from Penny. And they're flannel, so they're soft. But most importantly, they're warm."

He nodded to her feet. "And the pink flamingo slippers?"

"Warm."

He pointed to the couch. "The Nancy Drew blanket?"

"Warm."

"I'm sensing a theme here."

"Yes, I like to be . . ."

"Warm," they said together.

He laughed. "And you chose to be a flight paramedic. In the mountains of Asheville, North Carolina. Where it gets really cold."

Raina rolled her eyes. "It's where God planted me, so it's where I'm blooming."

She walked into the kitchen and he followed. "Sarcasm?"

"It was a meme I saw on social media when I first moved here. Bloom where you're planted. Or something like that. At the time, I took it to heart."

"And now?"

She opened the refrigerator and removed a bottle of sweet tea and a water. She passed him the tea and opened the water to take a long swig. "I don't think I should have ever let myself grow roots." The quiet words echoed around them. "Because," she said, her voice still low and soft, "it's going to hurt beyond belief when I have to yank them up."

Vince had no idea how to respond to that. So, he settled for reaching out and pulling her into his arms. She rested her cheek against his chest, and they stood there, drinks still in hand, the wall clock audibly ticking off the seconds behind him. "I wish I could help more," he finally whispered against her temple.

She sighed. "You are. Just by forcing me to allow you to stay."

He frowned. "Huh?"

A silent chuckle shook her shoulders and she stepped back. "I'm just kidding. Mostly. I know that if I sent you away, you would park yourself outside my door."

"Of course."

"Of course."

He reached out to stroke her cheek and she swallowed. "Raina, I have a confession."

She raised a brow, but he was grateful that she didn't seem to be too worried. "What is it?"

"In the effort to find Kevin Anderson—who isn't Kevin Anderson—I looked into your case."

"Oh, okay. And?"

"There are a lot of things about your attack that are very similar to four other unsolved cases out there. Granted, there are a few outliers, but there are enough things that are the same that make it worth looking into."

Raina gaped. "What? You mean he's done this before?"

"And since, but there's one thing that stands out more clearly than anything else."

"What's that?"

"You're the only one who survived."

CHAPTER
ELEVEN

Simon looked at the man on the large television screen used as a monitor for the FaceTime call. "Please tell me that this wasn't your doing."

"It wasn't."

"And yet the man is dead."

"Not by my hand. I may be willing to skirt the edge of the law occasionally, but even I draw the line at murder." Freddy turned from the screen and threw something into the suitcase on the bed behind him.

"I'm serious," Simon said. "I didn't hire you to . . ." Why was he bothering? He didn't have saints on his payroll and shouldn't get his britches in a twist when they occasionally went rogue—and lied about it. He shook his head. "The authorities had better not connect this back to me."

The man frowned. "Why would they? *How* would they? You have no connection to the man. I don't either. And like I said, I didn't kill him. He was dead when I got there, so there's absolutely no way to trace it back to either of us. Right now, the detectives are digging into Carter's background, looking for anything that might give them a clue as to who would want him dead—assuming they don't just decide it was a junkie

117

looking for some quick cash—and neither of us are in that background, so relax."

Relax. Right. Did he believe this guy? Did he truly not kill Trent Carter? Simon wasn't sure. And he didn't like being unsure. Because if Freddy didn't kill him, who did? And why? How would the person even know about Trent Carter?

Unease settled next to unsure.

"How did you know to go looking for this guy?"

"I have my ways. If you really want to know them, I'll tell you, but . . ."

"Right." Simon rubbed a hand over his head. "Okay. Just don't do anything else, you understand? We got what we needed. Back off and lay low. And yet . . . keep an eye on her."

"Of course."

Why did he have a feeling the man was placating him. "I mean it."

The sharp words echoed in the room and the man's eyes narrowed at him. "I got it. Have I failed you yet?"

"No." The reassurances helped. Somewhat. "No, you haven't. Thank you."

"I've got your back, Simon. I always have and I always will." A smirk twisted his lips. "Your success and well-being directly affect mine. And I always look out for me, so you can rest comfortably."

Simon barked a short laugh. "Rest comfortably. Right. Okay, keep me updated on any developments. And the investigation into Carter's death. I want to know why someone thought he needed killing."

"Absolutely."

The man disconnected the call and Simon leaned back in his chair.

"Dad?" Christopher stood in the doorway, dressed in the black tux and looking every inch the successful politician he dreamed of being.

"Yes, son."

"We're leaving in ten minutes. Everything okay?"

"Of course."

"What about Keith?"

"What about him?"

"He's been awfully quiet. It worries me."

Simon waved a hand. "I'll take care of him. You just focus on wowing your constituents. Especially the wealthy ones." Christopher smiled. A tight stretching of his lips that caused Simon's nerves to twitch. "Focus, my son."

"I am, Dad, I am."

"Christopher, honey," Leslie said from the door. "Are you ready?" She looked almost regal in her black-sequined floor-length dress. The sleeves encased her thin arms, and her right hand gripped a small black purse. The three-inch heels put her at almost even height with Christopher, and Simon smiled at the beautiful pair they made.

"You look lovely, Leslie," he said.

Her eyes warmed and she smiled, revealing her even, white teeth. "Thank you, Simon. Are you sure you're not interested in attending? I've no doubt we could find another ticket."

At fifteen hundred a plate? Not likely. Then again, if it would further his agenda in a more timely manner, it might be worth it. "Is Daphne's father going to be there?"

Christopher shook his head. "He sends his regrets. He's not feeling well. But he did offer a nice donation, so I'll be sure to mention that in any conversations I have."

"Good. Good." Simon rubbed a hand over his chin. "Sounds like everything is taken care of, so I think I'll take advantage of the evening to clear up some business before a meeting tomorrow, then call it an early night. You two go on and enjoy. I'll look forward to hearing all about it at breakfast."

Leslie shot him another brilliant smile and slipped her hand into the crook of her husband's elbow. They turned as one and walked out of the office. Simon's smile faded and his temple pulsed with a sharp pain. He pressed a hand to it and sighed before walking into his bedroom to find the pills in the nightstand. Swallowing the pain pill dry, he stood at the window and stared out over the vast estate that had been in his family for over fifty years. His father would be terribly disappointed in him, and that thought nearly took him to his knees.

But it was also the reason he couldn't give up. He couldn't be the one to lose everything.

■ ■ ■ ■

At his words *"You're the only one who survived,"* Raina had dropped into the nearest chair and fallen silent. And she'd been that way for the past—he glanced at the clock—fifteen minutes. He didn't mind letting her think, but the silence was getting to him. "Did you hear me?"

"I heard you."

She finally got up, grabbed her water bottle from the counter, and took a long drink. "Is this your way of processing?" he finally asked.

"Yeah." She took a deep breath. "Yes. Sorry." She turned and looked him in the eye. "So what you're saying is that I escaped a serial killer."

He shrugged and sighed, studying her and trying to read what was going on behind her eyes. "I can't say that for sure, of course, but all the evidence seems to indicate that you escaped a worse fate. Whether the guy fits the definition of serial killer is yet to be determined." But it sure looked like it to him.

She leaned against the counter. "I want to know the details of the cases. Can you tell me about them?"

"I'll have to find that out. Why?"

"Because I want to compare them to mine. I know you or Holt can do that, but I want to do it myself."

The look on her face brought a frown to his. "Tell me what you're thinking."

She rubbed her eyes. "I may see something the investigators missed. Something that only I would know that could possibly connect them."

Vince nodded. He'd been thinking the same. "All right. I'll talk to Holt since he was one of the federal agents brought in. One of the murders was on his turf."

When she pressed her palms to her eyes for the third time, he sighed. "You're wiped. Why don't you get some rest? I've got the couch."

"You can't sleep on that. And what am I saying? You can't sleep here at all. You have a home and a job. I can't expect you to be my personal bodyguard."

"You're not expecting me to do that. I'm offering. Just like I offered to try and find Kevin."

"Right."

"Go to bed, Raina. Sleep well, knowing that I'm going to be wide awake and watching out for you."

She sighed. "You know what? I'm not even going to argue."

He raised a brow. "Do you have a fever?"

"Ha-ha. You're cute."

And just like that, his heart tumbled a little harder in her direction. He cleared his throat. "Well, thank you for not arguing."

"But you can't function on no sleep. The alarm is on. No one is in the garage or the attic—yes, I know you checked—and we'll hear if someone tries to get in. So, you have to promise to sleep."

"I'll rest."

She crossed her arms. "That's as good as I'm going to get, isn't it?"

"Probably."

She nodded. "All right. Make yourself at home. Everything

you need, including a couple of pillows, is in the closet of the guest bedroom. Feel free to use the bed. It's clean."

"I'd feel better on the couch." If he positioned himself a certain way, he could see right into the kitchen and the front door as well.

"Suit yourself. Night."

"Night."

She paused, then walked over to kiss his cheek. "Thank you, Vince."

He gripped her biceps and lightly brushed her lips with his, then gazed into her wide eyes. "You're welcome, Raina."

She drew in a deep breath. "Well, that was unexpected."

He dropped his hands and frowned. "I'm sorry if I crossed a line."

"You didn't. Good night."

She walked through the living room and down the hall. Vince watched her go into her bedroom, then dropped onto the couch. He was an idiot. What had led him to kiss her? It hadn't necessarily been the physical attraction he certainly felt for her, but more of a desire to show her that he could be trusted. That she didn't have to worry about him pushing her or hitting her or anything else she'd feared when she'd been with Kevin. "And kissing her was the way to show her that?" he muttered.

Probably not.

Then again, she didn't seem traumatized by it either. She said he hadn't crossed a line and she hadn't told him to leave. Thank goodness.

But he'd watch his step from now on. Kissing her probably hadn't been the brightest next step in the process to gain her trust—and heart. She was fighting an internal battle and he'd have to let her work it out. In the meantime, he was a big boy and needed to keep a tight rein on his feelings, practice a little self-control. He'd protect her and make sure she was safe. After they caught this Kevin dude, then maybe he could be a little more open with her about the fact that he wanted to take her out and show her the most romantic night of her life.

And make sure she understood that she was someone to be cherished.

And that the relationship would move at her pace.

Assuming she wanted a relationship.

He bit off a groan, then jumped when his phone dinged with a text from Holt.

> You can share the cases with her. Just be sure to document anything she says and so on. You know the drill.

Vince tapped a quick reply.

> Thanks. Will do.

> By the way, have you talked to Penny?

> About?

> Anything. She's been acting a little weird.

> Weird how?

> Just . . . weird. Running a lot of errands lately. I've been working a lot so am just noticing it, but . . .

> But what?

> But nothing, I guess. If you haven't noticed it, then it's probably all my imagination. Talk later.

> Thanks again.

Now, he had to think. While it was good he'd gotten the clearance he needed to talk to Raina about the cases, he wasn't sure how he felt about showing her the information. Not because he didn't trust her. It was just once she saw the pictures of the dead women, she couldn't *un*see them. Then again, she did work with victims of severe trauma, some intentional, some not. But these pictures were different. They were personal. She'd suffered some of the same injuries as the women in these photos, and it was bound to trigger the memories.

If there was anything he'd learned about Raina in the months that he'd known her, she was stubborn and liked to do things her way. That wasn't necessarily a bad thing, but . . . it wasn't always a good thing either.

He sighed. And she'd be furious with him if he held something back from her. If she found out.

Which she would.

He didn't know how, but she would.

He stood and paced to the window. Then checked the alarm and the rest of the windows. All quiet.

After a check to find Raina already asleep with her door cracked, he made himself comfortable on the couch with his weapon close by. No one was getting near Raina. Not without going through him first.

■ ■ ■ ■

WEDNESDAY MORNING

When Raina walked into the kitchen the next morning, lured by the sound of low voices and the smell of fresh-brewed coffee and cinnamon rolls, she found Vince, Penny, and Holt sitting at her table. Covering a yawn, she blinked, then walked to the coffeepot, poured a mug of the steaming liquid, and sipped.

No one said a word, just watched her.

Finally, she lowered the cup to the counter and raised a brow. "All right. You can talk now."

Vince nodded to Holt, who cleared his throat. "How are you feeling?"

"Fine. The drug wore off long ago. I guess I was just exhausted from everything that came with it." Including the emotions that had swirled with that kiss from Vince Covelli.

She'd done her best to file that kiss in the "things to be processed later" part of her brain but hadn't been entirely successful.

Thinking about the call from her father and the murder of Trent Carter had taken precedence. A lump formed in her throat, and she swallowed it, then looked at Holt and Vince. "Do either of you guys have law enforcement connections in California?"

Holt nodded. "I do."

"Can you see what you can find out about the murder of Trent Carter? He's an attorney and good friend of my father's—stepfather's. He's the man I called the night we were at Julianna's and I kind of flipped out over seeing Michael on television." She rubbed her palms over her sweatpants. "I feel quite sure Kevin either killed him or had him killed."

"It's been over thirteen years since you last talked to anyone out there," Holt said. "You really think he was keeping tabs on Carter?"

"He's dead less than twenty-four hours after talking to me. What do you think?" She pressed fingers to her eyes. "I never should have called him." She dropped her hand and sucked in a steadying breath. "I just didn't know what else to do. He did say that he'd been getting yearly threats, so I have no doubt Kevin is behind his death. Either he killed him or had someone do it. And I led him to Trent." The guilt nearly choked her.

Holt raised a brow. "I think you have a point and it's worth looking into."

She took one of the gooey rolls from the box, wondering if she'd be able to eat it, but put it on a plate, then snagged her coffee. As she lowered herself into the empty chair next to Vince, she let her gaze touch on each of them. "I can tell you have something to tell me, but let me just say this. Kevin hated to lose. Anything. Before he started pounding on me that last night, he told me he was keeping tabs on everyone in my life, that there was nowhere I could run that he wouldn't find me. And if I tried, people I loved would die." The memories washed over her like it had all happened yesterday. "Kevin had money. At least he gave the appearance of having it. Once he found out I lived through the beating, he made it his mission to let me know that he might not be around, but he wasn't gone. He left messages at the hospital while I was healing." She sipped her coffee, letting it burn all the way down. "I wasn't supposed to know that, but I overheard the nurses talking. I also had two officers assigned to my floor and my stepfather hired my own private security detail. But Kevin knew about my stepfather and his inner circle of friends. Trent Carter is the family lawyer and Oliver Youngblood owns the largest private bank in Burbank. And, finally, John Tate, who is a US Marshal. The four of them all went to college together and remained friends. Kevin knew they would have the means and desire to help me should I ask for it." She gave a shuddering sigh. "I didn't ask, but my step-father did. I don't know how he made it happen without Kevin finding out, but John got me away and, except for one blip in Arizona, I've been relatively safe—or at least *felt* relatively safe. When I can ignore my paranoia."

"Until now," Vince murmured.

"Until now," she echoed. Everyone fell silent and she swept her gaze over the threesome once more. "And it started with that phone call to Trent. I'm telling you there's a connection there to Kevin. And that's why you need to stay updated on anything the detectives find about Trent's murder."

Vince leaned forward. "Have you contacted any of the others?"

"No. And I won't now. Not after what happened to Trent. I'm terrified someone will find out my father called me. I sure don't want to risk contacting anyone else. I'm telling you, Kevin is monitoring them somehow, someway. I don't know how, but . . . yeah."

"I'll have someone warn them," Holt said.

"I'm sure my father may have given them a heads-up by now, but thank you, an extra warning probably wouldn't hurt." She took a bite of the roll, washed it down with a swig of coffee, then said, "Your turn. What's going on?"

"The detectives found the guy who spiked your drink," Holt said.

Raina paused, fingers tightening around the handle of her mug. "They did? How?"

"Good police work. Once they had his name, it wasn't hard to find out he rented a car. He also used a credit card to buy a few meals and reserve a hotel room. They caught up to him about an hour ago. Looked like he was all packed up and ready to catch his flight. The detectives changed his plans and he's currently being interrogated as to who paid him to try to kill you."

"Let me guess," Raina said, "he's not talking."

"Right, except to protest his innocence. But they have him cold for the attempted murder, so he's not going anywhere anytime soon."

Raina nodded and took a bite of the cinnamon roll, letting the sugary sweetness coat her tongue once more and satisfy her taste buds. "So, what now?"

Holt rubbed his chin and glanced at Vince, who leaned toward her. "Now, we talk about the other cases that resemble yours." He paused, then looked at Penny. "Sorry, Penny, you can't be in on this."

Penny stood. "I know. I was just here for moral support until you guys started talking business. I've got some errands to run anyway." She planted a kiss on her husband's lips. "I'll see you at home."

"What kind of errands?" Holt asked.

Penny shrugged and smiled. "Just personal errands. I'll tell you later, Mr. Nosypants."

"Right. I'll text you," Holt said. "Love you."

"Love you."

The easy affection between the two grabbed at Raina's heart. What would it be like to have that kind of love? To marry your best friend?

She tossed the thoughts from her mind. Allowing herself to yearn for something like that was dangerous. Not just for her heart, but for the person she let get close.

After Penny gave Raina a quick squeeze, she left, and Holt looked at her. "You know what errands she's running?"

She frowned. "No. Why?"

Holt just shook his head and Vince reached into a briefcase at his side to pull out four folders. "Holt got these and the permission to show them to you. And me. Because it looks like the guy who attacked you fourteen years ago is the one who may be coming after you now—via hired help. But just because we got him doesn't mean the one behind it will be stopped. He can always hire someone else. But if we find a connection between the victims, then we might be able to figure out who he is."

Raina nodded, insides clenching. "Okay."

"You sure you're up to this?" Vince asked.

"Absolutely. Let me see."

He passed her the first folder. She flipped it open and her eyes landed on a woman who'd been severely beaten. Raina caught her breath and slapped the folder closed.

"Raina?" Vince gripped her right hand while Holt covered her left.

"I'm okay," she said. "I . . . it was . . . it was just a shock."

"I know. It's brutal."

"No." She shook her head. "I mean, yes, it is, but it's not the shock of the beating, it's the shock of seeing myself in that picture. It's like looking in a mirror."

"Take a deep breath," Holt said, "skip the photos, and just look at the reports and notes from the detectives."

Raina nodded, took the deep breath he recommended, then reopened the folder. She flipped the photos upside down and focused on the written words. "'Family reports that the victim had been distant lately,'" she said. "'They hadn't seen or talked to her in over two months.'" She looked up. "Well, that's familiar. It was about four months for me."

Vince frowned. "At the time, you were close to your family, right?"

"Yes. Mostly by then. I was a terror when my mom first married my stepfather, which resulted in my juvie stint." She grimaced. "I was caught in a stolen car. The judge knew who my stepfather was and assumed I needed some tough love. My lawyer overheard him saying that it was time to teach the prima donnas that they couldn't behave like that and expect not to have consequences."

"Ouch," Holt said.

"I'm surprised that your stalker would choose someone who had a support base," Vince said, "a strong family connection. Usually, these guys go for women who don't have that, who are a lot more emotionally vulnerable."

"I probably fit in that 'emotionally vulnerable' slot at the time. When I met Kevin, I had just reconciled with my parents—and yes, I call my stepfather my father—or Dad." She sighed. "I had a good birth dad. A wonderful dad. But one moment he was there, the next, he was gone. Killed in a car accident by a drunk driver. Mom and I reeled. Her parents were dead and my father's family lived in England. Still do. They came for the funeral, of course, then returned home and I haven't seen them since. So Mom and I were pretty much on our own. The more she had to work, the angrier I got. Angry at God, at life, at the drunk driver who chose his path that night that led him to run the red light. Just angry. And scared. So very scared. Without my dad, we were lost." She looked down at her hands, the memories sweeping over her. She cleared her throat and looked up. "Sorry. You're not here to relive my past."

When Vince's hand covered hers, Raina's heart picked up

speed. What would he think about her revelations? And Holt? She eyed the man who'd befriended her from the moment they'd met. He'd been clinging to life after being stabbed by a serial killer, and she'd been one of the medical personnel who'd helped save him. "I guess you think I'm awful for not telling Penny and the others about everything before now."

He frowned. "Aw, Raina, of course I don't think you're awful. I think you have your reasons and I'm not one to judge."

Something flickered in his eyes and she wondered if he was reliving his own silence when it came to parts of his past he'd kept from Penny. Parts that she'd only learned about a few months ago. No, he wouldn't judge her. She relaxed a fraction. "So, back to the files." She skipped the pictures again and went back to the written report. The men fell silent while she read.

The more she absorbed of the details, the more her stomach twisted into a tight knot. She finally closed the file and went to the next one, and then the next, and finally the last. Then she rested her clenched fists on top of the short stack. Short, but still four too many.

"Raina?"

She went back to the first file. "This one mentions a ring."

"Yeah, a little silver ring with an infinity sign."

"Did the others have one?" She took a deep breath and fanned the pictures out in front of her.

"Uh, I don't think it was mentioned," Holt said. "But that doesn't mean they didn't have one."

She pointed. "He gave me a ring just like that."

"What?" Holt and Vince spoke the word at the same time and leaned forward. Steeling herself, she flipped through the pictures of the other victims. "No ring, but like you said, that doesn't mean he didn't give them one." She paused and let out a low breath she hadn't realized she'd been holding. "He did this to these women and he did it to me. And we have to stop him."

CHAPTER
TWELVE

"We?" Vince raised a brow at her while, at the same time, clamping down on the desire to find this guy and give him a taste of his own medicine. But that wasn't how he operated. At least not up to this point. He wasn't sure what he'd do if he ever came face-to-face with the man who'd almost killed Raina.

"Yes. I told you that if you couldn't find him, I wanted to use myself as bait."

Holt held up a hand. "You gave us something we didn't have before. We now can investigate the ring. Do you still have it?"

"No. At least not with me. It . . . might be in a jewelry box I used to have. I honestly don't know what happened to all the stuff I had at the apartment I shared with Kevin. My dad said he'd get it, so he probably did. You can ask him, but I worry about you contacting him and Kevin finding out somehow."

"I'll manage," Holt said. "Will you trust me to do that?"

She bit her lip and glanced between the two men. "I guess, but doing that is going to take some time. I still think I should . . . do something."

Vince exchanged a look with Holt. "What does that *something* entail?"

She sat back in the chair with a huff. "I have no idea." But her eyes narrowed and she straightened. "Wait a minute. Maybe I do."

"What?" Holt asked.

"The guy the cops are questioning at the jail."

"Freddy Harper." Vince frowned. "What about him?"

"He's probably working for Kevin, right?"

"Possibly."

"What if I talk to him?"

"Uh . . ." Holt shook his head. "I think that's a bad idea."

"What's he like? His personality?"

"I'm not sure. They haven't said."

Raina stood. "I'm going down there. I want to see him."

Vince and Holt rose as well. "Raina, he's not going to talk to you either," Vince said.

"How do you know that? What if my appearance is a shock to his system or something? Maybe it will jar him into saying something."

"That's what the detectives investigating your case are trying to do," Holt said. "I'm buddies with one of them. His name is Ryan Byrd and he promised to keep me updated."

She hesitated, then lifted her chin. "I still want to go."

"Then let's go," Vince said, pulling his keys from his pocket.

Raina's eyes widened, but she nodded and headed for her bedroom. "Give me ten minutes."

Once her door was shut, Holt turned to Vince. "Are you sure about this?"

"Not at all, but nothing we said was going to keep her here." He jingled the keys. "At least this way, I can keep an eye on . . . things."

"You like her a lot, don't you?"

Vince shrugged. "Of course. What's not to like? She's become a good friend." He tried not to wince at that last statement. Then again, it was true. She was definitely a friend.

Holt's eyes narrowed. "Hmm." His phone pinged, pulling his attention away from Vince, who breathed a quiet sigh of relief. Of course he liked Raina. He more than liked her, but right now, she had to stay in the friend category. Especially after that kiss.

Holt looked up from his phone. "They've resumed questioning the guy, but while he refuses to disclose who hired him, he insists that he didn't put anything in Raina's drink and he was just there to watch someone for a client."

"Watch who?"

"Wouldn't say. Hold on, there's more. Ryan said even when they presented the video evidence to the guy, he stands on his claim that it's not him, but . . ."

"But?"

"But his cell phone pinged off the hospital tower."

"Of course it did. Because he was there to kill Raina."

Holt frowned. "Well, your phone would show the same information and you definitely weren't there to kill Raina."

"Cute. You know it's him." Vince curled his fingers into a tight fist. "And we both know he's the key to finding out who beat Raina within an inch of her life."

Holt nodded just as Raina stepped back into the kitchen. "I'm ready."

Vince turned to her. "Do you mind if I drive?"

She tucked a strand of hair behind her ear before shrugging. "I don't mind."

"All right." He looked at Holt. "What's your plan?"

"I have cases that need my attention, so Penny's choppering me to Columbia. I'll be there for the next few days, but just holler if you need something. I'll keep you up-to-date on anything that comes through. I'll also see if we can be clever about getting the ring from your parents' home."

"Okay. Thanks." They followed Raina out the door and Vince waited while she set the alarm.

■ ■ ■ ■

Raina walked into the police department with Vince at her side. She crossed her arms and scanned the area. Two front desk officers looked up at their entrance, and Vince showed them his badge. "We're here for Ryan Byrd. He's expecting us."

"I'll let him know you're here." The nearest officer picked up the phone.

Raina's gaze skimmed the two people sitting huddled in the corner in the hard plastic chairs. She couldn't help but wonder what their story was.

The side door buzzed and opened, distracting her from her musings. A man in his midthirties with a neatly trimmed mustache and sharp blue eyes waved at Vince. "Hey, man, good to see you."

"You too." Vince shook hands with the guy, then introduced her. "This is our friend Holt was telling you about, Ryan Byrd. Ryan, this is Raina. The one your prisoner almost killed."

Ryan's eyes softened with sympathy. "So sorry about that. You sure you're up to this?"

"I'm sure." The words rolled off her tongue, confident and assured, but the truth was, she wasn't sure at all. She just knew she had to do it.

With her heart pounding hard enough to echo in her ears, she walked between the men to the viewing area for the interrogation room. Ryan pushed the door open and held it for her and Vince. Once inside, she turned to see her attacker sitting at the table, handcuffed, fingers clasped. He was staring at the mirror as though he could see right through it. He couldn't, but she shivered anyway. "That's Freddy Harper?"

"Yes, ma'am."

"Ask him why he—or whoever hired him—wants me dead. I mean, I have a pretty good idea, but . . ."

"Trust me, we've asked him," Ryan said, "but he's insistent that neither he—nor his client—want you dead."

"But he *was* hired to find me? He admits that?"

"No. He says his presence in the hospital has nothing to do with you and that he was only there at the request of a client."

"But he won't give you the name of the client."

"No, but just before you got here, I got a text that the crime scene unit searching his hotel room and car found a burner phone. There were calls made to someone in California."

Nausea hit and she bit her tongue. "Kevin."

"We're not sure. The other phone was also a burner, but we've got detectives working on tracking down the location the calls were made to."

"It'll lead back to Kevin," she said.

Vince's hand rested on her shoulder, and after almost shrugging it off, she let it stay there, reminding herself she was going to trust him. Let him help. More than that, she was going to consciously make the choice to trust God. She wished it was an easy step of faith, but—

Ryan cleared his throat. "I'm going to go in and talk to him and let him know that he's running out of time, although the truth is, *we're* the ones running out of time. If we don't charge him with something in the next couple of hours, we have to let him go."

"He hasn't lawyered up?" Vince asked.

"No. Says it wasn't him that put the drug in the drink and he doesn't need a lawyer."

"But what about the security footage?" Raina asked.

"Unfortunately, the video doesn't give us a clear shot of his face in the ER, just coming out of the hospital, so it's not going to hold up in court. We were just hoping that when confronted with the video 'evidence,' he would confess. He hasn't."

Raina stepped closer to the window, studying everything about the man. He was midforties, blond hair, good-looking in a suntanned-surfer-dude kind of way. His blue eyes caught hers and she gasped, even though she knew he couldn't see her.

Vince's hand squeezed and Ryan walked out of the room.

Seconds later, he was in the interrogation room with her *alleged* attacker.

Ryan leaned against the wall and crossed his arms. "All right, Mr. Harper—"

"Freddy."

"Freddy. Now that we've all had a bit of a break, let's see if we can get a little farther in the conversation this time."

"If the questions are still the same, the answers are too."

Raina pressed her fists against her thighs. How she wanted to go in there and shake the man until the words spilled from his lips. But since that probably wouldn't work, she waited.

Ryan shifted. "So, you say you didn't put the drug in Ms. Price's drink."

"I did not."

"Then what were you doing there?"

"As I said before, I was there because a client asked me to check up on someone."

"But you won't tell us the client's name—or who you were checking up on."

"I won't. He asked for confidentiality. Made me sign a contract and I won't break it."

Raina stomped a foot and spun to glare at Vince. "This is going nowhere. I want to speak to him."

"That's not my call, Raina, you know that."

"Then talk to Ryan. Please?"

He sighed. "When he comes out."

"Thank you."

For the next thirty minutes, they listened as Ryan and Freddy talked in circles. Ryan finally shoved his hands in his pockets, the first sign of irritation she'd seen from him. "We've got you dead in the water here. I'll give you some alone time to think, then we'll do this again."

The man sighed. "Whatever, Detective. My answers will still be the same." He glanced at the clock on the wall. "And you can't keep me here much longer without charging me."

"I'm aware." Ryan left the room and seconds later stepped into the viewing area. "I'm sorry, guys, he's just not budging. Unless the search of his car and hotel room turn up something else, I'm going to have to release him."

"Raina wants to talk to him," Vince said.

The detective rubbed his chin. "It's not something that's really done."

"But you can make it happen?" Vince asked.

He paused, his concerned eyes narrowed. "Are you sure about that?"

"I'm sure."

"No promises, but let me see what I can do."

He left again, and in less than fifteen minutes Raina found herself outside the interrogation room door fighting off nerves and the desire to run—and wishing it was Vince by her side instead of the detective. But when Ryan pushed the door open and gestured for her to enter, she stepped inside.

The man chained to the table looked up. And frowned. "What's she doing here?"

"So, you know her?" Ryan asked.

He blinked. "No. Why? I just wondered why she was here. She's obviously not a cop."

"You're lying," Raina said, her voice low. "You broke into my house, and when you failed to kill me there, you came to the hospital and tried to kill me there. I want to know why." His eyes met hers, and she lifted her chin, refusing to be intimidated or back down. But a hint of uncertainty niggled at her. She wasn't a hundred percent sure she was right. Keeping those thoughts to herself, she pressed. "Why?"

"I don't know who you are or what you're talking about. I never broke into your home and I was at the hospital on business for a client. End of story." He slid his gaze from hers to Ryan. "And now, it's about time you let me out of here."

"We still have a few minutes," Ryan said.

"Then I'll just sit here and wait for those minutes to tick by." And that's exactly what he did.

Ten minutes later, to Raina's fury, the man walked out of the police department and climbed into an Uber. "Can't you follow him?" she asked, her gaze bouncing between Ryan and Vince.

Ryan nodded. "I've already asked for an unmarked to follow them. We'll see where he goes."

His words took the edge off her ire and she drew in a deep breath. "All right, now what?"

Vince took her hand. "Now, we regroup and plan, but first, I have a surprise for you."

CHAPTER
THIRTEEN

Vince refused to tell her his idea until they were buckled in his vehicle and heading out of the parking lot, then he glanced at her. "So, as far as the case is concerned, I've got calls in to my supervisor to have John Tate get in touch with me. He hasn't yet, but that doesn't mean he's not going to. Second, Holt is having a guy go undercover to meet with your dad and find out about the ring. Third, my buddy checked in and said Michael was doing fine and his family were still safe. Fourth, my partner Charlie said our protectee is recovering and he's called in another marshal to help out while I take some personal time off."

"Wait, what? Personal time? But—"

"I want to, Raina. I want to be there for you."

She let out a low sigh and Vince couldn't tell what it meant. Finally, she nodded. "Okay, thank you."

He raised a brow. That was it? He was making progress. "So, now that we've got business taken care of, I guess I should ask if you like the water."

"The water how?"

"Like boating, fishing, swimming, Jet Skis, et cetera."

"Sure. I love anything outdoors. Except the cold." She eyed

the sky. "At least at the moment. When that storm rolls in, it's going to be a bit colder than cold. Why?"

"I know a place by the lake. It's peaceful. Quiet. Surrounded by woods and lots of wildlife. Want to swing through a drive-thru, grab some food, and go sit out on the dock? With some-one on Harper's tail, we should be able to have some time to decompress."

"Decompress?"

"Some people call it relaxing, but after everything that's happened, decompressing seems like a better description."

She laughed. "True." Then nodded. "Okay. I like that idea."

"And I have blankets to ward off the chill if we need them."

Thirty minutes later, with the delicious smell of burgers and fries filling the car and the sun beaming through slightly gray clouds, Vince wound them up Bald Mountain, then pulled into the driveway of a large lake house.

Raina gaped. "Is this yours?"

He laughed. "I wish, but no. It belongs to a good friend. We went through the academy together, then he inherited a small fortune from his grandparents when they passed away. This was a part of that inheritance, and I have an open invitation to stop by and use it whenever I can. I texted him and asked if it was available this afternoon and he told me to help myself."

"Nice friend."

"One of the best." He grabbed the food. "Ready?"

"Absolutely."

They climbed out of the car and he motioned to the side of the house. "We can use the kitchen table or sit in the gazebo at the end of the dock. What's your preference?"

"The gazebo, definitely." She cast a glance at the sky. "And we'd have cover if it rains."

"Hopefully it'll hold off. I have plans."

"What kind of plans?"

"You'll see."

Vince led the way, following the stepping-stone path around the side of the two-story brick home and into a yard that sloped down to a wooden dock. A pontoon boat bobbed gently on the right side and a red ski boat did the same on the left.

"Nice," she murmured, stopping at the edge of the back deck.

"Chip loves the water. His wife hates it, but she loves him, so . . ."

"The things we do for those we love, right? The sacrifices we make?"

The abrupt sadness in her voice jerked his gaze to her in time to see the grief etched on her features. Then she blinked and it was gone. He took her hand and squeezed. "You okay? What was that look all about?"

She shrugged. "The past." Her lips curved upward, but he thought it looked forced. "And that's where it needs to stay, although it appears that's not going to happen."

"Well, for now we can just relax and enjoy the rest of the day, right?"

"We can?"

"Why not?"

She raised a brow. "Well, don't you have to work?"

"PTO, remember? When is your next shift?"

"Um, day after tomorrow."

"So, you have the time?"

A laugh slipped from her. "Yes, sure. I have the time."

"Then let's have fun."

Confusion flickered. "Fun?"

"You do know what that is, don't you?"

"Ha. Cute. I have a vague memory of it." She sighed. "Seriously, you just want to hang out?"

"Yep." He walked up the deck steps to the back door and ran his hand under the windowsill on his left. And . . . there it was. He pulled out the key, unlocked the house, and turned off the alarm. "Do you prefer the pontoon or the speed boat?"

"We get to take the boat out too?"

The twinge of awe in her voice made him feel like a superhero. "If you want."

"Oh, I want. The pontoon. It's more conducive to decompressing, I think."

"Great choice. It also has a cover in case it rains. As long as there's no lightning, we should be fine on the water."

"My dad had a boat." A pause. "My biological dad, not my stepdad." She followed him into the kitchen where he snagged a set of keys from the hook on the wall. "We used to take it out on the lake almost every weekend in the summer. I'd bring a friend and we'd swim, snorkel, ski, fish . . . I remember those days. I remember the fun." She smiled at him—a sad, wistful curving of her lips that appeared, then vanished. "And then," she said, "it was all over. He was gone and so was the house, the boat, the friends . . . and all the fun."

She was opening up to him, trusting him. Maybe there was hope after all. His heart pounded with the intensity of his emotions, and it was an effort to rein it in. He reached out to grip her fingers and give them a light squeeze. "Then let's have a little fun today."

She smiled and the shadows of her past faded from her gaze. "Okay, let's do that."

"I'm going to get some drinks from the fridge. Water or soda?"

"Water, please, but I can carry them."

He passed her two bottles and they walked out of the house and down to the gazebo. Vince nodded to the built-in benches attached to the interior perimeter of the small shelter. "I helped build those two summers ago. Chip and Donna kept having to haul a table and chairs down here, and it was getting old fast."

"This is lovely. I feel like I'm in a little valley with mountains surrounding us."

She slid onto the closest bench, and he set the food on the

table in front of her. "Napkins and everything should be in there."

"Perfect." She passed him a water bottle, then unwrapped her burger and waited for him to do the same.

Vince gripped her hands and bowed his head. "Lord, thank you for your protection over us and please continue that. Thank you for the gifts of the beauty of nature and the chance to have fun. Keep our hearts centered on you and let us rest in the assurance that nothing can happen without your permission. Bless this food, thank you for this time together. Amen."

"Amen." Raina's low murmur of agreement. She hesitated, hand holding her burger, eyes on him. "You really believe that?"

"What?"

"That nothing happens without his permission?"

"Absolutely. You ever read the book of Job?"

"I have. It just all seems like he asks too much of people sometimes."

"Like what?"

She shrugged. "I don't know. I think about what my friends have been through over the last couple of years. Penny and Holt had to deal with a serial killer, Julianna with someone who wanted her dead, and then Grace and Sam and everything they dealt with when it came to his father." Her eyes narrowed and she shook her head. "I think I'm going through a questioning phase right now. Like I believe God is who he says he is. I do. I guess I just don't understand why some people seem to have perfect lives where nothing bad ever happens, and other people seem to walk under the proverbial rain cloud."

He leaned back, thinking about her words, wondering how to put his own thoughts into something that would make sense. "No one has a perfect life, but I agree, some seem to have it easier than others. I think a lot of things come down to choice. People make choices that have consequences. I'm not even necessarily talking about bad choices. Sometimes good choices have lousy consequences. You do something you think is right and wind up with it coming back to bite you in the end. Then there are the bad choices. Those consequences usually aren't great either."

"Like the drunk driver who chose to get behind the wheel and killed my dad."

"Exactly. It didn't just affect his life, but it sent yours and your mother's spiraling as well."

"Like ripples on a pond." She drew in a deep breath. "Tell me about your life, Vincent Covelli. We've certainly talked enough about mine. What choices did you make that came back to bite you?"

■ ■ ■ ■

Raina caught his micro-flinch and frowned. "I hit a sore spot, didn't I? I'm sorry."

"No, you don't have to apologize. You're right. I haven't shared much of my past. I'm like you in that regard."

"Playing your cards close to the vest?"

"Yes."

"Why?"

"It's not something I like to revisit, mostly because it hurts to talk about it."

A breeze could have knocked Raina over at that point. She'd never known a man so open with his feelings, so willing to admit to something that could be construed as a weakness. "Does it have to do with your sister?"

"It does."

"What happened?"

"Let's eat and I'll tell you in the boat."

Raina wondered if he was avoiding talking to her, but went along with his wishes. She was hungry, so it didn't take long to finish off the burger and fries and half the water bottle.

Vince finally stood. "Ready?"

"Sure."

Five minutes later, Vince sat behind the wheel and she'd chosen the seat next to him. With steady hands, he steered them toward the middle of the lake. The wind whipped the strands that had escaped her ponytail around her face.

"If you get cold," he said, "the blankets I mentioned are in that storage bench." He pointed to it and she shook her head.

"I'm fine right now."

Once they were a good distance from the shore, he turned off the engine and the world went silent. Peaceful. Chilly.

"Raina?"

"Yeah?"

"You're cold."

A shiver swept over her at just that moment and she laughed. "I am."

He rose and grabbed a blanket from the box and wrapped it around her, his head dipping close to hers. For a moment, their eyes clung, then he smiled and pressed a button. A whirring sound reached her, and she realized he was closing them in with the canopy. "For warmth. I know you hate to be cold."

His kindness touched her. "Thank you." She cleared her throat and moved to the table under the canopy with dessert that neither of them had wanted after the burgers and fries. "You were going to tell me about the choice that came back to bite you in the rear."

"I guess I was."

He took a long sip of water. "My sister's name was Eden. She was four years older than I and I adored her. She was one of my best friends when we were younger. One of our favorite things to do was build a blanket fort in the middle of the den, move the TV inside, and watch cartoons on Saturday mornings. It was kind of our weekend thing—at least until she got older. Then those times got fewer and fewer, but every once in a while she'd come over and we'd have our fort time. I miss that. I miss *her*." He shot her a sad smile. "She was great. But . . . she also liked attention. She'd do outrageous things sometimes just for kicks. I loved her, but she embarrassed me sometimes too."

"What happened?"

"She got involved in a relationship with a guy. A guy who treated me like a brother and—on the surface—treated her very well."

"On the surface?"

He frowned. "When no one was around, if something triggered him, he'd go off and take it out on her."

Raina nodded, her eyes sad and knowing. "Like how?"

He lifted a shoulder and looked away from her. "One day, I asked her about the bruise on her cheek and she said Matt had hit her. I asked her if it had been by accident, and she said no, he'd punched her." Vince shook his head and rubbed a hand down the side of his face. "There's more to the story than what I told you earlier. She did refuse to let me help her, but it was because of how I responded when she told me that. Something I'm very ashamed of and is my biggest life regret."

"What do you mean?" She couldn't imagine him being anything but supportive in that kind of situation.

"Let me just give you some background. I'd always wanted a brother, and Matt, her husband, had stepped into that role. We did a lot together. Pickup basketball games, fishing, hiking, just hanging out watching sports. So for her to say something like that . . . it just floored me. Completely stunned me." He drew in a deep breath and closed his eyes. "I called her a liar."

Raina's heart dipped. "Oh, Vince . . ."

"I know. Told her that if she wanted attention, she needed to find another way to get it, but saying Matt was an abuser was a lousy thing to do."

"Oh no . . ."

He pressed fingers to his eyelids, then dropped his hand and looked at her. "It wasn't until she landed in the hospital with broken ribs and a concussion that I believed her. She'd been asking for help without asking. When I approached the hospital room, I could hear arguing. When I rushed in, Matt had a grip on her hair with one hand and was in a downswing with his other. He landed the blow and I saw red. I went after him and punched him so hard, it knocked him out. He dropped to the floor, and it was only the sound of Eden's sobs that kept me from . . . doing more damage to him."

"I don't know what to say," Raina whispered. She truly didn't.

"The police were called. It was a mess, but thankfully one of the nurses had followed me in and saw the whole thing. Matt was arrested."

Raina swallowed and took a sip of her drink. "So, he went to jail?"

"For a few days, then was released. I tried to convince Eden to file a restraining order, but she refused. Said there was no point, he'd just ignore it. I demanded to know why she didn't get help, and she just looked at me and said she didn't think anyone would believe her." Tears filled his eyes and he rubbed them away. "It was because I didn't believe her. Anyway, she told me to back off, that I'd done enough damage."

"Oh, Vince . . ."

Her soft words seemed to bounce off him. "I asked her why she didn't insist that she was telling the truth. I mean, if she hadn't just let it go when I accused her of lying, she would have convinced me. She knew it and I knew it. But she didn't bother."

"She was afraid for you," Raina said.

He frowned at her. "Afraid for me? I was the one with the gun."

"But I bet he had one too and wasn't restricted to the confines of the law when it came to using it."

Vince fell silent, the anguish on his features reaching right through her chest to wrap itself around her heart and squeeze until she thought it might rupture. But he was nodding. "Yes.

All true. I went over to her house the night he was released, knowing he was going to show up and she was going to let him in."

"And she did."

"I tried to stop him before he got to the door and she came outside, told me to leave them alone, that she'd never ask me for help again. Told me to get off her property or she'd call the cops and have me removed. Finally, I left and he shot her in the face approximately thirty minutes later." Tears tracked his cheeks and Raina brushed them away, feeling the roughness of the stubble on his face. "I shouldn't have left," he whispered. His agonized eyes met hers. "Why did I leave?"

"I'm so sorry," she whispered.

He pulled her into a hug the same moment a bullet whipped through the plastic cover and out the other side.

CHAPTER
FOURTEEN

Vince threw himself backward, arms still locked around Raina, emotions scattering while he went into defense mode. They fell to the deck of the pontoon as more bullets peppered the cover. She might be small, but her full weight landing on top of him stunned him for a brief second.

"Vince?"

"Not hit." He sucked in air. "You?"

"N-no. Just slightly terrified."

"Same here." He snagged her hand. A bullet pierced the deck. Another pinged off the motor. Hit it again. Smoke billowed. So much for driving out of there. Even if he could get to the key to crank it without catching a bullet, he was sure the motor was shot. Literally. "He's changed positions. I didn't hear the shots," he murmured.

"Meaning?"

"He's a long-range shooter and we need to get some help." He pulled his phone from the clip on his belt.

A bullet whizzed past her head and she gasped and ducked. Vince left the phone on and tucked it into the zip-up pocket of his vest. Unfortunately, not the bulletproof kind. At least it was waterproof, though. "Come on."

"Where are we going exactly?" But she scrambled after him, mimicking his army crawl.

"Can you swim?"

"You know I can. But usually in ninety-plus-degree weather. That water is cold. Cold's not really my thing, remember?"

"We can do cold lake water or cold morgue. You pick."

"Lake water it is."

"Give me your phone." She passed it to him and he added it to his pocket.

The gunfire stopped and he froze, listening, wondering if he dared to lift his head to try and spot the shooter.

Then three more bullets bit into the boat's cover, and two sent shards of the boat's decking spitting into the air.

"Over the side on three," he said. "Aim for the little island. It's the closest piece of land."

"Vince, I can swim, but that's a long . . ." She swallowed. "Never mind, let's go."

He hurried to the box he'd pulled the blanket from and snagged a life jacket before a round of bullets sent him scrambling backward. "He's looking for us on this end and I think he's shooting from the garage of that house."

"Which means we go to the other side?"

"Yep. We'll be exposed for a second or two, so don't hesitate once you're out from under the canopy. Just go over. Understand?"

"I got it."

"Go. I'm right behind you."

Raina went. Army crawling herself to the other end of the boat. As soon as she got to the end of the canopy, she pulled her feet underneath her. Vince did the same, staying right with her, doing his best to use his body as a shield. She launched herself to the bow, then over. Shots rang out. Vince felt a burning sting just below his right shoulder, then he was in the frigid water, doing his best not to gasp as his body instantly turned to ice.

He opened his eyes and the life vest in his left hand pulled him toward the surface.

Raina!

A cold hand grabbed his and he jerked toward the right.

Oh, thank God. Raina.

Her eyes were wide with fear, but also filled with determination and fight. He let the life jacket go, looked up, and spied the pontoon float. He swam toward it, pulling her after him. Together, they surfaced underneath the boat, between the pontoons. Raina gasped, spit water, and swiped a hand down her face. Her teeth chattered. "You okay?" she asked.

A shudder racked him and his shoulder burned with a fire that not even the freezing temps of the water could put out. "Me? Yeah, just fine." Their voices sounded weird, hollow, in the small space between the water and the bottom of the boat.

"L-liar," she stuttered. "Y-you're bleeding. You got shot!"

"Eh, just a graze, I think." Another shiver swept over him. "At least there are no sharks to come investigate." His little joke fell flat. "But you were right. It's definitely cold. We have to get out of the water."

"Thought we were swimming for the island."

"We are. I just don't want to get shot doing it." He leaned back, keeping the pocket of his vest above the water, and dug his phone out. "F-figured it was better to take shelter under here where he c-can't see us and take stock of the situation." He tapped 911, then looked at her. "Can you make it if we have to swim for it?"

"Sure." She raked a trembling hand over her hair, slicking it back. "Where is everyone? You think anyone called the cops? Or is this place deserted this time of year?"

"Definitely less traffic around here than in the summer, but there are a few year-round residents." Very few. Vince could kick himself. What had he been thinking bringing her out into this semi-isolated area?

"911. What's the address of your emergency?"

"We're out on Lake Giselle. Someone's shooting at us. We're hiding under a pontoon boat but may have to swim to the island."

"I'm sorry, did you say you were *under* a boat?"

"Exactly. It's a pontoon."

"Got it." He could hear the keys clacking in the background. "All right, sir, could I get your name—"

A round of bullets pinged off the pontoon's float, and Raina flinched, pulling him away from the area. He tucked the phone back in his pocket and sealed it.

"He knows we're under here," Raina said. "He's trying to do enough damage to the floats to sink it? To force us out from under it?"

"That's what it sounds like to me." His brain raced, desperate for a plan. "How long can you hold your breath?"

"Probably not as long as I need to."

"As soon as he stops shooting, we're going to swim for it. Hopefully, he'll be changing positions." The bullets still thudded and thunked on the float and the boat listed.

"And if he's not?"

"Let's just pray real hard that he is." His hand gripped hers. "You ready?"

"S-sure. How's your arm? Can you swim?"

"It's pretty numb at the moment. The absolutely only good thing about the temperature of this water." As soon as he warmed up, it was going to be a different story. For the next fifteen seconds, they waited. Listening. "All right," he said, "I think we're up. Take a deep breath and swim under the sinking side. Hopefully, he'll be so busy shooting out the other side that we'll be out of his line of sight and halfway to the island."

"Only halfway?"

He squeezed her cold hand. "At least the swimming will keep us warm."

"Right. Okay. L-let's go."

Together, they inhaled, then ducked below the surface. Vince almost wondered if he was just getting used to the temperature because he didn't feel quite as cold anymore. The fact that his movements were more sluggish than he'd like registered. But Raina needed him to get her out of this.

And he wasn't failing her.

■　■　■　■

Raina seriously didn't know how much longer she could swim. In spite of the medical knowledge that told her otherwise, she was quite sure her blood had frozen in her veins and the weight was going to drag her down to the bottom of the lake if she even thought about stopping.

But at least no more bullets were—

Thwack.

"Dive, Raina!"

The bullet had struck the water to her side. The next one followed her down. She kicked with leaden legs and spun to see Vince beside her, pointing. With an inward groan and dread pushing her to the edge of tears, she dragged her arms through the water and swam until she had to surface or pass out.

Raina aimed herself up, tilted her face toward the sky, and as soon as she broke through, gasped in a lungful of air.

And waited for another bullet to slam beside her.

Or into her. But she couldn't go back under. Not yet.

Vince did the same next to her, sucking in air and treading water.

Raina was so tired, so cold, so sleepy. She stopped trying to stay above the surface and let herself sink so she could be still just for a brief moment.

A hand yanked her back up. "No, no, no, Raina," Vince said,

his warm breath fanning her ear. "We've come this far, we just have a little bit farther to go."

She sputtered water, then dragged in another ragged breath. "He didn't shoot us, right? We're breathing and he's not shooting. So, what's he doing?"

"I don't know. Let's get to land. Hopefully, the 911 operator is still on the other end of the line."

"I'm not sure I can—"

"You can. You don't have a choice, so swim."

"B-bossy, aren't you?" But she knew what he was doing and she was grateful for it. She swam. And prayed. And swam some more. And envisioned a blazing fire with s'mores—

"Raina!"

She gasped, swallowed a mouthful of water, then choked and spit it out. She'd been sinking again.

"We're almost there," Vince said, his voice faint. "Don't stop now."

This was her fault. Her fault Vince was in danger. Her fault someone was shooting at them. Her fault. She should have told him no, pushed him away and refused to allow him to help. *God, you were supposed to keep him safe!*

Fueled by a growing anger, Raina pulled on every last shred of energy she had and finally found the bottom of the lake and walked, the murky mud trying to suck her boots from her feet.

Vince's hand gripped hers. "Ten more steps."

She took five and went to her knees.

Vince did the same. Swayed forward like he might face-plant. She managed to lean and push her body into his while water lapped around his upper thighs and her waist. "Vince?"

"I know. I'm good. Just had a moment there. We're too cold."

"Hypothermia is . . . is . . . a danger. And I'm sleepy. I just wanna sleep."

"Can't sleep. Gotta get warm."

"Which means moving. Right."

With a pained grunt, he rose and grasped her hand to pull her to her feet. On legs that didn't feel strong enough to hold her, she forced one foot in front of the other until she reached the shore.

"Don't stop," he said. "We have to keep moving to warm up."

"I know. I know. Where we going?"

"Doesn't matter. Just move."

He looked back over his shoulder and she followed his gaze.

"Think he's gone?" she asked.

"I see flashing lights. Cops are there. They'll send someone to come get us, but I'm going to build a f-fire. We need heat. But first . . ." With clumsy fingers, he finally managed to pull the phone from his pocket and press it to his ear. "You still there?" He listened and nodded, his body shaking and shivering. "Send someone to pick us up. Hot coffee would be a good thing to bring with them." He hung up. "Someone should be here soon, but for now, grab some sticks, whatever you can find that looks like it might burn. The movement will be good for us."

Her head knew that, but her body was protesting. It wanted her to sink to the ground, curl up in a ball, and go to sleep. She ignored it and moved, her hands like frozen blocks of ice. She flexed her fingers, thankful she could do so. No frostbite yet. "You d-don't think we're too exposed out here?"

"I think the shooter's gone, thanks to the arrival of law enforcement, but we're tucked into this little horseshoe area with trees surrounding us, so I think we're all right."

"Okay." She stood shivering, trying to work up the energy to move.

"Raina?"

"I know, I know. Move."

"Yes, ma'am."

All she wanted was to be warm again. Okay, mostly, she wanted to stay alive, but getting warm was a very close second. If gathering sticks would lead her to that outcome, she was all in. She stomped her feet, glad she could feel them, but the wet clothes were driving her nuts. "Sticks. I need sticks." Could she find anything dry? It still looked like it might rain but so far had held off.

Ignoring her physical discomfort, she walked to the edge of the wooded area and found as many pieces of dry wood or kindling as she could carry. On her search for small or broken limbs, she spotted an empty two-liter drink bottle in the underbrush. She hurried over to it and grabbed it to add to her stack of wood, noting there were three more in the same spot. She scurried back to where Vince had made some kind of bow out of a broken tree limb and a shoelace.

"You have a p-pocketknife? That's handy. Were you a Boy Scout?" she asked, dropping the armload on the ground next to him. She picked up the bottle and slid a dirty fingernail under the label.

"Eagle Scout."

"Of course you were."

His eyes landed on the bottle. "Plastic label?"

"Yup."

"You're a genius. That's going to make things a lot easier." He took it from her and added it to his little teepee-shaped pile of sticks, then went back to his bow and another piece of wood he'd notched a small hole in. "This is the fireboard." He nodded to the bow. "That's the drill. It's what's going to help create enough friction to start the fire."

"Great." She honestly didn't care how it was done, she just wanted to see flames. She was wet and cold, and for some reason, it was taking a really long time for anyone to start heading their way. "Where is the rescue boat? Isn't there some kind of water police or something out here? We shouldn't even have time for this kind of thing."

"No idea. We're going to need some larger pieces of wood. Wanna see what you can find while I get this going?"

"Sure." Raina did as he asked, finding that he was right about moving. The more she moved, the warmer she stayed—although the term *warm* was a stretch. The wind whipped around her, chilling every inch of exposed skin. She gathered a few larger tree limbs and returned to find the wood smoking. Then a tiny spark caught, and Vince blew gently, holding the label to it.

At first there was just some smoke, then a tiny flame nibbled at the label. "It's working," she breathed.

He continued to baby the small flame, then transferred it to the area he'd prepared. Within a few short minutes, large flames reached higher and finally started putting out enough warmth for Raina to feel it against her palms.

She eyed him as she dropped to the ground next to the fire. "You did it."

"Yeah." He drew her closer, squishing the wet clothes against her. She grimaced but didn't pull away since he was huddling next to her. "Look." He nodded to the officers gathered on the shore in the distance. They looked like tiny specks, but she thought she could see them backing a boat into the water. "They're coming."

Feeling was returning to her face, but her body was still chilled to the bone. "Awesome." She paused and looked him in the eye. "Thank you, Vince."

"For what?"

"For pushing me to swim. For keeping me safe. I know you didn't have to build a fire. I suspect that it was to give me something to do to make sure I kept moving."

A small smile curved his lips. "To make sure we both kept moving. Working that bow takes a lot of effort and exertion. I didn't exactly start sweating, but it kept my blood pumping."

She leaned her head against him. "I want a hot bath, my fuzzy Wonder Woman pj's, and warm slippers. And a cup of hot chocolate. In that order."

"I wouldn't mind that myself. Minus the Wonder Woman. I think Iron Man would be appropriate though."

Raina laughed. A long burst of sound that was too loud and on the verge of tears, but it still felt good. Then she sobered. "I'm sorry, Vince."

"For?"

"For dragging you into this. For asking you for help. For you almost getting killed." A tear trickled down her numb cheek and dropped from her chin. "I'm sorry. I should have—"

"Hey, no should haves." He tilted her chin toward him. "Remember our conversation? God is in charge, not you."

"But God isn't doing a very good job of keeping you safe!"

He stilled, his eyes dark with compassion. "I'm still alive, Raina, the bullet didn't hit anything vital, and we've got a big fire going to keep us warm while we wait. I'd say he's doing an exceptional job."

Her jaw dropped at his assessment, then she snapped it shut. "I guess it's all about perspective, isn't it? My perspective is, he could just stop the whole thing and make everything better. Stop the bad stuff before it even starts."

"If he did that, we wouldn't get to see him work, would we? What good is faith if you have no opportunity to exercise it?"

Good point. "Maybe so, but I think this is a bit excessive."

The roar of the boat engine caught her attention, and she noticed it skimming the water toward them. "They're almost here."

"Just as we almost got thawed out."

"You have a real gift for exaggeration. How's the arm?"

"Numb at the moment."

"Let me take a look at it?"

"No. If you start poking around at it, it's just going to start hurting. I'd rather just sit here and hold you for a bit."

Raina started to protest, then thought better of it. She didn't have any medical supplies, so what was the point in aggravating the injury? It obviously couldn't be too bad.

She snuggled against him, deciding to share his gratitude that they were alive, with the opportunity to be warm just around the corner. Because while the fire was nice, the wet clothes were not. Nor was the fact that a killer was out there most likely planning his next attack. "I hate being cold," she muttered. He chuckled and kissed the top of her head. She looked up. "But there's no one I'd rather be cold with."

This time his lips grazed hers just as the boat arrived and it was time to go.

CHAPTER
FIFTEEN

Simon disconnected the call with a one-finger punch to the screen, longing for the days when he could actually slam the receiver down. He settled for tossing the burner phone on his desk with harder than necessary force.

"Dad?" He looked up to see Christopher standing in the door, brow raised. "Bad news?"

"Something like that." Simon forced a smile with a shrug. "Just business. I'll get it sorted out later." He stood and walked toward his son. "Come on in the kitchen. I want some ice cream."

"Ice cream, eh? Must be serious."

Once they had the two bowls filled to overflowing, Simon looked up. "Where's Leslie?"

"She's meeting some friends for a girls' day out thing. And I have the night off." Christopher shoveled a spoonful of the sweet coldness into his mouth and grinned. Simon shook his head and grinned back. For a nanosecond. The weight of his worries was too great to hold the expression any longer.

"What's going on, Dad?" Christopher asked.

Simon looked at his son and debated whether or not to say

anything. Then he sighed. "That phone call that irritated me was my private investigator, who let me know that Daphne's father is snooping around into Keith's background."

Christopher pushed his ice cream bowl away. "Does it matter? There's nothing for him to find."

"I don't know. And that's the problem. I just don't know."

"And how does your PI know that anyway? That Daphne's father has someone looking into Keith?"

"We have our ways."

"You bugged his office?"

"And his home." Simon wasn't going to try and cover it up. No sense in that. "I need to know that Daphne isn't ready to change her mind or anything."

Christopher frowned at him. "That's illegal, Dad. If you get caught . . ."

"I know, but it's also providing me a special advantage that I need right now. Like the ability to head off trouble at the pass."

"There's more trouble?"

"Not yet."

His son pulled his bowl back and rubbed his temples like he had a headache. "Well, I'm certainly not one to throw stones. Just don't tell me anything else."

"Nothing to tell. Daphne is still googly-eyed over your brother and talking about the possibility of a wedding with her girlfriends. I'm going to tell Keith it's time to pop the question."

The kitchen door opened and Keith stepped inside. He took one look at their bowls and headed for the freezer. "Thanks for the invite."

Simon exchanged a look with Christopher, then forced a smile. "Glad you're here, Keith. Grab a bowl and pull up a chair. It's time for us to talk about your upcoming nuptials."

"I haven't even asked her yet."

"Exactly. You need to get that done."

Keith swiped a hand down his chin in an uncharacteristic

display of . . . nervousness? Or was it something else? "I . . . I don't know. I think it might be too soon. I don't know that she'd say yes."

Simon wanted to pound something. Mostly some sense into his son's head. "She'll say yes. Any fool can see she's head over heels for you." That's one thing he could say about Keith. He knew all the right words, body language, and more to make the ladies fall for him.

"Right, but what's she going to say when she learns I want to find my son?"

Simon bit his tongue and stood while Christopher went into a coughing fit. He finally released his tongue before he drew blood. "Son? Keith, do you hear yourself?"

"I do. I've decided to go after my kid. I'll keep it quiet, but I'm going to get him. He belongs to me, and the sooner you two come to terms with that, the happier we'll all be."

"And what about the child's family? He's happy where he is. Leave him alone."

Keith shook his head. "No. I've had time to think about this and I've got a plan."

"What kind of plan?"

Keith finished off the ice cream in one big bite that made Simon's head hurt. "A plan to get my son back and make sure the people who kept him from me all these years pay. Big time."

Leaving his bowl on the kitchen table, he stood and walked out of the kitchen without a backward glance.

Christopher groaned and dropped his chin to his chest. "What now?"

Simon blew out a low, frustrated huff of air. "He's going to ruin everything. We have to make this go away."

"How?"

"I'll think of something."

■ ■ ■ ■

Once again, Vince found himself sitting in the hospital, only this time, he was perched on the edge of the bed, waiting for someone to come stitch up the groove in his arm. The bullet had gouged out a nice chunk of flesh but thankfully, as he'd suspected, hadn't hit anything serious, and the cold water had stemmed the blood flow.

He stood, grateful his legs held him. By the time the boat had arrived, they'd been more unsteady than he would have liked to admit. And he needed to know how Raina was. His phone buzzed, and seeing his supervisor's name on the screen, he swiped it. "Covelli here."

"Vince, it's James. I heard about your little adventure. How are you doing?" The words were light, but Vince could hear the concern behind them.

"Doing okay. Got grazed by a bullet and need a couple of stitches, but I'll be fine."

"And the woman you were with?"

"Raina Price. She's okay too, thanks." He hoped. She was in the room next to him and he was about to go check on her.

"Glad to hear it. I tracked down John Tate. He's going to be calling you in a couple of hours."

"That's great. Thanks. And what about Freddy Harper? How did he get away from the tail?"

"He didn't. He went straight to the airport, hopped a private plane, and took off. Flight itinerary said he was landing at a private airfield near Burbank."

"So, there's no way it was him shooting at us," he murmured.

"No, wasn't him."

"Then who was it?"

"Good question. Authorities are investigating, of course, but if you have any thoughts, now's the time to give them."

"I don't, but I'll . . . think."

"I'll let you go. Keep me updated. Charlie and Fiona are on Fedorov, so you use your medical leave to recover."

"Thank you. I think I'll do that."

Just as he hung up, a knock on the door jerked his gaze up to see Raina enter. "I was just getting ready to come find you," he said. She wore scrubs—long pants and sleeves—and hospital socks on her feet. Her hair was dry and hung down her shoulders in waves. He found himself wanting to run his hands through it and, instead, clasped his fingers together and resisted.

"I was with the officers giving my statement," she said. "I was fine."

He nodded to the clothing. "You didn't have anything at base?"

"I didn't want to take the time to go up there." She chewed on the side of her cheek and Vince recognized that as a sign she was thinking.

"Spill it," he said.

She raised her brows and tucked her hands into the pockets of the shirt. "Sorry?"

"You're thinking."

"Oh. Yes. I am."

"About?"

"Freddy Harper."

"What about him?"

"His nose wasn't bruised."

It was his turn to raise his brows. "Was it supposed to be?"

"If he'd been the guy in my house, it should have been. I got in a good hit. I mean, I guess it's possible it wasn't as solid a hit as I thought it was, but . . ." She shrugged.

"So you've got two people after you?"

"I don't know. I was convinced Kevin sent him, but now . . . I don't know. What if Harper's telling the truth and he didn't have anything to do with coming after me?" She walked over to sit in the chair next to the bed. He'd rather her sit on the mattress next to him but shelved the thought as soon as it popped in his head.

"I think he is. Telling the truth, I mean." He told her about the conversation with his supervisor. "It wasn't Freddy shooting at us."

She blinked and paled a shade. "Then who was it?"

"That's the question of the hour." His phone rang once more. "It's Gabrielle."

"Clay's detective friend that came to the hospital?"

He nodded and swiped the screen. "Covelli here."

"Hi, Vince." Gabrielle's smooth alto was a pleasant sound. "I've got some interesting news for you that I thought you might like to hear."

"What's that?"

"The guy that was nabbed, Freddy Harper? It wasn't him who drugged Ms. Price."

"What do you mean?" He frowned. "We have him on video."

"He was there at the hospital, but he wasn't the one you saw at the counter. There was another guy of similar build. If you look at the mask on the guy in the ER and then the mask Freddy takes off when he exits the hospital, they're very close to being the same but are two different ones. And before you ask, yes, I'm sure. We've had experts weigh in and they've pointed out the differences. Even the color is different. It's subtle, but it's there."

Vince ran a hand over his head and glanced at Raina, who was looking at him like she'd really love to be listening in. "All right, thanks. I'll pass that on to Raina."

"We're doing our best to track the guy down. We got him leaving the hospital through a different exit about thirty minutes after the other guy and getting into a black pickup truck— which we discovered was stolen around eight that morning."

"Of course it was."

"I'll keep you updated."

"Wait, Gabrielle?"

"Yeah?"

"Can you find out who Freddy Harper is working for? I still think it's important to know that."

She went silent for a moment. "I guess we could, but right now it's not a priority. He was there, but it didn't have anything to do with Raina."

"And that's where I have to respectfully disagree. He was watching her at the restaurant and ran from us when we tried to catch up to him. He definitely has something to do with Raina. Even if he wasn't the one who drugged her or shot at us earlier. You really need to look into him."

Another pause on her end. "I'll mention it to my partner and the others and see what they think." She fell silent and he waited because he didn't think she was finished. "I'm not saying it's not kind of weird that he was at the restaurant," she finally said, "because it is. And I can see why that bothers you, but—"

"And he ran."

"Yes. And he ran. All good points. All right. I'll see what we can dig up."

"Right. Thanks."

He hung up and filled in Raina, who let out a slow breath. "Wow. That's not what I expected to hear."

His phone buzzed and she laughed. "You're one popular man today."

He glanced at the screen. "It's a California number. I'm guessing this is John Tate."

The smile slid from her lips and she swallowed hard. "Oh. Okay."

He tapped the screen and lifted the phone to his ear. "Covelli."

"This is John Tate. I hear you've been looking for me."

CHAPTER
SIXTEEN

The nurse with the suture kit, whose nametag read Barbara, chose that moment to step inside, and to Raina's frustration, Vince ended the conversation, with the promise to call right back as soon as he was released.

"Hey, Raina, how are you doing?" Barbara asked while she laid out her supplies. Barbara was in her midsixties, tall, with her salt-and-pepper hair cut in a fashionable style. She was one of Raina's favorite people in the hospital.

"Doing all right." Still alive, so more than all right, but she bit her tongue on those words. "Barbara, this is Vince. He's a good friend. Vince, this is Barbara, the best stitcher in the hospital. You'll be impressed at her needle-wielding skills."

"Needle-wielding skills. Right." Vince shot Barbara a weak smile. "Nice to meet you."

Since he was going to be a little while, Raina decided it was a good time to run an errand. "I'll just leave you to it."

"Wait, where are you going?" Vince's almost panicked question stopped her.

"I'm going to see someone who's a patient here." She'd already learned he was on the orthopedic floor.

"The DUI guy?"

She nodded and Barbara moved in, syringe in hand. "All right, Raina, why don't you go visit your patient while I take care of this young man." She turned to Vince. "This is just going to numb up the area before I give it a good cleaning and sew it up."

His eyes widened and he cleared his throat. "Um . . . Raina?"

"Yes." He looked really pale. What in the world—

"I . . . uh . . . tend to pass out when needles are aimed my way." He swayed and Raina rushed in to catch him against her before he fell off the bed.

"Vince?"

Barbara had set her syringe down and hurried to help.

"He's out cold," Raina said. They got him horizontal, elevated his feet, and she checked his pulse. "Steady and strong."

"Not the first time I've had that happen," Barbara said. "Let me just get this done while he's unconscious. Trust me, it'll be better for both of us."

"Go for it. I'll hold his hand in case he wakes up." It wouldn't be long before he'd stir.

"What about going to see the other patient?" Barbara worked fast, numbing the area and taking the first stitch.

Raina gazed at the man on the table, who was already blinking. "This guy is more important right now," she said, her voice low. "Hey, Vince, look at me." His eyes locked on hers. "You're fine."

"I passed out, didn't I?" A red flush climbed up his neck and into his cheeks, chasing away the pale gray color.

"You did."

"Great. There goes my superhero status."

She grinned at him. "Never. You'll always be a superhero in my eyes."

"I don't know. That's a pretty big thing to live up to."

"I'm not worried." She held his gaze, her heart thudding at

the look in his. He cared about her. The knowledge was daunting. Scary. Exhilarating.

She lost track of how long they simply looked at one another before he cleared his throat. "Don't tell me when she starts. I don't want to know."

Raina kicked herself. She was not a "get lost in someone's eyes" kind of person. At least not usually. She was the one who made fun of those kinds of people.

Not anymore.

"Raina?"

"Oh, sorry. Right. I won't tell you when she starts." She glanced at Barbara, then back to Vince. "But can I tell you when she's finished?"

"Huh?"

Barbara stepped back. "All done, big guy. You only needed ten."

Only ten.

Vince threw his good arm across his eyes. "I feel a little sick. Think I'm just going to stay right here for a few minutes."

"Want some Zofran?" Barbara asked. "Could be the local giving you some trouble."

"No, I'll be okay. I don't need anything that'll make me sleepy. Oh wait. Your phone is in that vest pocket. You need it."

She retrieved it and stuck it in her scrub pocket.

At the knock on the door, Raina opened it to find a hospital worker with a bag in her hand. "Raina Price?"

"Yes."

"Someone dropped this off for you. Said it was stuff left on a boat?"

Her purse and everything in it. What a relief. "Thank you."

"No problem." She left and Raina looked inside the bag. Everything was dry. She pulled out the picture she'd taken from the car wreck and stuck it in her pocket. She closed her eyes a moment and pulled in a deep breath. Okay, then. It was now or never.

Raina walked back to the bed and patted Vince's hand. "You stay here. I'll be back shortly." If she didn't take care of this now, she'd chicken out—or revert back to making googly eyes at Vince. And that wasn't going to happen again.

She fingered the photo in her pocket and knew she'd have to resist smacking the DUI dude in the face with it. No, she'd keep her cool and let him know her thoughts from a victim's point of view. He was probably going to prison for a while, so she'd give him some things to think about while he was incarcerated.

"Be careful, please," Vince said. "Watch your back."

"Always."

The door burst open and Penny's wide eyes landed on Raina, then Vince, then back to Raina. "What in the world? Y'all are just trouble magnets of the most powerful kind, aren't you?"

Raina snorted. "You're one to talk."

Penny waved a hand. "Aw, that's all in the past. I haven't had a lick of trouble since Rabor's been behind bars. But I'm not here about me. I'm here about you." She hugged Raina and gestured to Vince. "I can't believe all of this."

"I know," Raina said, "but right now, I don't have time to worry about someone out to kill me. I have an errand to run, so . . ." Another delay and she *would* lose her nerve. But she wasn't going to keep the picture, so that meant she had to go visit the owner and give it back to him.

"And I have to get back to work," Penny said.

"I thought you weren't working today? What happened to taking Holt to Columbia?"

"I thought I wasn't working as well, but tell that to the sick pilot. Holt found another ride."

"Sorry."

"Me too."

"Hey, do you have a spare pair of shoes in your locker? I can't keep walking around in these little booties."

"Yes, boots. What size you wear?"

"Seven and a half."

"They're sevens."

"I'll make them work."

"Then have at it." She gave the locker key to Raina. "Just leave it at the nurse's station. Gotta run." And then she was gone.

Raina smiled at Vince, who'd been watching the whole thing with avid interest. Now he frowned. "Raina—"

She walked over to him, kissed his cheek. "I'll be back."

"Raina—"

"See you in a few."

She slipped out the door before he could talk her out of it.

He didn't like her going off on her own, but she was in her second home. She wasn't worried. She made a quick stop by Penny's locker where she grabbed the boots, then her own locker where she found a pair of jeans, socks, and a sweatshirt. She changed faster than Superman in a phone booth, then shoved her feet in the boots. They were a little tight, but they'd do. She then made her way to the floor where Felix Hamilton was recuperating and aimed herself toward his room. Once he was released, he'd be transported to the jail to await his time in front of the judge.

"Hey, Raina, wait up."

She turned to see hospital security officer Lenny Maxwell ambling toward her. "Hi, Lenny, I'm sorry, I'm kind of busy. Can we chat a little later?"

"Not here to chat, just going to hang close by."

"Oh?" The light dawned. "Oh. Let me guess. Vince asked you to keep an eye on me?"

"Not exactly how he put it. Just asked me to hang around a specific room number."

"Funny how I'm going to that room." She shook her head. "All right, come on. I just want to check the waiting area first, okay?"

Lenny shot her a grin and followed her to the waiting room. "You looking for someone?"

"His wife and kids."

Raina stepped inside, scanning for the faces in the picture. Not there. Maybe the kids were with relatives and the man's wife was back in the room with him—or maybe they were all with him. She was kind of surprised he wasn't in the ICU, but keeping the piece of the steering wheel lodged where it was had been the right thing to do. So much so that he got a regular room.

Lucky him.

The television in the corner caught her eye. A ski slope and the Olympic Rings in the upper-right-hand corner of the screen. Captions scrolled across the bottom relaying the words of the reporter. "The Olympic team is gearing up for the charity benefit they've been asked to participate in. From downhill skiing to snowboarding to ice skating, it should be a fun afternoon that will raise a lot of money for the local Children's Hospital. One fun piece of news is that Michael Harrison has been asked to join in the event. I know I'm looking forward to watching that and I'm sure you are too." A picture of Michael on his snowboard popped up and then flashed to replay the interview that had started Raina's hunt for the man who'd almost killed her.

"Oh boy," she whispered.

"What is it?" Lenny asked.

"Nothing." Something. But she had to focus. She needed to get in the room, say what she came to say—without saying anything she'd regret—and get out.

She approached the guard and flashed her hospital badge at her. "Can he have visitors? I'm a paramedic and was one of the people at the scene. I also worked on him in the chopper."

"No kidding. Yeah, the doc came out just a few minutes ago. Said he was awake. His lawyer stopped by and they talked a long time—until the nurse came and chased him off."

"Then it's okay if I go in?"

"You're close enough to being considered hospital personnel and you were a part of saving his life, so . . ."

"Right. Thanks."

Raina pushed the door open. "Mr. Hamilton?"

No answer.

She stepped into the room and found the man alone and sleeping. His pale face was turned toward the window and one wrist was shackled to the bed frame.

Pity swept over her and the sudden surge of emotion caught her by surprise. Here was a man who'd caused a disaster on the highway, put several people in the hospital, and nearly killed himself. A man with a family who loved him if the picture was any indication. Why was she feeling sorry for the guy? He needed to be put away for a very long time and—

His head rolled toward her and his eyes flickered open. When they centered on her, he frowned. Licked his lips. "Who are you?" The words were no more than a whisper.

Against her better judgment, she picked up the Styrofoam cup that probably had held ice but was just water now and held it to Felix's dry lips.

He sucked on the straw and swallowed three times before pulling away and nodding. "Thanks," he croaked.

"I was one of the paramedics on the scene." She kept her voice neutral, devoid of the emotions she was doing her best to suppress. "How are you feeling?"

A tear leaked out of his left eye and he drew in a shuddering breath. "I don't think I have the words for that."

"Yeah. I imagine not. You're incredibly fortunate no one died because of you. At least you won't be looking at manslaughter charges."

He flinched and blinked. Then shuddered. "Yes, at least there's that." His low voice held shame, grief, and disbelief that he'd found himself in this situation. "At least there's that."

She pulled the picture from her pocket and slipped it into his free hand. "I thought you might want that."

He lifted it to stare at it while more tears flowed soundlessly down. His hand shook. Withdrawals?

"She would be furious with me," he whispered.

Raina raised a brow. "Would be?"

"She's dead. Six months ago. Her and our son. Killed by a drunk driver." He scoffed and looked away from the picture while Raina stood frozen solid in utter shock.

What did she say to that? How did she respond? She finally found her voice. "And yet you go and—"

"I know." He ran a hand over his face. "I had no intention of driving, but when my sister called—"

The door opened and a young woman in her midthirties stepped inside, stopping when she saw Raina. "Oh, I didn't realize you had company."

Raina needed to escape. To breathe. To think. "I was just leaving."

"Are you a friend of Felix's?"

"I was part of the rescue team."

Her eyes narrowed. "Okay. And you're here because?"

"There was a picture in the car he wrecked and I wanted to return it."

"Liv," Felix said, "how's Hannah?"

"She doesn't need the ventilator."

The breath whooshed from the man in the bed and Raina frowned. "Ventilator?"

"Hannah's his daughter," Liv said. "She was having trouble breathing so I brought her in. She's been diagnosed with pneumonia. Since she's asthmatic, they're watching her carefully. On Monday afternoon, they were discussing putting her on a ventilator. At that point, I called Felix."

"And that's when he climbed in the car after having too much to drink," Raina said.

"Apparently." She pursed her lips and shook her head. "I didn't know where he was or I never would have called him."

Raina cleared her throat. "I . . . uh . . . need to leave. I hope . . . Hannah gets better soon."

"Thank you for bringing me the picture," Felix said.

"Yeah. Sure." Raina practically ran out of the room, stopping only when she was inside the nearest bathroom. After splashing water on her face and drying it, she pulled in a ragged breath and blew it out slowly. "Unbelievable," she whispered. "Absolutely unbelie—"

A knock on the door echoed around her. "Raina?"

"I'm okay, Lenny. I'll be out in a minute." She looked at herself in the mirror and refused to talk to her reflection. Taking two more minutes to try and sort through her emotions and finding it impossible, she turned and strode to the door, opened it, and found Lenny waiting. "You don't have to babysit me."

"I'm not. I'm just the messenger."

"Oh. Sorry. What's the message?"

"Your man is trying to get in touch with you. Says he's ready to go."

"My ma—? Never mind. Thank you. I'm ready to head back down to the ER."

■ ■ ■ ■

Vince didn't like having Raina out of his sight but had to trust the security officer would keep an eye her. His thoughts went to his truck? He needed a plan to get it from the lake house. Someone had brought Raina's stuff to her, but he'd had the keys in his waterproof zip-up pocket along with his and Raina's phones, and he and Raina had ridden to the hospital in the ambulance. He checked the app on his phone, and it told him his truck was in the hospital parking lot. "Huh."

He'd worry about how it got there later. Right now, he just wanted the queasy feeling to go away. And he still needed to call John Tate back, but that was going to have to wait until he could talk to the man without puking. He closed his eyes, wishing he could work up the energy to go after Raina, but Lenny had texted to assure him that he had her in his sights. Two minutes later, knuckles rapped on the door.

"Come in."

Clay Fox stepped inside. "Hey there. I hear someone mistook you and Raina for targets. You two okay?"

"We're fine. You didn't have to drive all the way over here."

"Penny called and told me what was going on and that your truck was still at the scene. Figured since I had your only spare key, I'd put it to good use. Julianna was with me and we picked it up." He dropped a bag on the bed next to Vince. "Thought you could use a dry change of clothes too. Unless you prefer the hospital gown."

"Always the comedian. Thanks, man."

"Welcome." Clay leaned against the wall and crossed his arms. "Anything else we can do for you?"

"No, I'm just waiting on—"

Two knocks cut him off. "Come in."

Raina swept inside. "I hear you're ready to go. Hey, Clay."

"Hey, Raina."

Vince noted that while he didn't feel great, he wasn't going to hurl anytime soon. Improvement.

Raina handed him a bottle of ginger ale. "Thought you could use that."

"Yeah. Thanks." He studied her, trying to read beyond the surface. "How'd it go?"

"Weird. I'll explain later. I've got to take a little trip to Colorado."

Vince blinked. "Huh?"

"What?" Clay raised a brow.

"I'm going to see if Penny can fly me. If not, then I'll just catch a commercial flight."

"Um . . ." Vince really needed to find his tongue. "Why?" Good enough.

"Because I figured out how to catch Kevin."

"And he's going to be in Colorado?" His brain was kicking in.

"Yes. At some fundraiser thing for the Children's Hospital. There's no way Michael Harrison won't be there. He may have protection around him—and that's good, but also bad, because Kevin will know exactly where he is and how to find him. And I feel sure Kevin will show up." She hesitated. "Okay, I know to you guys it probably seems like a long shot, but I'm still going. Somehow."

"When is the benefit?"

"Two days from now, but they're practicing tomorrow, so I'm sure Michael is already there. Or soon will be."

"I can call my buddy and see what the family's status is," Vince said. "Don't go anywhere until I find out, okay?"

She hesitated. "I won't leave without talking to you first. Did you call John Tate back?"

"Not yet." Vince stood and waited to see if another wave of nausea was going to take him down. After a few hairy seconds and several swallows, he kept everything where it belonged and nodded. "All right, I'm going with you."

"I figured you'd say that, but you need to stay here and rest—"

"That's really not an option. Think about it. What would you do if the situation was reversed? Would you seriously let me go off on my own?"

She bit her lip, started to say something, glanced at Clay, who still had that annoying brow up toward his hairline. She snapped her lips closed. Finally, she sighed. "No, of course not."

"Then you'll spare me the energy of arguing with you?"

Her own brows rose, but she gave a short nod. "Fine. I'm going to grab some stuff out of my locker and find Penny while

I'm there. I'll let you know what the plan is and the time of departure—or if we need to get tickets."

"O—kay." He finished the word while watching her sweep back out the door.

His gaze landed on Lenny and the man saluted him. "Right behind her."

"You deserve a raise."

"I sure do."

And then Lenny was gone too.

Vince blew out a breath, lay back on the bed with a relieved groan, and snagged his phone.

"You're looking really rough, my friend," Clay said. "Are you sure this is a wise decision?"

"If it was Julianna, what would you do?"

"I see your point. Okay, what can I do to help you?"

"Catch me if I pass out mid-call." He dialed John Tate's number and let it ring until it went to voice mail. He left a message for the man to call him back and sighed. "Great."

CHAPTER
SEVENTEEN

Raina ignored Lenny's heavy steps behind her and raced to base, where Penny was lying on the couch, fingers flying over the screen of her phone. Probably texting Holt. "Hey."

Penny looked up. "Hey, what are you doing here?"

"You're off tomorrow and the next day, right?"

"Yes. Why?"

"I need a favor. And it's a doozy of one."

Penny set her phone aside. "Okay. What can I do?"

"Fly me—and Vince—to Frisco, Colorado. In your chopper. The one you built, not the hospital one, of course."

Her friend's eyes widened. "Uh . . . what?"

"Or Denver. Whatever is easier. Frisco would be better because it's closer to Copper Mountain where the event is, but—"

"Raina!"

Raina fell silent. "Sorry. I'm babbling, aren't I?"

"A bit. Take a breath and tell me what's going on?"

She explained the situation. "And I need to get there because apparently, I'm the only person alive who can point the finger at Kevin Anderson—or whoever he is." Raina pinched the bridge of her nose. "I'm willing to bet he's going to be there."

Penny frowned. "Raina, you can't go with no plan. Or backup. Or whatever."

"I know. Vince is working on that."

"You said you're willing to bet Kevin's going to be there. What about Michael? Do you even know for sure that he's going to be there? His parents may decide his safety is more important."

The air left Raina's lungs. It was possible Michael might not be going and she was off on a fool's errand anyway. Could she trust her memories of Kevin from over a decade ago were still accurate? Kevin could have changed during the past fourteen years. She sure had.

But men like him didn't change, did they?

Not without divine intervention and a serious "come to Jesus" moment. It was possible, of course, but she wasn't going to take that chance.

The same man Grace had profiled for her, describing him as a narcissist and probable sociopath.

A man who wouldn't care one bit about the harm he would cause a boy and his family if he decided Michael belonged to him. "I know it seems crazy. But on the off chance that Michael and his family decide the risk is worth him performing at the event, I have to go."

Penny glanced at the clock on the wall. "Okay, first, we can't take my chopper. Denver is just too far without fuel stops." She wrinkled her nose and squinted at the ceiling. "Like four stops if I did the math right. And it would take us about nine hours to get there."

"Oh." Raina's shoulders slumped. "Of course it would. We'll just have to fly commercial, but that will take so long too." She pulled her phone from her pocket and started searching for flights. "Well, it is what it is."

Penny sighed. "Maybe not."

"What do you mean?"

"I have a friend who has a jet at the same hangar."

"The hangar on top of the mountain?"

"A flat top of the mountain with a runway, yes." She shook her phone at Raina. "Let me see if I can get in touch with Bob and ask him if I can use the jet."

Raina blinked. "Are you rated to fly that?"

A slow grin curved her friend's lips. "I am."

"When did that happen?"

"It's a surprise. Or it was. I was going to fly Holt and me to the Dominican Republic for a special weekend."

"So, those are the errands you've been running."

"Yes. Flying lessons and then the test. I passed a while ago, but have been flying every chance I got to get hours in." Her fingers flew across the screen of her phone.

"And you can fly solo?"

"Well, of course." Her phone buzzed and she glanced at it. "That's Bob. He says it's fine."

"Fuel's expensive, isn't it?"

"Yeah, but we'll worry about that. Bob gives me a special rate on it because I'm letting him use my chopper for his lessons."

"Awesome. Penny, that's amazing."

Her friend scowled. "But not a word to Holt."

"You don't think he's going to find out that you're flying us to Denver?"

"Not if we're sneaky. Now, assuming we don't get a call, I can meet you at the hangar in three hours. From here to Colorado is about a three-hour flight. However, that timetable will change if we get a call . . ."

"Right." It would have to do. "Thank you. If Vince tells me Michael is going to be there, I want to get there ASAP. I'll find a hotel or something for the two nights—I'll pay for yours too. If you get a call, then you get a call." She'd be praying for no call.

"But," Penny said, "if the competition's not for two days, what's the rush?"

"Because he'll be practicing. Kevin could decide to strike any moment. I feel like . . . like . . . I'm racing against a ticking clock—and Kevin. I have to beat him there or things could go south very fast." She pressed a palm to her forehead. "Look, I know I'm making a lot of assumptions." A whole lot. "But I just have to follow my gut on this one. We could get there and everything could be just fine, but with someone out to get me, I'm thinking my gut may not be too far off. If I'm wrong, I'm wrong." But she really didn't think she was.

Penny raised a brow. "All right, then. I'll see you in three hours."

"Thank you." She gave her friend a quick hug and hurried back to find Vince. Lenny dutifully pounded behind her. They'd just announced the fundraiser and the fact that Michael would be participating in the event. Hadn't they? Or had this been on the news before and she was simply spinning her wheels?

She didn't know. A quick Google search showed Michael Harrison on the list of snowboarders to participate.

But would he really show up?

Even if he didn't, the fact that he was on the list meant Kevin might.

With Lenny behind her, she returned to Vince's room to find him ready to go. "Did you get Michael's parents?"

"Yeah, they said they're not letting him participate."

Her shoulders wilted. "Seriously?"

"They said his name was supposed to be removed from the list of participants."

"Oh. Okay then. That's a relief." She chewed her lip for a thoughtful moment, then shrugged. "I think we still need to go. I think this is my best shot at finally finding Kevin."

"I agree." Vince glanced at her empty hands and raised a brow at her. "I thought you were grabbing stuff from your locker."

Raina followed his gaze and sighed. "I'm losing it."

Lenny held up a hand. "I got this. Come on."

Once Raina had her bag from her locker—the one her friends jokingly called her "go bag" for good reasons—she and Lenny returned to the ER.

Clay glanced at his phone, then nodded to the exit. "Vince said for me to escort you to the passenger seat when he pulled up."

"He did, huh?"

"Yes, ma'am." Lenny nodded.

A light drizzle fell outside the glass doors and Raina grimaced. "Great," she whispered. "Cold and rainy."

Clay side-hugged her. "You need to move to Florida. Or the Mojave Desert."

"Ha-ha."

"It'll be warm in the truck and the plane. You'll be fine." He cleared his throat. "Someone will keep me updated, right?"

"Of course." Raina turned to the guard. "Thank you for all your help today, Lenny. I really do appreciate it."

The man turned scarlet and he ducked his head. Looking up, he patted her shoulder. "Happy to do it, Raina. Be safe."

Vince pulled to the curb and Clay opened the door for her. She tossed her bag in the back and slipped into the passenger seat.

Clay nodded and met Vince's gaze. "Let me know if you need anything."

"Will do. Thanks."

He shut the door and Raina buckled up. "You sure you're up for driving?" she asked.

"Yeah. I didn't take anything that I shouldn't be driving with."

"And the nausea?"

"Almost gone."

She narrowed her gaze and studied him. He did look like he was feeling much better. "I'm glad, but don't hesitate to let me drive if you need to."

"Noted."

Raina tapped the address to the hangar into her GPS. "I never can remember how to get there," she muttered. "Who keeps a helicopter—or a plane—on top of a mountain?"

"Only Penny." He laughed. "Guess it makes sense, though. Climb in and you're already halfway to your destination. Saves on gas too."

She grinned. "Cute. And not totally wrong." He reached for her hand, his eyes suddenly serious and on hers for a split second before he looked back at the road. She frowned. "What's with the sober expression all of a sudden?"

"I just realized how rarely you smile. Like that full-blown grin."

"Oh." She sighed. "I guess I haven't had much to smile about lately."

His hand squeezed hers. "We're going to change that."

Her heart trembled at the care on his features and the warmth in his touch. But a little voice reminded her that she hadn't been completely honest with him and didn't need to be having feelings for the man—because when he knew the truth, he might just walk away. The thought doused her budding feelings as effectively as a firehose aimed at a firepit.

She removed her hand from his and clasped it with her other in her lap. He shot her a questioning look but didn't say anything.

"I saw Felix Hamilton," she blurted, "the drunk driver."

"I was hoping you'd tell me how that went."

"It went."

"Ah. I see."

He didn't see, of course, but how could she put into words what she was thinking? Feeling? To try or not to try? She glanced at him. He met her gaze with a brief, warm look. But he would understand in a way most people couldn't. "I've hated the man who killed my father from day one," she finally said, her voice low, gaze on the passing scenery. "I don't *want* to hate him, but I'm not sure I want to forgive him either, although I know that's what I'm supposed to do. Forgive your enemies, right?"

He nodded. "I get it."

"Have you forgiven your brother-in-law?"

Vince blew out a low breath. "I think it's a process. Some days forgiveness comes easier. Other days, like holidays, the resentment and anger want to surface, and I have to make a conscious effort not to dwell on it. To give it back to God."

"I think that's part of my problem too. I think deep down, I'm still not sure I can trust God. Mentally, I know I can. But sometimes my heart doesn't line up with that."

"Better to go with what you know than what you feel."

Raina shot him a small smile. "I know that too." The smile faded. "I judged him, Vince. I judged him and found him guilty. In my head, even when I was saving his life, I had put him on trial, with me as the sole judge and jury. If I'd had the power, I would have sentenced him right then and there."

"Did that change after you met him?"

She sighed. "Yes. Sort of. I felt compassion for him, and that felt like I was making less of what happened to my father. Like I was cheating him from having his justice."

"Didn't the guy who killed him die?"

"He did. And I've been glad ever since. But meeting Felix Hamilton has given me something to think about."

"Like what?"

"He was a mess, Vince. He was in pain, hurting and grieving the loss of his wife and son. He had no intention of driving home, but then he got word his daughter was in the hospital. And he acted. How can I sit in judgment of him when I've done things that resulted in terrible consequences for others? Like Mrs. Atwater? If I hadn't allowed Kevin into my life, she would still be alive. So would Trent Carter." Tears clogged her throat and shame coursed through her. She blinked at the onslaught of emotion and pulled in a deep breath. "Sorry, I didn't mean to lay all that on you."

His hand gripped hers. "I want you to, Raina. It actually helps me to hear you voice that. It helps to know I'm not alone in my thoughts when I want to storm the prison and put a bullet in Eden's ex. It helps to remember that he's human just like I am. My choices didn't result in my sister's death, but they didn't prevent it either." He paused. "I think that's where faith comes in. We just have to trust that God is still in control even when it looks like he isn't and we don't understand why he does or doesn't do something."

She squeezed his fingers. "Easier said than done."

"Yep."

They fell silent, but he didn't let go of her hand and she didn't pull away. Twenty minutes later, they were on a mountain road heading toward Penny and Holt's vacation home that doubled as a hangar for Penny's hand-built chopper.

Only Vince's eyes were on the rearview mirror.

"What is it?" she asked. Her gaze went to the side mirror, noting the green truck behind them.

Traffic was light, but people were out despite the rain and below-freezing temps. She was glad they were going to be off the road shortly.

"That truck's been behind us a while."

"You think it's following us?"

"I don't know. Could be just a little paranoia on my part."

"But you don't like it."

"I don't. I'm going to take the next turn up—" No sooner had the words left his lips than the green truck accelerated and slammed into the back of them.

■　■　■　■

Vince registered Raina's gasp as he jerked the wheel to the left to keep his vehicle on the road, but hit a patch of black ice.

He brought his foot off the gas and tried to steer into the slide, but the hit had him going too fast and he spun a one-eighty onto the shoulder. Rocks and other debris crunched under the tires. Traction. He pressed the brakes. The truck hit them again and the seat belt locked. Pain sparked in his shoulder, then shot across his torso.

"Vince!"

Raina's sharp cry seared him almost as bad as the shoulder injury. "Hold on!"

Another spin of the wheel and he shot off the shoulder, bounced over the raised grassy area. He did his best to keep the truck level, but the left front tire blew, sending them into the flooded ditch. They tilted, then rocked back so the driver's door was against the side of the ditch closest to the road. Muddy water raced below them. It wasn't deep, but it did look like a small river.

Dazed, he shook his head, trying to get his brain working. "Raina? You okay?"

"I . . . I think so. Are you?"

"Yeah. But we need to get out of here and call for help." He hadn't heard an engine speeding away, which meant the pickup might still be out there. He looked around for his phone and couldn't see it.

Thwack.

Vince jerked.

Raina's gaze slammed into his. "Was that a—"

"Yes!" The back windshield shattered. "We're sitting ducks. Get out!"

Without hesitation, she grabbed the door handle and shoved. Another bullet whizzed past his cheek. "Raina, go!" He reached into the back and snagged her bag.

"I'm trying! The door won't open!"

With the truck greatly slanted toward the driver's side, Vince could see that gravity was going to win against her strength.

Since the truck was still running, he lowered the window and she hauled herself out while more bullets peppered the side and roof of the vehicle. He lunged after her, pulling her duffel with him.

As he hung halfway out the window, a sudden sting in his calf made him gasp, but he kept going, both of them landing on the hard, wet ground. Water sloshed to his ankles, rolling over the edges of his boots and turning his feet into blocks of ice. The cold wind and rain bit through the sweatshirt and heavy vest, chilling him to the bone, and the smell of earth and rain filled his nostrils. "Go up," he said, "but stay low. Army crawl."

"Right. That sounds like so much fun."

He ignored the coping sarcasm, but was grateful she scrambled to do as ordered while the rain came down, sluicing over them, turning the normally grassy ground into quicksand-type mud that sucked. A pasture lay in the distance, with trees beyond it. A barn, a house, and two other outbuildings dotted the landscape.

The shooting had stopped, but that didn't mean the shooter was gone. "Stay low. Roll under the fence and use the post for cover." Not that it would provide much, but she was small, so maybe it would at least cover her back.

"Where's he shooting from?" She rolled, the grimace on her face saying more than words what she thought about the current situation.

"I can't tell." He followed her, figuring the look on his face probably mirrored hers. He ignored the burning in his shoulder and the fiery sensation in his calf. Scrambling, he leaned his back against the fence's thick wood beam. "Maybe from across the street in the other pasture. How far are we from the hangar?"

"A good three miles." She patted her pocket. "Oh no."

"What?"

"My phone's gone."

He pressed cold-numbed fingers to his eyes. "And I think

mine went flying out of the cupholder when he hit us the first time." He'd been hoping she had hers.

"Great."

"Yeah, but the shooting's stopped." Because the person was scouting for a better angle?

"I'm really tired of being sh-shot at. And cold. I'm tired of that too."

"I'm with you on that."

"S-sorry, I'm complaining. I'll sh-shut up now."

"I get it, Raina." And he did. Law enforcement personnel used all kinds of coping mechanisms, including sarcasm, a morbid sense of humor, and so on. During the verbal sparring, he'd been watching the home. "Okay, I don't see any cars in the drive or lights on in the house. No one came out to investigate the shots. The barn is the closest place for some good cover. Let's make it there and regroup."

"Okay."

He crawled over to her, ignoring the squishy mud and the rain sliding down under his collar. Shivering, he shook his head. Unbelievable.

"At least we're n-not trapped on an island this time," she said.

"You read my mind." With her cold hand tucked in his almost-frozen one, he squeezed, then pulled his weapon from his holster. "When I say run, get to your feet as fast as possible and aim yourself to the barn. I'll be right behind you."

"O-okay."

It was only about twenty yards away, but bullets could still do their damage before they got there. And while the shooter wasn't shooting . . .

"Run."

She lurched to her feet with his help, and together they raced to the door of the barn, with him aiming his gun in the direction the bullets had come from.

But they made it and Vince sent up a prayer of thanks that it was unlocked. They slipped inside with no more bullets coming their way.

It had been too much to hope the building was heated, but at least they were out of the rain. His shoulder and leg throbbed, but he and Raina were alive—which meant they had the chance to stay in the fight. He swiped the rain from his face and shook his head. Water flew from the strands and slid under the collar of his shirt to make its way down his back while goose bumps pebbled his skin. He tucked his weapon back into his holster.

A violent shudder rippled through Raina and he placed a hand on her shoulder. "Come on, let's get you warm." The barn was a simple layout. Six stalls, three on each side. The doors on each end mirrored one another. Four horses peered curiously at the newcomers. Two stalls were empty. Four windows—one in each corner— offered some natural light. He hesitated to flip the switch on the wall.

"Didn't we just live this?" Raina asked, sweeping a hand over her sopping head. "I feel like I'm in the twilight zone. Or that old movie, *Groundhog Day*." He raised a brow and she shivered. Her jaw trembled and her teeth chattered. "Apparently, I'm destined to be freezing. I'll get warm later. Think there's a phone in here?"

"I'll look. But if you'll dig in one of those hay bales, you could get enough to cover up with. Might help. And there are probably some horse blankets somewhere."

"I'm fine. Let's just focus on getting out of here. Penny's going to be at the airfield in"—she nodded to the clock on the wall—"two hours. I don't want her to have to wait on us."

"We have to report this, Raina."

"I know, but let's just try to wrap this up in less than two hours—with us alive at the end of it, of course."

"I love your optimism."

Ignoring the pain in his limbs, Vince scanned the area for a phone—and came up empty. Not that he was surprised. Most people had their cells and didn't bother with a landline any-more. "Well, there's enough hay in here to keep about ten horses fed for a few years, so if we get hungry, I guess we can chow down."

"Yay." She sounded so forlorn, so opposite from only seconds before, he couldn't help but smile in spite of everything.

He pulled the bag from his uninjured shoulder and tossed it to her. "Anything in there you could use?"

Her eyes widened. "You grabbed my bag? We don't have to eat hay, I have protein bars and trail mix. You're my hero. Thank you."

Despite the chill invading every inch of his body, heat crept up from his neck into his cheeks. He cleared his throat. "You're welcome." He walked to the window next to the door and looked out in the direction they'd run from. He could see his truck listing in the ditch. Probably totaled. Rats. He'd liked that truck.

The rain still fell, creating small rivers in the muddy field. But he didn't see any evidence that someone had followed them. Not that that was a good indication. The water would have washed away any footprints.

He started to turn, but movement near the truck whipped him back around.

"What is it?" Raina stepped up next to him, a blanket wrapped around her, and her hair pulled back in a ponytail tied at the nape of her neck. She looked beautiful, vulnerable, scared . . . and strong all at the same time.

He swung his gaze back to the area where he'd seen the shadow but was now wondering if he'd imagined it.

Sure hadn't imagined the bullets that had come their way.

Doing his best to ignore the cold—yet again—and the pain in his leg, he stayed focused and . . . yes, there. The rain had slowed to a drizzle and Vince could make out the figure in the truck bed. "He's going through my truck," Vince murmured.

"What?" She scooted closer, trying to see.

He made room for her, breathing in the scent that was uniquely hers. A mixture of strawberry body wash and vanilla shampoo. A scent he didn't think he'd ever get tired of—*Stop it!*

"While he's distracted, now might be a good time to head to the house," Raina said. "See if there's a phone there?"

He really didn't think there would be, but . . .

The guy stood, yanked his ball cap lower with a movement that indicated frustration. He had a bag over his shoulder—probably loaded with ammo—and turned to survey the area, gun in his right hand, left hand on his hip. "He's mad we're not there," Vince said. "He thought he got us. The good thing is, I don't think he saw us run for the barn."

"How is that possible?"

"I don't know. Something distracted him? He assumed his bullets hit their mark?"

The man's gaze landed on the barn and Vince ducked back. In time? He eased back to the window. "But it's safe to assume that since we're not dead in the truck, he'll know we got away and are hiding somewhere close by. Won't take him long to figure that out and start looking. Probably here first."

Their attacker walked through the flooded ditch to the side they'd exited. His gaze swept the ground and he punched the fence post with a fist.

After several seconds, he walked back to Vince's truck.

"What are you doing, dude?" Vince whispered aloud.

Raina reached out and took his hand, her fingers spasming around his. The guy stuck something in his bag, checked the weapon, then aimed himself at the barn.

"What's he doing?" Raina asked. "He's carrying something. I can't tell what it is."

"I don't know, but just like I figured, he's coming this way."

CHAPTER
EIGHTEEN

She still held his cold hand and found herself not wanting to let go. "Any thoughts on what to do?"

"I've got my weapon, of course, and will use it if necessary, but I honestly want to talk to the guy more than I want to shoot him."

"So, how do you want to make that happen?"

"I'm thinking."

A loud thud against the side of the barn jerked her heart into a gallop. "What was that?"

"No idea."

Seconds passed, then another thump on the other side of the building echoed the first one. "Vince?"

His frown didn't bode well. He raced to the window nearest the last thud and looked out. "Nothing."

A third clunk hit the door behind them.

The horses, who had lost interest in their unexpected visitors, now came back to hang their heads over the doors of the stalls. One thumped his feet. Another whinnied.

"Something's wrong," she whispered. "They sense something."

"Yeah, but what?"

She sniffed. "You smell that?"

"No, what?"

"Gas? And . . . smoke! Look!" She pointed at the gray ten-drils curling under the barn door, then threw off the blanket and ran to the nearest stall. "Get the horses out!"

"He's smoking us out." Vince opened the second stall and gripped the halter of the animal inside.

"What are we going to do? As soon as we step foot outside, he'll pick us off." Flames licked under the door at the end, and she wouldn't have thought it possible, but her heart ticked a little faster.

"He came prepared to burn something down?" Raina led the horse to the exit. "I'm finding that a little hard to believe."

"Most likely he found the gas can in the back of my truck and improvised."

"Fabulous."

The first two horses raced out the other end, away from the smoking door. Raina gripped the halter of the third animal—Benji was carved into the side of it—and led him behind Vince. Benji tossed his head and whinnied, not liking the building smoke. He was antsy and wanted out. She did too, but not at the expense of getting shot. Then again, she didn't want to die from smoke inhalation either. She sent him thundering out.

The silence enveloped her and she glanced out the window. "The rain slowed. It's just a drizzle now." Dumb observation maybe, but the words slipped out. The open door revealed dark clouds, a wet pasture, and trees in the distance. "As soon as we go, he's going to shoot at us."

"Not if he can't see us," Vince said. "I think he's on the other side of the door waiting for us to come out that way. He deliberately left it open—no flames coming from that way—so we're going out the other way."

She gaped. Then coughed when the swirling smoke dipped into her lungs. "Through the flames?"

"Yep. We'll send the last one out the same way," he pointed, then he turned. "And we're going that way."

In the opposite direction.

At the burning door.

"We're soaking wet," he said. "Maybe that will work in our favor."

"Maybe?" She squeaked the word and didn't even care. But knew he was right. The smoke was building and the horse she held was trying to pull her to what he considered safety.

Vince nodded and slung her bag over his shoulder. "But before we do that, I'm going to soak that blanket with the water in the pails in the stall. You keep holding the horse." Working fast, he soaked the blanket until it dripped, then handed it to her as he took the horse's halter. "It's going to be cold, but put it over your head." She did so and he slapped the animal on the rump. The horse didn't waste a second and galloped after his buddies. Vince ducked under the blanket with her, took her hand, and aimed them at the other exit.

"Hold your breath and just run. Ready?"

She wasn't. "Go. I'm right with you."

He ran and hit the wall of flames. She did the same, feeling the intense heat, then Vince tossed the blanket and kept going, Raina doing her best to keep up, slogging through the soggy pasture. The mud sucked at her boots and she was thankful she had laced them tight.

Finally, they reached the tree line with no bullets fired their way, and he pulled her to a stop behind a large oak. "I think it worked," she sputtered, gasping, a stitch in her side telling her she probably needed to up the intensity of her workouts.

Keeping himself shielded behind the trunk, he peered around the side. "I don't see him."

"You think he figures we're still in there?"

"I don't know. If he looks around, he'll see the blanket." He sighed. "I should have brought it with me."

"That fire is pretty intense. We dropped it close to where we ran out. It's probably incinerated. And my guess is, he's not getting near the area for a while to check anyway."

"True."

She paused. "Think anyone's seen it and called it in?"

He closed his eyes. "I don't hear any sirens yet." He grimaced. "Man, I hope they have good insurance on that barn."

Raina nodded. But a barn could be rebuilt. "At least we got the horses out."

Vince swiped a hand over his cheek. "So, what do you think? Wait for the fire department and cops to show up? Because they will eventually. Or hike until we come to another house with a phone?"

"A ph-phone sounds good. I know we need to tell them what happened, but . . . I don't want to waste any time getting to Colorado. Maybe you can call Holt—once we find the phone—and tell him what happened?"

"Yeah. Okay." His eyes swept the area once more. "Let's just hang out here for a few more minutes. I want to make sure the shooter is well and truly gone."

Raina shivered as another gust of wind blew over her neck. She pulled her hair out of the ponytail and let the weight fall over her neck. It offered only a modicum of warmth, but she'd take what she could get right now.

"How are you feeling?" Vince asked.

That was a loaded question. "I'm not exactly sure how to answer that."

"Try?"

"I'm cold—yet again—scared—yet again—and wondering if this will ever end. Wishing I had made different choices in my past." She paused and decided to be straight-up honest. "Mostly I'm feeling fear. But not for me. I'm scared to death that Kevin is going to get to Michael before I can get there and point the finger at him."

"He's got a ton of protection around him," Vince said. "He'll be okay."

She shook her head, not convinced. "You don't know Kevin. He has influence and time and everything else."

"He's not God," Vince said. "He's a human. He makes mistakes. He'll get caught."

"Oh, he's going to get caught. I'm not stopping until I find him this time." She couldn't. Not now that he knew about Michael. "When he seemed to drop off the planet fourteen years ago, I didn't know what else to do, I just knew I had to take care of myself. Survive and heal. And make it to fight another day, so to speak." She shot him a tight smile. "Looks like that day has come."

They fell silent a moment, then Vince looked at her.

"He's yours, isn't he?"

"What?"

"Michael. He's . . . yours."

She hesitated, swallowed, then nodded. "When did you figure it out?"

"I suspected almost from the very beginning. I know that you would be concerned about any child in danger, but the way you reacted when you saw him on the television and then you were so worried about Kevin getting to him, well . . . it was more than just a concern. It just seemed like it was a mother's worry."

Raina blew out a low breath, then lifted her eyes to meet his gaze. "Are you mad I didn't tell you?"

"Mad? No. A little disappointed you didn't feel you could trust me with the information? Yeah, maybe."

"I know. I'm sorry. I thought you might judge me. At least that's what I told myself, but I think it went deeper than that."

"Like how?"

"Like I was judging myself." She let out a hard laugh. "And, I think I was afraid to say it out loud."

"Oh. Why?"

A shrug. "Because then I'd have to admit that I gave my child away and . . ." Tears climbed from her throat into her eyes, her nose burned, and her breath caught. She pressed her fingers to her eyelids and fought the onslaught. "And . . . what kind of mother gives her baby away?" The last word was a mere squeak.

"Why?" he asked, his voice so soft she almost missed the question.

"Why what?" she said with her eyes still closed.

"Why did you put him up for adoption?"

The tears dried up like someone flipped a switch and she dropped her hands to narrow her eyes at him. "To keep him safe. I desperately didn't want to give him up, but I saw no other option."

"I think that answers your question."

She sniffed. "What do you mean?"

"You sacrificed your own happiness to keep him safe. That's what a mother does. That's what any good and decent parent does for their child. They do whatever it takes to keep them safe. To make the hard choices for the good of their child. And I think, deep down, you know that. What would you say if it was someone else?"

She stayed silent. Thinking.

"Raina? Seriously, answer the question. What would you say to someone else who found themself in your situation, faced with making that kind of decision?"

"I would say she did the right thing." The low words slipped from her, but she also found herself believing them for the first time. Believing that what she had done was brave, not selfish. That no one would hold it against her. Except Kevin, and he didn't count.

"Exactly. You did the right thing."

She nodded, dislodging a few tears hovering on the edges of her lashes. They slipped down her cheeks, and Vince used a cold thumb to swipe them away, then gathered her closer to him. "Before all of this, I was doing so good," she whispered. "I thought about him every day, but I knew he went to a good family. I picked them out. I didn't know their names, I didn't even know what they looked like, but I knew they were good people and would love him like he had their blood. Maybe even more. Some people can take their kids for granted, but I knew they would never do that to him. And then I saw him on TV and maybe it's crazy to assume he's the one I gave birth to. Maybe he's not. Maybe it's all just some wild coincidence, but . . ."

"But you don't think so."

"I don't. And I can't just dismiss the possibility or hope Kevin or someone Kevin knows never sees him. I can't."

He kissed the top of her head. "I know."

Raina's heart tumbled all over itself with conflicting emotions and feelings, and she dragged in a ragged breath. "Okay, sorry. I didn't mean to lay all that out there. We have someone trying to kill us. We don't have time to dissect my personal issues."

"Thank you for sharing with me. For telling me about him."

She shrugged. "I wasn't going to deny it. And to be even more honest . . . in spite of how I thought it would feel, it's good to finally admit it." She raked a shaky hand over her hair. "But I can't meet him, Vince." She lifted her gaze to his. "If I see him, meet him, talk to him . . . I don't think I'd be able to walk away from him again."

■ ■ ■ ■

Vince almost couldn't stand the agony in her eyes, his heart twisting into a painful knot on her behalf. Almost as painful as the incessant throb in his right calf. "Ah, Raina, I'm so sorry. But I'll be frank with you. You're stronger than you give yourself credit for."

She sniffed and swiped her eyes. "It doesn't matter right now. All that matters is getting there and finding Kevin, having him arrested, and removing the threat to Michael. Then we can all return to our normal lives."

He could only hope it would be that easy. For some reason, he wasn't compelled to hold his breath. Just his tongue. Another few minutes of scoping the area, then he frowned. "He's gone, I think."

"Where are the fire trucks? Surely, someone's noticed all the smoke and—" Wailing sirens in the distance cut her off. "Well, okay then. About time." She glanced at him. "I think instead of hiking the rest of the way to Penny's hangar, we hitch a ride with someone down there."

"Good thinking. CSU will take care of the truck, and we can give our statements to the officers, but it's going to take a while. We'll need to call Penny and let her know what's going on and ask her to wait on us."

"She can also get us some clean, dry clothes to change into and a couple of phones to get us through the next few days—assuming we don't find ours."

"Even if we do find them, there's no guarantee they'll be in working order if they've been submerged."

Raina grimaced and nodded. Fighting the cold and the wind, they retraced their steps back across the field, giving the burning barn a wide berth. Although Vince didn't mind the blast of heat he got from it. From Raina's expression, she was fine with it as well.

Firemen worked quickly, aiming the streaming hoses with precision. With each step, the ache in his leg intensified and he wondered if he'd been shot. Again.

"Hey." Raina grabbed his arm, distracting him a moment from his pain. "I know that officer. That's Kira."

"You know everyone."

"Just about. You do what I do long enough, you meet a lot of people. Especially the ones who work a lot of hours." Vince followed her as she hurried over to the dark-haired officer speaking into her radio. "Kira."

The officer looked up and her green eyes widened. "I've got to go. I'll report back shortly." She lifted her thumb from the side button of the radio. "What's going on, Raina?" Her gaze traveled to Vince, then swung back to Raina. "You guys are soaking wet and freezing."

"It's a long story," Raina said, her teeth chattering and shivers racking her once more. "B-but can I borrow your phone to make a call?"

The woman, who appeared to be in her late thirties, unhooked the device from the clip on her belt and handed it over. "You were in the truck?" She walked to the trunk of her cruiser and opened it, reached in, and pulled out two blankets. Vince took one and wrapped it around Raina. Then did the same for himself.

Raina nodded, pulled the blanket tight beneath her chin, and held it with one hand while she dialed with the other. "This is Vince Covelli. It's his truck."

"Whoever peppered you with bullets didn't want you walking away."

"No kidding," Vince said.

"People are crazy." Kira motioned to someone behind them. "You'll need to talk to the leads on this one. Give your statements."

"I know." Raina gripped the phone and hit Send. "I just need to call Penny and let her know we're running late."

As soon as that was done, she handed the phone back to Kira. "Penny's not there yet," she told Vince, "but promised to wait."

A large van pulled to a stop behind the last police car in the line and four people climbed out. "Crime scene unit is here," Kira said.

"Good." Vince pulled the blanket tighter, but they were both still wet and cold. Only dry clothes and a big mug of coffee were going to help them warm up again. "Since it doesn't look like we're going to be leaving anytime soon, I'm going to see if I can find our phones. I'll be right back."

Looking resigned at the delay, Raina nodded.

He headed to meet CSU, badge in hand. "Excuse me." He introduced himself. "That's my truck. You mind if I get my phone? It's got nothing to do with this crime scene and I'd like to see if it's still working."

The older man nodded. "Not at all. Follow me."

Vince fell into step behind the man, gritting his teeth at the shooting pain in his leg. "And I think you'll find my gas can if it hasn't completely melted. The guy who set the barn on fire stole it out of the back of the truck." He shook his head. "There's a lot of dry hay in there. That fire's going to burn hot and hard for the next few hours despite the rain." Some people didn't realize it, but a light rain could actually cause the fire to spread more rapidly, depending on certain conditions.

Leaving the problem to the professionals, Vince waited while the investigator crawled through the shattered rear windshield and searched the truck. Now that the adrenaline was fading, all Vince wanted to do was climb in a warm shower, then slip between his sheets and sleep for a few days. He glanced back at Raina. She was still wrapped in her blanket and talking to Kira.

"This it?"

Vince whipped his head around to find the man popped out of the back windshield, holding his phone. "How bad is it?"

"With the truck tilted like it was, I don't think the water touched it. It was wedged between the console and the driver's seat."

Vince took it and tapped the screen. He had voice mails and

texts he'd answer when he had a moment. "I really appreciate it. You see another one? My passenger had it in her pocket. Could be on the other side."

The man ducked back into the king cab and seconds ticked past while he looked. Vince couldn't stop his gaze from scouring the area. Was the guy out there reveling in the chaos he'd caused, or was he just mad that he'd missed once again and had to come up with another plan? Vince knew what he'd put his money on.

"Got it." The guy made his way back out of the vehicle, joined Vince, and handed him the device.

"Thanks." Vince took a step toward Raina and grimaced. Just a few more things to take care of and he'd get his leg looked at.

CHAPTER
NINETEEN

Raina had given her statement while Vince busied himself with whatever he needed at the truck. It looked like the officer had found his phone, which was great. She hoped it still worked, but right now, she just wanted to get to Penny's hangar. Wanted that more than she wanted a hot shower and dry clothes. And she wanted those two things pretty bad.

Vince walked toward her and she noticed his limp. He favored his right leg with each step, the lines around his tight mouth and furrowed brow letting her know something was wrong.

She hurried to him and pointed to the ambulance. "Come with me."

"What?"

"You need to get your leg looked at it and I'm not taking no for an answer."

He shot her an amused smile tinged with pain. "I'm not going to argue. It's starting to really bug me."

That he would allow himself to say so worried her. Once he was in the back of the ambulance, Raina stayed outside, restraining herself from taking over. In spite of Vince's assertion that she knew everyone, she didn't know these two paramedics and was reluctant to release him into their hands. She wanted to be the one to examine him, make sure that no one missed anything.

Vince lay on his stomach, and the paramedic nearest her, who'd introduced himself as David, cut away his pants leg from the knee down.

Raina caught a glimpse of a small object protruding from his calf and gasped. "What in the world?" How had he managed to do all he'd done with that kind of wound? "Vince!"

He glanced back over his shoulder. "Is it that bad?"

"Um . . . yeah," David said. "Looks pretty bad. You're definitely going to need stitches."

Vince flinched. "No stitches. Just stick some butterfly bandages on it and we'll call it good. I need to get on the road."

"Um . . ."

Raina stepped up. "You need to stay here, Vince." Her heart was still in her throat. Twice he'd been hurt because of her. Because he wanted to *help* her. His reassurances came back to her. *"God's in control."*

But still . . .

"I'm not staying here," he said. "Stop thinking whatever it is you're thinking. We've already been down this conversational road. This is not your fault."

"I know that. Mentally."

He started to sit up, his wince stabbing her more effectively than a knife. "Vince, please . . ."

"I'm going with you. I won't leave you on your own."

David's gaze bounced back and forth between them before looking at his partner, Lisa, who shrugged.

Raina sighed. "Long story short, someone's trying to kill me. Vince is trying to make sure that doesn't happen, and I want him to stay put so he'll be out of danger."

Their jaws dropped in sync. "Well . . . huh."

"Exactly. And if he gets killed, I have to live with the guilt."

"Told you I'm a big boy," Vince grunted. "I can handle it."

"But I don't know if I can," she whispered.

"Well, we don't have time to argue," David said. "Are you riding to the hospital or not?"

Vince stuck out his chin. "Not."

Raina planted hands on her hips. "He is."

The two paramedics sighed.

"You really think you're going to convince me?" He asked the question in a low voice.

"I—"

"Think about it while you pull that thing out and stitch me up."

Now both paramedics sputtered protests, but Raina knew when to concede. "Fine. I can stitch it. Do you have a kit?" David blinked at her and she shot him a tight smile. "I'm an AEMT. I can suture." Advanced EMTs had more training than the average EMT, and with those few words, Raina finally got her wish to take over. "I can't believe I'm letting you win."

"It's not a win/lose situation, Raina. It's an I'm-your-*friend*-and-I-care-about-you-so-what-kind-of-person-would-I-be-if-I-just-waved-you-off-on-this-little-adventure kind of situation."

"I get it." She heard the emphasis on the word *friend* and ignored it. For now. "Are you going to pass out?"

"Not if I don't look and you don't tell me what you're doing."

He sounded a little weak, so Raina got busy.

Once the piece of shrapnel—at least that's what it looked like—was removed from the wound, she numbed the area, cleaned it, then started stitching, wishing she could sew up the gaping hole in her heart just as easily.

"And besides, you asked Penny for help," he said.

"I asked Penny for a ride." She looked up for a brief second, but he had his head turned and eyes closed. His pale face said he was probably on the verge of passing out. She glanced at the other paramedic. "Cold cloths on his face and smelling salts."

Vince huffed a weak laugh. "Smelling salts? What year are we in? The 1800s?"

"Zip it, Covelli." But she knew what he was doing. Distracting himself from what *she* was doing. She could help with that. "And to circle back to the whole 'asking Penny for help' thing, I asked her for transportation. That's it. She's not going to be dodging bullets, forced to swim in a freezing lake, and barely missing out on being roasted alive or smoked to death."

He groaned. "Just keep sewing."

"So stubborn," she muttered. When he gave a weak groan, she barely refrained from rolling her eyes, but within a few minutes, she had the wound closed and bandaged. The sight turned her stomach. Not because of the wound itself, but because it was on Vince's flesh. "I have no idea what that metal was that caused that gash, but glad it was your leg and not your head," she said. Just the thought nearly did her in.

"God was looking out for me." He turned his head and winked at her.

"Yes," she said, his words penetrating her heart. "I guess he was. Looking out for both of us."

"Glad you're starting to see things my way—which of course is the right way."

"Ha-ha."

He sat up and swallowed. "Whoa."

"Feel sick?"

"Yeah, just like last time. It'll pass."

David raised a brow. "Want some nausea meds? I'm qualified to give those out." His partner snickered. Vince held out his hand for the little white pill.

Raina ignored them. She knew they didn't mean anything by the teasing but wasn't in the mood.

Vince stood and she grabbed his arm. "Can you walk?"

"I think so."

He made it out of the ambulance without falling and she

looked up at him. "You do realize I can outrun you at this point."

"And I'm the one with the badge that you might find beneficial. Just think. If you happen to run into Kevin, I can make the arrest—and you will have the satisfaction of watching me do it. Just sayin'."

Raina closed her eyes for a brief moment. "Why do you have to be right about *everything*?"

"It's the way God made me. What can I say?"

Raina snorted and ignored the paramedics' guffaws. "Fine. Let's go, Mr. Right About Everything. We have a plane to catch, and Kira said she'd drive us to the hangar."

"Right behind you." He paused. "As long as there's no running involved."

■ ■ ■ ■

"Where is he!" Simon's shout outside the restaurant turned heads of those seated in the covered area. He pulled in several deep breaths before forcing a smile and waving to the lookie-loos that he was fine. They returned to their meals and Simon focused on his call, thankful he'd arrived at the restaurant early.

"He wasn't really my assignment, remember?" Freddy Harper's unflappable voice made Simon want to chew and spit nails at the PI.

"I thought you had someone watching him."

"That kid travels all over the place. You don't pay me enough to keep track of him that well. It's all I can do to keep up with the woman—who is also causing problems."

"What do you mean?"

A pause. "Nothing really. She's just a pain to keep track of. As for your kid . . . I know he got on a plane not too long ago."

"Like you said, he travels. Where was he going this time?"

"Flight plan said Colorado."

"What hotel would he be overseeing in—" Dread curled inside him. "No. Please tell me he's not—"

"What?"

Simon hung up and dialed Christopher's number. "Answer the phone, son. Please," he whispered.

"Hello?"

Simon gasped at the relief that flowed through him. "Can you talk?"

"Um . . . hang on a sec." Simon heard the door shut. "What is it?"

"Your brother has taken off to Colorado."

"So?"

"So? Are you not keeping up with the kid? Michael Harrison? Even I have an alert on my phone that lets me know when his name is mentioned in the news or if there's anything going on with snowboarding."

"Tell me."

"He's going to be at some snowboarding event in Colorado. Keith has hopped a plane and is headed there. Probably to see the kid. We need to catch up to him and stop him from doing anything stupid."

Christopher's groan echoed the one Simon wanted to release. "We? I thought you had someone on him!"

"So did I, but apparently I don't pay well enough to—"

He broke off when heads turned again and realized his voice was once again louder than it should be.

"Simon?"

He turned to see his lunch appointment eyeing him with a raised brow. Simon waved, indicating he'd be right there. "I've got to go. Can you find someone there to stop him?"

"I'll see what I can do." A pause. "I'm very sick of cleaning up his messes, Dad. Just letting you know that."

"I know, son. I know." He hung up and walked into the restaurant.

■ ■ ■ ■

After Kira had dropped them at the hangar, Penny presented them each a bag of clothing she'd had her friends put together, then pointed them to the locker rooms—his to the right, Raina's to the left—and instructed them to shower and change, and when they were ready, they'd take off.

Thirty minutes later, they were in the air.

Vince closed his eyes and refused to hurl. He hated flying to begin with, but combined with the meds, his stomach was decidedly unsteady. At least the throbbing had eased.

"Here." Raina held out a barf bag.

"I look that green?"

"More like a sickly pale yellowish green."

He took the bag. "Wouldn't want to mess up my clean, dry clothes."

"Exactly."

"Or this plane," Penny said, her amused voice coming through the headset. "Please, not the very expensive *borrowed* plane. You know, the one that doesn't belong to me?"

Vince rolled his eyes and Raina shot him a sympathetic look.

When he finally felt like he could move without puking, he dug into his pocket. He passed Raina her phone. "He found both of them. Said yours got a little wet, but it was still powered on, so maybe it's okay."

She took it from him. "Thank you." She tapped the screen and smiled.

"What?"

"It's Mrs. Gibbs's eightieth birthday next month. Penny, Jules, and Grace and I have all been invited to celebrate with her—along with our plus ones—in California." Her eyes widened. "At a resort. Wow. Her family is going all out, and she's asked for us to be there if we can make it. It's the weekend after the Super Bowl."

"Mrs. Gibbs . . . she's the psychiatrist from juvie?"

Raina nodded. "She's the reason we're the people we are today. I think her prayers alone have sustained us in some ways." Regret flickered in her gaze. "She'd be sad about my doubts."

"What would she say about them?"

"Hmm. Probably the same thing you have."

"She sounds like an amazing person."

"Ha. Cute. But in all seriousness, she is. I haven't seen her since I walked out of juvie, but she sends cards to the others every birthday and Christmas."

"Not you?"

She shot him a sad smile. "She didn't know where I was, and I wouldn't let the others tell her."

"Just in case?"

"Yeah. Just in case." She sighed and leaned her head back against the headrest and Vince wished she'd keep talking. It took his mind off the pain in his leg and shoulder.

"Did you ever talk to John Tate?" she asked.

"No. I called him back from the hospital, but he didn't answer." He glanced at his phone. "And he hasn't called me back since."

"So, let's recap."

He raised a brow at her. "All right. Recap what?"

"Everything. Starting with the night I saw Michael on the television. It wasn't long after that, everything started going crazy. My calls to Trent let Kevin—or someone—know where I was. If I hadn't called, none of this would be happening."

"That's an assumption. It makes sense, but you can't say for sure that's how someone found you."

"I think it's a pretty safe assumption."

He sighed. "Probably."

"I think Kevin has been looking for me all these years—and monitoring the people that I told him about. He used to pump me for information. Of course, I didn't realize it at the time.

211

I thought he was being so attentive and loving. That he was interested in everything about me. And he was. Just not for the reasons that I assumed."

"He wanted to figure out how to control you."

She nodded.

"I'm sorry, Raina."

"I've never been able to trust a man since then," she said softly. Then her gaze lifted to meet his. "Until you."

He reached over and took her hand. "I'm honored."

A throat clearing reminded him that Penny could hear every word. He didn't care, but Raina's pink cheeks said she'd forgotten too.

"Love the fact that I can be totally invisible," Penny said. "And just for the record, I didn't know about the birthday party. Sounds like fun."

Raina laughed and Vince grinned. Then he leaned his head back against the seat and closed his eyes.

With Raina's hand still gripped in his.

CHAPTER
TWENTY

Raina wasn't sure how she'd managed to sleep, but she was awakened when Penny's voice came through the headset. "Wake up, sleepyheads, we're landing." Raina blinked and glanced out the window to see a landscape of white. "Where are we landing?"

"Closest I could get you to Copper Mountain. We're in Denver and you have a rental car waiting—in Vince's name. I put it on my card since I wasn't sure if you had a wallet."

"Thank you, Penny, you're the absolute best. Don't worry about waiting or coming back to get us. We'll get a regular flight home."

"Just text a few hours before you're ready to leave and I'll see what I can do."

Vince stirred and Raina finally pulled her hand from his grasp. With one indrawn breath, he was instantly alert. "We're here," he said.

"We are," Penny said. The wheels touched the tarmac, then settled while the engines wound down. "How are you feeling?"

"Like I've gone a few rounds with a pro boxer. And lost. But the nap helped."

Penny pulled her headset off and turned to Raina. "Here."

"What?"

"It's a credit card. Use it if you need it."

"Penny, I'm not taking your card. I have cash in my go bag."
She glanced at Vince. "The one he rescued from the fire."

"Just keep it. If you have to charge something, you won't
want to use one of your cards. You know. Because you don't
want anyone to be able to trace it?"

"Oh." Raina huffed a sigh, then smiled, her heart tender
at the love of her friend. "As much as I hate to admit it, that's
good thinking. Fine. Thank you."

"And one more thing." Penny dug in the small bag next to
her. "Altitude pills." She pressed them into Raina's other hand.

"I didn't even think about that, but thank you. You've
thought of everything." After a hug and another thank-you,
Raina and Vince climbed out of the plane and headed for the
rental car counter. "She put the reservation in your name but
used her card. I'm going to owe her big-time by the time this is
all over. Assuming I'm still alive."

"You'll be alive."

If the sheer resolve in his voice was anything to go by, she
would be. That gave her comfort. "Well, if Kevin doesn't get to
me, the lack of oxygen here might. What's the altitude? Holy
smokes, I should have brought an air tank."

He laughed. "Drink water and take the pills. You'll get used
to it."

"It's not bothering you?"

"It is, but like I said, you get used to it." He nodded to the
pills in her hand. "And I plan to take those." She gave him one
and he downed it.

"Ugh." She did the same, hoping they worked fast.

Once they were loaded into the rental with the go bag, and
other items supplied by Penny, Raina's heart thudded in anticipation of coming face-to-face with the man she'd never really

been able to release and leave in her past. A man she'd dreamed of seeing behind bars.

And now she was very close to helping make that happen. *Please let it happen.*

Vince rounded the car toward the driver's side and Raina laughed. "Um. No. You get to ride this time."

"Sorry?"

"Your calf has to be hurting. Not to mention your shoulder. I'll drive."

She thought he might protest, then he shrugged and limped around to the passenger side, climbed in, and buckled up.

Raina tapped the resort address into the vehicle's GPS and followed the directions to Pena Boulevard. Then headed for I-70. "It's about a two-hour drive," she said. "Lean back and relax."

"I'm thinking."

"About?"

"Where we're going to stay. Did you get us a hotel or anything?"

She glanced at him. "Um. No. I didn't."

"So, we're going to sleep in the car?"

"Of course not. Why don't you find us a place? And . . ."

"And?"

Raina sighed. "Use Penny's card. I'll pay her back."

Vince did as she asked, scrolling on his phone. "Got it," he said ten minutes later. "This is perfect. It's a two-bedroom condo. We'll have privacy and still be able to have each other's back. Not to mention, a good view of the slope and the event."

"Sounds perfect. But what you mean is that you'll be able to keep an eye on *me*, right?"

He snagged her hand and she looked at him for a fraction of a second before turning her eyes back to the road. "I meant exactly what I said, Raina. I don't discount your ability to have my back should I need it."

She swallowed. "Thanks. Sorry."

"No need to apologize."

While Vince dialed and made the reservation, Raina's thoughts flipped to Michael and his family. Thank goodness they'd declined to bring him. Nerves skittered in her stomach. What had his parents told him about her? His birth mother? They hadn't told him anything about his birth father because they hadn't known much about him. Or her, really. She'd left a short letter expressing her love for the baby and her desire for him to have the best life possible. Had they shown him the note?

Did it matter?

"Raina?"

She blinked. "Sorry. Again." She'd been driving on autopilot. "I've got all kinds of emotions warring inside of me and it's caught me off guard." A sigh slipped from her. "I guess I should have expected it, but it's not like I had a lot of time to prepare."

"Once you get there and you point out Kevin, you'll be able to breathe a little better."

"Right. Yeah." Hopefully.

"And now, I'm going figure out how we can work with security on-site." Because this was an Olympics-related event with a huge crowd in attendance, the FBI would be heavily involved and coordinating with local law enforcement. Denver's SWAT and other personnel would be on location and the Command Post would be set up on-site. "Once you ID Kevin, they can move in and arrest him."

"I'm happy with that plan. What do you say we get some rest? You're obviously exhausted and I am too. Tomorrow's going to be a long day. I know it's probably wishful thinking, but a good night's sleep sounds like something I need to attempt to get or I'm going to be no good to anyone tomorrow."

"Ditto. Let's get checked in and crash."

■ ■ ■ ■

THURSDAY MORNING

Michael Harrison stood on the balcony of the condo he and his parents had just checked in to. He wasn't sure he understood exactly why they'd run from their home when the two marshals had shown up—no one had bothered to share the details—but he got enough to know that he and his family were believed to be in danger.

But were they? Really? From who? And why? He'd overheard his parents questioning the validity of the threat, but they finally decided he shouldn't compete. He'd managed to talk them into bringing him to just watch, but now that he was here, he was itching to be on that slope.

Michael loved his parents and knew they just wanted the best for him, but how was keeping him out of the event the best thing?

Anger swirled, mixing with confusion at the out-of-the-blue threat. "So weird," he muttered.

The sliding glass door opened, and his father stepped out, blanket in hand, to join him. "You okay, son?"

"Fine."

His dad settled the blanket around his shoulders, then slid a strong arm around him and led him to the chairs facing the snow run. Michael sat and his father pulled the other one around to face him.

"I thought it would be enough just to be here to watch, but it's not, Dad. I need to be out there," Michael said. The argument had been going on since he'd stashed his stuff in his room—including the gear he'd insisted on bringing.

"We're talking about it. Your mom and I understand that this is an amazing opportunity for you, but we also don't want anything to happen to you."

"Like what? What exactly is the threat?"

His dad looked at him through his lashes as though debating something with himself.

217

"I'm old enough to know what's going on. This is affecting my life too."

"True." His father pulled in a deep breath. "You know how you asked us to find your birth parents?"

"Yes."

"The threat has to do with your birth father. Apparently, he never knew about you. But after you appeared on national television, it's possible that he's come to know that he has a son."

"Okay. Does he want to meet me? I mean, why would he be a threat?"

"He's not a nice person. I've learned from one of the marshals that your birth mother gave you up because she never wanted your birth father to know about you. She said he's dangerous and would come after you. He beat her and put her in the hospital. He thought he'd killed her, but . . ."

"But he didn't." Michael swallowed. "Okay, I can see why she wouldn't want me near him."

"But when you did the interview on television—"

"But . . . how would he know it was me?"

"You look just like him. Right down to the birthmark on your chin."

Michael touched the brown patch of skin that he never really thought about. "Wow. So, all of this protection stuff is because you're afraid he'll come after me at the benefit?"

"Yes."

"Thank you for being honest with me." He lifted his chin. "But I still want to be a part of it."

"Michael—"

"I know you're worried, but do you think that I'm supposed to be doing this? Snowboarding?"

"Of course. We've often talked about how God has gifted you, not only with an amazing brain, but also with athletic ability."

"And it's your job as my parent to help me grow into that, right?"

"Yes." His father looked wary now.

"I think I need to do this, Dad." His father's furrowed brow didn't bode well for the response. "Think about it. I'm not saying I should go out there without a plan, but I already have marshals watching out for me. I have no doubt that security is aware of the situation and will be alert to any trouble. Why should we let the possibility of this threat keep me from doing what I've been born to do? You've always taught me we're not to live in fear but to embrace life and all it brings—including the challenges. I don't want to hide from this, but I do want to be safe. Isn't there some sort of compromise we can come to? A way to do both?"

A soft puff of laughter escaped his father's lips. "We've done too good of a job with the parenting, haven't we?"

Michael grinned. "Of course."

"I'll talk to security and see what they have to say."

"Are the marshals still here?"

"Just one." He stood. "Stay tuned. I'll be back." He walked to the door. "Come inside where it's warm. You're going to be cold soon enough on the slope."

"I'm never cold on the slopes. I don't even feel the chill."

"Just the exhilaration of the run?"

"Exactly." But Michael followed his father inside and went to change into his gear. The practice started in less than an hour.

Fifteen minutes later, he exited his room and found his parents sitting on the couch, expressions sober. "What is it?"

"We talked to security and they don't think you should participate," his mother said.

His heart dropped. "*They* don't or *you* don't?"

"Mike—" His dad pointed to the recliner and Michael dropped into it.

He let his gloves fall to the floor. "I thought we were okay with me doing this. Why else would you bring me here?"

"We were hoping that the danger would be over by the time

you had to get out there, but it's not. And," his father said, "while you made a good argument, your mother made a better one. We don't know what the threat entails, and while there's still a chance this guy could show up, we can't risk something happening to you."

"But all the security . . . I have so many people watching out for me that he wouldn't be able to get to me anyway."

His mother dropped her chin to her chest, then looked him in the eye. "We're sorry, Michael, but we're going to have to veto this event."

He wasn't going to change their minds, not when they had those identical "this subject isn't open for debate" looks on their faces. He grabbed his gloves and stood. "I'll be in my room. Please don't ask me if I want anything to eat. I've lost my appetite."

"Hold on a second."

Michael paused and his father exchanged a glance with his mother before pulling a piece of paper out of his pocket. "We think you should read this."

"What is it?"

"A note from your birth mother."

Michael took the letter, then picked up his gloves and returned to his room. He stood there for a moment, then opened the letter.

Dear Son,

I don't know if you'll ever read this letter, but I'm going to write it in the hope that your parents will share it with you one day should they feel the need. Giving you up for adoption was the hardest thing I've ever had to do. If I could keep you, I would in a heartbeat. At first, when I found out about you, I was terrified. Not so much at the thought of being a mother—although, at the age of nineteen, there was some of that—but that your birth father would find out about you. I hate to admit it, but I made some pretty stupid choices. I'm not a stupid person, but my choices have not been good. As a result, I'm on the run from the man who fathered you. Oh, my dear boy, giving you up is killing me, but I've picked out a couple who will cherish you and raise you to know only love. They love Jesus and they'll share that love with you. You're going to grow up strong and brave and amazing and I'd give anything to see it happen. But it's not possible and because your safety, your very life depends on me being willing to give you up, that's the decision I've made. I will think about you and miss you every day of your life. I love you.

Mom

With shaking hands, Michael folded the note and tucked it into the pocket of his snowpants. Time to be brave and strong and amazing. He walked over to the window and raised it, thankful they were on the first floor.

■ ■ ■ ■

As Raina nursed a third cup of coffee, staring out the restaurant's wall of windows, Vince reached over to give her hand a quick squeeze. "You ready?"

She gave him a tight smile and set down her mug. "I've had enough caffeine to keep me up the whole day."

They pulled on their parkas and headed out to the deck overlooking the slope, Vince a little more slowly than she. He pressed a hand to his shoulder and looked around.

The place was packed with eager snowboarding fans, the media, and more tourists. A team of vans shuttled people from the parking lot to the lodge every few minutes. From there, they would make their way to a location where they could watch the fun.

"Where do we even start?" she asked.

"The security team. The guy I'm looking for is Joseph Helms. He's the sheriff here and will be working with the FBI. He'll be able to get us clearance and a badge that will allow us to move in secure locations if we need to."

Vince led the way with Raina beside him. He noted her eyes studying the faces she passed.

It didn't take long for the crowd to shift and the mood to swing into an energy-laden atmosphere. Spectators lined the slope behind the barricade that had been set up to keep them separate from the competitors. He tried not to compare it to crime scene tape.

"Okay, well, I guess the boarders are up there and getting ready to practice," she said.

"And our condo is right up there too." Vince pointed just as his phone vibrated. He pulled it out and glanced at an incoming text. "Joseph said Michael and his family were already here. They're allowing him to watch, but not participate."

"Wow. At least that's one less worry for the moment."

"I know. Anyway, Joseph said he'd meet us at the entrance here, so let's head over there. Just keep your eyes peeled for Kevin."

"I have been, but everyone is all bundled up. Hats, sunglasses, heavy coats. Kevin doesn't need a disguise. He just has to dress weather appropriate. I'm never going to be able to find him. Not this way. We're going to have to figure out a way to lure him out."

"No luring. At least not yet. Let's talk to Joseph and see where we go from there."

Vince and Raina met with Joseph and got two earpieces that would allow them all to be able to stay in touch with one another. They even had badges pinned to their coats identifying them as part of the security team. They'd have access to any area they needed. And as soon as Raina saw Kevin—assuming she spotted him—she would alert them and they would close in. Raina caught the sheriff's eye. "You're sure Michael's not participating." It was a statement, not a question.

"That's what they said."

She nodded. "Okay then. Good."

"You want to go see him?" Vince asked.

She bit her lip. "I want to, but not just yet. The first priority is to find Kevin. As long as Michael's safe, I can concentrate on that."

"He's safe as long as they stay put," the sheriff said. "I've got to get moving. Stay in touch."

They thanked him, and once the sheriff left, Vince led her to the lobby of the condo complex and up to their unit. While Raina was in her room down the hall, he stood in the galley kitchen and tried once more to call John Tate, only to get the man's voice mail yet again. "Call me back, please. I've got questions that only you can answer. Thanks."

He hung up and tucked the phone into his pocket, then headed out to the balcony. The crowd had grown and was dispersed along the run the snowboarders would use.

Raina joined him, her gaze scanning the people.

He wrapped an arm around her shoulders and tugged her closer, gratified when she didn't pull away. His shoulder throbbed in time with his leg, but he'd put up with it all as long as he could hold her close. "They said he wasn't."

"But he's still on the program, so Kevin—or whoever he is—probably thinks he's here."

"Right." He nodded. "Which is why we're here. What's going on in that head of yours?"

"Just thinking. They call out names of the snowboarders before they go down, right?"

"Yes."

"Then," she said, "we'll just watch and see who leaves when they skip his name."

"That's actually a great idea." He pointed. "The parking

lot is at the base of the run. If I were Kevin, I'd be down at the bottom so when Michael finished, I'd have a better chance of having access to him."

"So we just watch the people at the base of the run."

"It's just a guess, but an educated one."

"A smart one. Let's go." She made sure the comms unit was tucked into her ear, then grabbed the heavy coat, gloves, and hat Penny had provided, and Vince did the same.

They headed for the door, and Vince let her take the lead while he glanced at his watch. "They're getting ready to start."

They made it out of the condo and onto the slope. Steps led to the base of the run and they hurried down them.

"All right, everyone, the countdown is on!" The voice boomed from the speakers and Vince flinched and stopped.

He grabbed her hand. "Raina. Hold up."

With a frown, she turned. "What is it?"

"Let's just stand here and watch a second. It's a good view. Some of the spectators aren't wearing hats. Focus on them."

She stood beside him, scanning faces, while the voice over the speaker continued. "Are you ready to say hello to your Olympic team?" A deafening cheer rose from the crowd. "All right, here we go. First up, the superpipe . . ."

"I don't see anyone that could be Kevin." Raina pointed to the schedule on the board. "Michael is still listed as doing the halfpipe. I don't think Kevin would be here at this event. He'd be at the other run, waiting. Which is . . ." She turned, looking. "Over there."

Vince nodded. "Yeah. I can see that. Let's get to the other slope and you can scope it out. It won't be long before they're done with this one."

While the announcer continued, Vince let his gaze roam the crowd. The first athlete swooped down the slope, impressive with his skill and awe-inspiring stunts. Vince shook his head.

He'd never be able to judge them, as they all looked amazing to him. "All right, let's go."

With Raina's hand still in his, he led her through the crowd toward the other halfpipe. Thankfully, they reached it ahead of the mass of bodies, and Vince edged closer to a security officer on the other side of the fencing. He showed him his badge and introduced himself and Raina. "We're looking for someone who may be a threat to one of the snowboarders." He didn't mention that the kid wasn't there. "Do you mind if we stand on the platform so we can get a good look at the other side as well? We're working with Sheriff Helms." Vince gave him their information and the man studied the badges for what seemed like an eternity. Finally, after a verbal check with the sheriff, he nodded and opened the gate to let them through.

Vince led Raina to a set of steps that took them up to a covered area. And a perfect view of the slope once again and all of the people converging on it. "It's incredible," Vince murmured.

He'd done his homework. The twenty-two-foot-high U-shaped walls were sixty-four feet apart from lip to lip and towered over the onlookers. It was a six-hundred-foot-long run at an eighteen-degree pitch. Perfect for maintaining the speed needed for the tricks the participants would do.

"Awe inspiring," Raina agreed.

"Next up, we have the halfpipe," the announcer said. "We'll give everyone a moment to get settled, then our contestants will start their show."

"He's last," Raina murmured. "Or he would be if he was here."

"Yeah. Take note of the crowd. You watch for Kevin. I'll watch for someone moving out of the ordinary."

Raina tapped an impatient toe through the performances, and finally, the announcer's voice boomed over the loudspeaker. "And now, what you've all been waiting for. The seemingly overnight snowboarding sensation, the youngest American to ever earn enough points that, should he be old enough to go, he'd be heading for the Olympics, Michael Harrison!"

Cheers erupted and Vince spied the movement at the top of the run.

Raina gasped and her hand shot out to clasp his bicep. "He announced him? He's here? Vince, he's not supposed to be participating!"

"I know." But he was, and just like all the other competitors, he balanced himself on the board, waved, and shot down the slope into the halfpipe.

"There's that puff of snow at the takeoff, folks. Perfect conditions today for this event. Look at that boy go! Right into a Method air. This kid has got mad skills, people."

"There," Vince said. He pointed to a man who'd shoved closer, not seeming to care about the dirty looks he was getting. "Maybe?"

Raina's gaze was frozen on the boy. Her son. The child she'd carried in her body for nine months and given birth to. Then gave up to protect him.

"Raina?" He kept his voice low. Soft.

She jerked her gaze to his, tears glistening, determination in the set of her shoulders. He squeezed her fingers, then gestured with a subtle point in the direction of the guy he wanted her to look at.

She narrowed her gaze on the man. "I don't know, Vince. No, I don't think—" She pointed. "Him."

CHAPTER
TWENTY-ONE

Raina spotted the man moving toward the boy who'd just finished his run. But he stopped and crossed his arms as another man raced to Michael, anger in every step.

"That him?" Vince asked.

"No. He's too short and his skin is too dark." The man grabbed Michael by the bicep and spun him around. Michael's eyes went wide, then his chin dropped to his chest.

"I'd be willing to bet that's his father," Raina said. "I'm guessing Michael snuck out."

"But why are they even here? If they weren't going to let him participate, why bring him? That just seems cruel."

"I don't know. Parenting is tough enough, but when you have a kid as gifted as Michael, it was probably a compromise. Right now, I'm thinking Michael's okay, which is great, but I don't see anyone who even remotely resembles Kevin. I thought it might be that guy over there, but . . . it's not." She sighed. This was a bust. But she wanted to get close enough to hear his voice. Just once.

Vince's phone vibrated and he pulled it from his pocket. "It's Gabrielle," he said.

"Okay, see what she wants. I'm just going to get a little closer."

"Don't go too far."

"I'm not." She slipped closer with Vince right behind her, his phone pressed to his ear.

"No!" The boy's shout pulled her to a stop.

Vince said, "Uh-huh. Okay. Raina?" She looked at him. "Does the name Simon Baldridge mean anything to you?" he asked.

Raina turned the name over in her mind while she kept an eye on the scene unfolding between the father and son. "No, never heard of him." She hesitated. "I've heard of Christopher Baldridge. I think he's the guy running for governor of California. Any relation?"

Vince spoke into the phone once more, and she focused back on Michael. He pulled away from his father's grasp and shoved his board into the man's hands, before spinning on his booted heel and exiting through the gate, straight into the thick of the crowd. Raina gasped and darted after him.

His snow boots didn't slow him down one bit.

"Michael, wait!"

He either ignored her or couldn't hear her, as he never slowed. The crowd didn't seem to understand what was going on, but they didn't stop the boy's forward momentum.

"Raina!"

Vince's voice in her ear nearly caused her to trip. Then she remembered the device. She looked back over her shoulder and spotted Michael's father trapped by a line of reporters, who'd descended like vultures. She didn't see Vince either. "Where's security for Michael? He's all alone and running off!"

"They're looking for him. How far ahead is he?"

She darted around a mother and child. "I don't see him! Vince, I've lost—no wait. There he is." A figure dressed in a ski patrol jacket broke off from the crowd and fell into step behind Michael. But something was wrong with his uniform. His pants didn't match the others'. Goggles were raised and on top of his head. A head she recognized. Raina knew exactly where Kevin Anderson was. "I see him, Vince. I see Kevin! He's going after Michael!"

"Where? *I* can't see *you*!"

"Head toward the ski lodge. The one near the parking lot." An event van pulled up next to Michael, and the driver got out to open the door to unload his passengers while Kevin closed in from behind. "Hey, Michael," Kevin called. "Wait up."

The boy stopped and turned.

"Kevin!" Raina's shout echoed and people stopped to look. "No! Michael, run! Get away from him! Someone get Michael Harrison now!" From the corner of her eye, she saw a man she recognized. John Tate. "John!" The word was a gasp, but her attention quickly swung back to Kevin, who turned. Familiar eyes locked with hers, and for a brief moment, time stood still while Michael froze, unsure what was going on.

Then Raina was within ten feet of the man who'd almost killed her. The man who planned to kidnap her son.

Security and John Tate pounded toward Michael and Kevin. When Kevin realized he was almost surrounded, a snarl curled his lips, and he lifted his hand with something in it. He aimed it at Michael, but Raina lunged the rest of the way and threw herself into Kevin. His scream of rage mixed with Vince's holler for her to stop.

Then something liquid hit her in the face. Her muscles went weak and she wobbled. Hard arms hoisted her over an even harder shoulder, then she was falling, felt the thud of her body hitting the floor of the van. She heard the door shut, tried to call out, but the darkness swept over her, and she had no choice but to give in.

■ ■ ■ ■

Vince was in shock. That was the only word he could come up with to explain the paralyzing numbness that rendered him unable to move for a good second. Then he grabbed the nearest security officer and pointed. "Radio someone and tell them not to lose that van! He just kidnapped a woman." The officer was on his radio almost before Vince finished speaking. "Raina, can you hear me?" He could only pray she still had her comms in and her abductor hadn't noticed it. "Raina?"

Silence, then static answered him. She was already out of range. The radios for the security team probably only reached around the perimeter of the event and not beyond.

"What happened?"

He turned to find the sheriff running toward him. "He took her."

Joseph tensed. "Her?"

The driver of the van hurried over to them. "He stole the van!"

"She saved me," Michael said, his eyes wide, voice shaky. Michael's father didn't look much better, his dark skin pale, brows furrowed in a deep frown. "Did you see what she did, Dad? She pushed the guy away from me, and he sprayed her with something, then took her."

"I saw, son." He pulled Michael into a tight hug, and even in his panicked, distracted state, Vince noticed the boy didn't pull away.

Local police on scene and part of the security descended, and Vince got on the phone with Holt.

It only took him a few seconds to bring the man up to speed. "There's a BOLO out on the van, of course, but I need you to use any influence you have with the Bureau in this location to get them looking for Raina."

"Of course. I'll make some calls."'

Vince's phone beeped with an incoming call. "I've got to go."

"I'll be in touch."

He tapped the screen. "Gabrielle, I'm here. Just so you know, Raina's been taken."

"What?"

He gave her the short version. "What do you have?" *Please have something that'll help find Raina.*

"I looked into the Baldridges and you might find it interesting. He has two sons. Christopher and Keith. No rentals, hotels, or plane tickets that would raise suspicion—nothing."

"Why did Simon hire a PI?"

"I don't know. One thing interesting, I can't find any pictures of Keith Baldridge other than a fuzzy driver's license photo."

"Send it to me." Unfortunately, he hadn't gotten a look at the guy who'd stolen the van and taken Raina away.

"Sending."

His phone pinged. "Keep digging, please. Find whatever little detail you can about every single family member. I feel like the answer's there, it's just going to take some effort." And time. Time Raina might not have.

"Will do. Also, something interesting. That lawyer who was killed in California. The one Raina called?"

"Yeah."

"I asked to be updated on anything as it could be related to cases here, and they said they found a whole drawer full of threats addressed to Trent."

"What kind of threats?"

"Pictures of his family with their heads cut off, notes saying, 'I'm still watching' and 'It may have been ten years, but I'm still here,' 'If you help her, your family is dead,' and so on. Creepy stuff."

"Unbelievable. And he never reported it?"

"No, doesn't look like it. He was just too afraid, I guess." A pause. "And looks like he had good reason to be."

Vince shut his eyes, forcing his brain to think. If he wanted to help Raina, he had to think. "See if other people had those same threats. Including Raina's parents." It hit him that he didn't know her birth name. Chopper blades beat the air and he found himself impressed at how fast law enforcement had mobilized to find Raina. "I've got to go, Gabrielle. Text me anything else that you find?"

"Will do. But one more thing. Holt let me know they were able to trace the jeweler who made the rings Raina told you about."

"They found hers?"

"No, but they got the one from the family of one of the victims. They found the organizer of an annual jewelry convention and snagged the email distribution list. Had them send a blanket email with a picture of the ring and received an almost instant response."

"No kidding. That's brilliant."

"It was a very high-end jeweler who custom designed that piece for a man named Kevin Anderson. Even though it's been years, he remembered the transaction, because the guy wanted ten rings of the same design."

"I wish I could hug you. We're closing in on him."

"Go get him. I'll text if I wind up with anything else."

Vince hung up and found himself in the midst of the officers, trying to give as many details as he could remember, even while he kicked himself for letting Raina get away from him. He hadn't thought—

No sense in going there. Regrets and beating himself up wouldn't find her. She'd reacted and in all probability kept Kevin from snatching Michael. The timing of the van's arrival was just one of those things. If it hadn't been the van, it would have been something else.

They just needed to focus on getting her back, because leaving her in the hands of a possible serial killer wasn't an option.

■ ■ ■ ■

The knock on the door didn't surprise Simon. Finding two federal agents on his doorstep did. He'd been expecting Freddy Harper.

The first agent showed his badge and identified himself as Special Agent Lance Gresham and his partner as Haley Fleming. Simon dug deep and found his poker face. "What's this all about?"

"Do you mind if we come in?"

"I guess not. Follow me into the sitting room."

Once they were in the room, he motioned for them to sit, but they declined, so Simon stood as well. "Again, what's this about?"

"We're here about a private investigator you hired. A Freddy Harper?"

Chills danced up Simon's spine.

Footsteps in the foyer distracted him for a moment, and he pulled in a breath at the reprieve.

Christopher stepped in the room and stopped. "What's going on here?"

"I was just getting ready to find out," Simon said. He introduced the agents to his son, then cleared his throat. "They're asking about the private investigator, Freddy Harper."

"Oh. And?"

"That's what we'd like to hear," Agent Fleming said. "Go on."

"I don't know what you're looking for. Freddy's been on my payroll for a while. I have him scout various real estate properties around the country. He does a lot of the background searches for titles and that kind of thing. Looks into the owners and why they're selling."

"Thought that's what lawyers were for," Fleming said.

Simon shrugged as though none of this was important to him. "PIs are cheaper by the hour."

"I see. Have you ever heard of a woman by the name of Raina Price?"

He met the agent's eyes. "No. I haven't."

"Your PI was in the hospital the same day she was drugged and almost killed."

"I'm sorry, I really don't see what this has to do with me. I didn't send him to the hospital."

"But you knew he was in North Carolina."

"To look at a property there. Property out east is cheaper and the dollar goes a lot farther."

All of that was actually true, and if they searched his laptop, they'd find evidence to back up his story.

"You have another son, Keith Baldridge."

"I do."

"Is he here?"

"He's not. He doesn't live here. He has his own place. But I think he's traveling for work. Why?"

"We'd just like to speak with him," Agent Gresham said.

"Well, you can try his cell phone, but there's nothing I can help you with other than to give you his number."

The agents nodded. "Thank you for your help."

CHAPTER
TWENTY-TWO

Raina groaned and lifted a hand to her head, wondering what band had taken up residence there. Or what truck had she walked in front of?

She blinked and her surroundings came into focus. A wood ceiling, wood walls, wood floor. A cabin? A very nice cabin with a floor-to-ceiling fireplace, a grand piano in the corner, and a kitchen to her right. She was on a sofa, the cushions beneath her comfortable, inviting her to drift back to sleep. But—

Michael!

Kevin!

She sat up with a gasp, then lay back down fast before she lost the contents of her stomach. Two deep breaths and a few minutes later, she sat back up and her eyes landed on the man in the recliner opposite her.

Kevin Anderson. He looked slightly older with a little gray at his temples and a few lines at the corner of his eyes. Eyes she wished she could forget about, but he was watching her, a gun resting in his lap. "Welcome back."

"How'd you find me?" She flexed her fingers. He hadn't used

any restraints. Of course he hadn't. He wouldn't think he'd need them.

"I didn't. I found Michael. Imagine my surprise when you yelled at him to run, and I turned to see the woman I've been searching for the past almost fourteen years." His right eyebrow lifted. "But that's not important at the moment. Just tell me, he *is* my son, isn't he?"

"Would you believe me if I said no?"

"No."

"Then why ask?" Something dark and furious flickered in his gaze, and Raina decided if she wanted to live, she was going to tell him. "He's yours."

"And you didn't think that was something I needed to know?"

How to answer without setting him off? That one thought took her back to the days where that was the filter through which she lived her life. "You killed Mrs. Atwater, didn't you? My parents' housekeeper? And left the black roses as a warning to me?"

"I did. I was going to give you some time to heal, then come back for you, but you dropped off the planet. I searched all over the place for you."

And he had no intention of letting her get away a second time. "Did you kill the others?" she asked.

He stilled. "Others?"

"Apparently, according to the research done by law enforcement, my case—being beaten within an inch of my life by an ex-boyfriend who no one ever met or could identify and disappears without a trace—was not an isolated incident."

He sat a little straighter. "No kidding."

"No kidding. Unfortunately, the other victims didn't survive. Only I did. I'm guessing that was a mistake on your part?"

"I don't make mistakes." His hand tightened around the grip of the weapon. With her mind clearing as the minutes ticked past, she had one thought—escape.

But how?

At least it seemed like he wanted to keep talking a bit before he killed her. She shuddered, memories of her last encounter with him crowding her mind and wanting to paralyze her.

Focus. If she let her fear take control, she'd die. *God, please, show me what to do.*

"Well? Did you kill those other women?" she asked.

"They weren't the right ones. They always wanted to leave me."

Pointing out that he was the reason they wanted to leave—why *she* wanted to leave—would do no good. "Why do you think that is?"

He drew in a deep breath and his eyes narrowed. "Because she couldn't help it."

"That's confusing. Kevin—"

"Keith."

She blinked. "What?"

"Keith. My name is Keith Baldridge. No sense in calling me Kevin anymore."

"Okay. *Keith.* Can you please explain?"

Raina shifted as though to get more comfortable. In truth, she needed to see if her legs would hold her. Seemed they might.

Kevin—no, Keith—lifted the weapon, then lowered it when she did nothing else.

"My mother died when I was young," he said. "My father was furious for her leaving us but kept saying she couldn't help it. That she'd loved him so much, the only way she'd ever leave was if she was dead."

It clicked. "So, when a woman decides to leave you, the only way you'll let her go is if she's dead?"

"It's the only way she's *allowed* to leave me."

Trying to wrap her mind around his sick reasoning wasn't going to work. It was what he believed no matter how twisted, and she was going to have to ignore that and figure out how to get away from him. "Why did you kill Mrs. Atwater?"

"She was in the way."

Don't throw up. Don't throw up. "In the way?"

"She served her purpose. I went to her house and could tell she was baking something. Then I overheard her talking on the phone, telling someone she was going to take the cake to the house and wait for you to get home. That you would be there in just a few minutes. I decided to hitch a ride. I hid in the trunk. Then once she parked, I followed her inside. I let her put the cake on the island before I took her out because I wanted you to have the cake. I knew it was your favorite. And of course she would make your favorite. Because you were always everyone's favorite. I've never been anyone's favorite. Even when Christopher was helping me, he hated me. He didn't help me because he loved me. He only helped me to keep his name clean. He wants to be governor, you know."

Raina was doing her best to follow his ramblings. "I know. And you were keeping tabs on all of my family and friends, all these years," she whispered, still shocked at the idea.

He shrugged. "It wasn't hard. Just planted a few bugs here and there and made sure they knew I was watching."

"You killed Trent Carter."

Keith raised a brow. "Actually, no. I didn't. I have no idea who killed him, but I can't say I was sorry to see him go. It was getting tedious keeping him in line." He raised the weapon. "Enough. I want to know about my son and who helped you hide him."

Okay, so if he didn't kill Trent, who did? And why? Raina was fighting to keep the facts straight but wasn't having much success. "Today was the first day I'd seen him other than on television. No one helped me hide him, I gave him up for adoption."

"Someone helped you do that!"

"Yes! Trent Carter! The man you killed."

"I didn't kill him!" He stood and looked like he might punch her. She refused to flinch but steeled herself for the pain. Surprisingly, he took a deep breath and settled back into the chair. "How did he help you?"

"He arranged the adoption. A private adoption. I picked out the couple who got Michael."

"You just gave him away like he was a puppy? And I never got a say in the matter?"

He was flat-out crazy.

"I looked for you, Kev—Keith," she said, her voice low.

That stopped him. "You what?"

"I looked for you, but you were nowhere to be found. I mean, granted, I was looking for Kevin Anderson, but I looked for you. I even talked my stepfather into hiring a private investigator to track you down and got nowhere." No need to mention that she'd planned to have him arrested and press charges as hard as they could be pressed.

Keith straightened. "You were going to tell me about the baby? That you didn't really want to leave?"

She had no idea what the right answer was. "I . . . wasn't sure what I was going to do, I just knew I needed to find you. So I tried."

He sat back with a huff. "Well, this does complicate things a bit, doesn't it?" After several seconds of silence, he stood.

"Keith—"

"Don't say anything. I need to think."

■ ■ ■ ■

"We really need to find her." Vince stated the obvious, pacing the floor at the command center set up in the lodge. Michael's father had taken the young man back to finish the event now that the danger for Michael had been averted.

As for Raina . . .

Security footage was pulled on the van and everywhere someone could find the guy dressed like the one who snatched Raina.

Unfortunately, that was every ski patrol man. "Focus on the pants," they'd been told. The pants were different. But all the footage was that of a man dressed for the weather at the base of the run. He'd gotten there early for a good spot, waited for Michael to do his thing, then simply followed him. The argument with his father and the van pulling up all worked in his favor.

"Ugh. Even the pictures of him spraying her and dumping her in the van don't give us anything to go on." He refused to say it was hopeless, but . . .

No. It wasn't hopeless. God knew where she was. Vince just needed him to share the information by guiding them in the right direction.

"They found the van," Joseph said. "CSU is on the way and will go over it with a fine-tooth comb."

Vince started to pace again, but stopped when he came face-to-face with a man who seemed to recognize him. Dressed in warm jeans with boots and a flannel shirt over a black turtleneck, the man stood in a casual pose that Vince recognized. Relaxed, but ready. "US Marshal John Tate?"

He quirked a brow. "How'd you know?"

"Raina said your name right before Kevin—or whoever he was—snatched her."

"Can we talk?"

"We sure can. Any idea where this Kevin guy would take her?"

"No. My job has been just to keep an eye on her all these years."

They stepped out of the command center, and the wind gusted down the back of Vince's jacket. He could see the benefit of a turtleneck. Turning up his collar, he kept his gaze on Tate. "How do you mean?"

"Brianne's father, sorry, Raina's father, hired me away from the marshal service years ago. He and Raina's mother were terrified Kevin would find her and she'd be on her own against him."

"You kept him updated on Raina, didn't you?"

"On most things. I never told him exactly where she was, but he could find out easy enough if he wanted to"—he shrugged—"if something had happened to me . . ." He waved a hand. "Anyway, he wanted me to be there should Kevin show up."

"Well, according to Raina, the guy who attacked her in her house wasn't Kevin. We assumed the guy who drugged her at the hospital was Freddy Harper, but it wasn't. So, my guess is, Kevin has someone working for him, and when that guy failed to kill Raina, he came to finish the job himself. Where were you for all of that?"

The man nodded. "I confess, when I noticed your attentiveness to her, I backed off a lot. I let her parents know that you were watching out for her."

Fat lot of good he'd done with that. "And now she's in that maniac's hands." Vince studied him for a brief second. "You know about Michael."

"I do. But I wasn't worried about him until Trent Carter was killed, his office ransacked, and his laptop stolen. He handled Michael's adoption. I just learned about the threats Trent was dealing with, but I should have guessed. I knew the man was wound tighter than a spring, but I honestly had no idea he was being threatened. I thought it was just Raina's family."

"You didn't get threats?"

"No."

"Probably didn't want to mess with law enforcement. So, this guy was threatening her parents?"

"Yep. Two or three times a year. Her father always called me to handle it, and every threat has been documented, just waiting for the time we can use them in court against the sender. But, as long as the threats kept coming, he knew Raina wasn't safe from this Kevin character."

"Right." Another short pause. "You're not a marshal anymore."

"I'm not. I couldn't do this for Tyler and still work for the marshals full time. I talked to my supervisor and told him that I wanted to do this for my friend. And"—he smiled—"it was a pay raise."

"I'm surprised Kevin didn't come after you. He had to know you were the one who helped Raina."

He shrugged. "Again, his distance could have something to do with the badge."

"True. But you've been waiting for him to show up, haven't you?"

"Every day." He pursed his lips. "And the fact is, I never would have known the man was in her house that night. I'm really glad you were there."

"Well, that answers a few questions, but right now, we have to figure out where he would take her."

Joseph stepped out of the command center. "We got a hit on a facial from a street camera. Looks like the guy's name is Keith Baldridge and he landed in Colorado yesterday. Rented a car and drove here."

"Can we track the rental?" Vince asked.

"First thing I checked. It's parked at the lodge right where he left it when he drove up. Crime scene unit is going over that too. Rental agreement is in the name of Kevin Anderson."

The breath whooshed from his lungs. "So Kevin Anderson is really Keith Baldridge?"

"Looks like it."

"He thinks he's unstoppable. Why would he use a name that he has to know everyone is looking for?" It didn't take a psychiatrist to answer that one. Kevin Anderson was Raina's boyfriend. He couldn't use another name or it wouldn't be "right" for him.

"Hopefully his arrogance will help lead to his downfall," John said. "Wouldn't be the first one to happen to."

Vince googled Keith Baldridge. Surprisingly very little came up. There was one family picture of him at his brother's wedding. He studied the face of the man and his family, then tapped the screen shut.

Sweat dripped into his eyes in spite of the outdoor temperature, and he needed to think. "I'm going to the restroom. I'll be right back."

Vince stepped into the men's room, grateful to find it empty. He went to the sink and splashed water on his face, his mind racing.

The bathroom door opened, and he glanced up to see a man enter, eyes on his phone. Vince swiped a hand down his face, said a prayer for Raina, and headed for the exit.

As soon as he stepped through the door, something stung the back of his neck and he whirled to see the man who entered seconds ago.

"Might want to lean on me so you don't fall," the guy said.

"What?" Then the dizziness hit him, and his legs went weak. He stumbled toward the main area, arm outstretched, but the man simply grabbed the back of his jacket and yanked him toward him. Vince had no strength to fight.

"Not that way," his attacker said. "We're going out the back." His hand gripped Vince's upper arm and he led him to the emergency exit.

"Did you take Raina?"

The man shot him a funny look. "No. That's why we need you."

"What'd you give me?"

"Scopolamine."

No wonder he was as obedient as a well-trained dog.

Fight it!

But he couldn't and he walked out the door, vaguely wondering why the alarm didn't sound, climbed into the car, and passed out.

CHAPTER
TWENTY-THREE

Raina stayed seated while Kevin—no, *Keith*—paced. If she moved, he spun with the gun and she was terrified it was going to go off. She finally had enough of being silent. "Keith, please . . ."

"No." He whirled on her once more, but at least he left the weapon pointed at the floor. "I'm thinking. If you didn't mean to leave me, then that changes everything."

She wasn't sure she wanted to know what he meant by that. "What were you going to do once you took Michael?"

Her question seemed to throw him, and he paused for a moment. Then shrugged. "I was going to bring him here for a bit. Get to know him. Let him get to know me. After that? I'm not sure exactly. I guess I was going to take him home to California."

His answer sent chills up her spine. Was he really that far gone mentally? "And what about when the BOLO went out on him and the AMBER alert with his face all over national television. What were you going to do about that?"

"I have a whole team of lawyers. I'd let them figure it out. The adoption can't be legal because I was never given a chance to say I wanted him. Not to mention Christopher can fix any trouble I get into."

"Christopher?"

"My brother. He's the one who always helps me."

"Helps you . . . what?"

A cold smile tilted the corners of his lips. "Clean up the mess."

Okay, Raina had had just about enough, but she needed to be careful. Rein in her fear and desperation to get away from this man. "So, do you plan to—"

"It doesn't matter right now. At the moment, I have a kid to find." He aimed the weapon at her. "And the security is going to be ridiculous now, thanks to you. Go down the hall into the first bedroom on the left."

She held up her hands in supplication. "Keith, no. Leave Michael alone. He's a happy, well-adjusted kid. If you care so much about him, you'll want what's best for him."

He slapped his chest with his free hand. "I'm what's best for him! A complete family is what's *best* for him. If you tried to find me, you must have planned to stay." He paused. "And now I know." He spoke the words low, as though to himself.

"Know what?"

"There was a reason I couldn't ask Daphne to marry me, no matter what my father demanded." His eyes lifted to meet hers. "It's because I never forgot you or stopped looking for you and this was meant to be. So, I'll get our son and we'll be a family. Now walk down the hall into the room or I can just knock you out and carry you there. Your choice."

Wait. What? He wasn't going to kill her? He was leaving?

To go find Michael.

"Fine." The last thing she wanted was to be unconscious. "I'll go." At least she'd have a fighting chance to get away if she was awake. Once she was in the bedroom, he shut the door and she heard the deadbolt lock. No doubt this was where he planned to keep Michael.

"Don't worry," Keith said, his voice carrying through the

door, "I'll be back soon. I'm just going on a little recon mission. I need to get the lay of the land, so to speak. You won't be alone long."

Raina rested her forehead against the door and closed her eyes. She refused to respond, and soon, his footsteps headed away from her back toward the den. She gulped in a steadying breath and turned.

The room was simple, with a queen bed, two end tables with lamps, a dresser on the opposite wall, a closet, and an en suite bath with all of the toiletries one would need.

She didn't plan to be there long enough to need them.

Raina went straight to the closed curtains and yanked them apart. Only to come face-to-face with a piece of metal in place of a window. "What in the world?" Her whispered words still echoed in the room.

Now what?

■ ■ ■ ■

Simon paced the den while his son tried Keith's phone once more. After leaving a blistering message to call, he hung up and tossed the device on the end table. "He's not answering."

"I noticed." That earned him a dark look, but he didn't have time to baby anyone's feelings. "He went after the kid, didn't he?"

"That's probably a safe assumption."

"I should have smothered him as a baby," Simon muttered.

"Dad!"

"Well? If I had, we wouldn't be in this situation."

"No, you'd be in prison!"

Simon waved a hand. "I'm not serious." Much. "But we've got to get him back here ASAP. He's going to ruin everything."

"I thought you had someone watching him." Christopher rose to pour himself a splash of whiskey and downed it in one swallow. Which brought on a coughing fit. Simon raised a brow. His son never drank. Ever.

"I thought I did too," Simon said, "but apparently, not close enough." Freddy Harper had ghosted him. "Where's Leslie? I haven't seen her lately."

"She flew out this morning. She wanted to visit her sister to help her pick out furniture for her new house. It's probably good that she's not here for all of this."

"No kidding." Simon wished he was anywhere but here as well.

"Try Freddy again. Maybe he's following Keith and just can't answer his phone at the moment."

Simon grunted and made the call. It went straight to voice mail. He disconnected the call without leaving a message. It was kind of odd that the man didn't answer. But Keith was just flat-out ignoring him. He looked at Christopher. "Can you track his phone?"

"Keith's? Or Freddy's?"

"Keith's, son, Keith's." He was running out of patience with both of his offspring.

Christopher studied him. "Yes, I can track him, but I can't make him answer the phone."

"Then where is he?"

"At Copper Mountain by now."

"You couldn't stop him?" Simon gritted his teeth and pulled out his phone, dread in his gut about the search he entered. "He went after the kid. I'm going to kill him."

"Not if I see him first."

■ ■ ■ ■

Vince woke slowly, his head pounding in time with his heart. What had hit him? Keeping his eyes closed, too afraid of what added pain a bright light might bring, he raised a hand to his forehead, trying to think. The last thing he remembered was walking into the men's room, feeling something sting him in the neck, and then . . . what? Nothing.

But . . . Raina! He touched his ear, looking for the comms. It was gone. Of course it was. Next, he patted his pockets and vest looking for his phone. Again, nothing to be found. Surprise, surprise.

He started to sit up and banged into something solid over his head. He yelped as pain shot through his skull.

Startled, he opened his eyes and inhaled. Darkness greeted him, along with the smell of old tires and oil, but soon his eyes adjusted and he could tell by the faint light that he was in a trunk. He wasn't tied up, which would save time in executing his escape. Wondering how he'd come to be there was an exercise in futility with the gap in his memory. The main thing was to get out. And keep the sickness swirling at the base of his throat from coming up.

He raised his foot to kick out the back light when a voice caught his attention. He stilled and waited, willing the nausea to pass.

". . . mess up everything. We can't use him for bait if we can't find her to pass the message on to!"

Vince frowned and shifted, grimacing at the shooting pains in his calf and shoulder. No one responded to the statement, then the man spoke again. "I'm telling you, I don't know! And you will pay me or I'll come after you and you know it." More silence. "I broke into her house, but she fights like a ninja, I poisoned her at the hospital, but help was right there. I did it all! Everything you asked. So, you better have my money or . . ." Pause. "You're here? Why?" The person on the other end talked for a minute, then, "No, you do not have to take care of everything. I'm telling you, I've got this . . . What? A cabin? How do you know that's where he is? Uh-huh. Yeah. Fine. So, what do I do with this guy?" Vince strained to hear as the man paced. "Right. So, you don't need him anymore? . . . Fine . . . yeah . . . I'll get rid of him and meet you there and we'll take care of her." Silence. "Right. Him too. And you'll make the transfer as soon as it's done . . . Good. Then I'm on the way."

Vince felt around the trunk for the emergency release, but couldn't locate it. However, his fingers brushed something hard, and when he explored the item, he discovered it was a wrench. Perfect.

Footsteps crunched on the ground. Gravel road or just frozen ground? The guy got back in the vehicle and the engine started. Soon, they were moving once more.

Fear for himself grabbed at him, but it was the one thing he couldn't give in to. Other emotions swirled within him as well, such as desperation to find Raina. But apparently, whoever this guy was, he wanted Raina too. And he couldn't find her.

Because Kevin had taken her. So, Kevin and this guy—and the person he was on the phone with—weren't working together.

Who else could possibly want Raina out of the picture other than Kevin?

Questions and more questions spun in his mind while he worked on the carpet, pulling it back from the taillight. He maneuvered his body around the small space, trying to give himself room to kick the light. It took two tries, but finally, the light gave way and disappeared. Cold air rushed in and he breathed deep, relishing it on his sweaty face. Once again, he had to move slow so as not to alert the driver that he was awake, but he shifted so that he could see out the back. They were on a winding road, trees lining each side while they climbed.

And no cars in sight behind them. Great.

Vince clutched the wrench. It was time to get the upper hand and figure out what was going on. If he understood the one-sided conversation correctly, they were going to use him as bait to get to Raina. He snorted. Not in this lifetime. And now they didn't need him because they'd found her.

When the vehicle pulled to a stop, Vince ignored his cramped muscles and aching wounds while he readied himself for when the trunk opened. Through the broken taillight, Vince would be able to see the man coming. His biggest concern was if his kidnapper noticed the light, then he'd know Vince was awake—and ready to fight.

The door slammed and footsteps headed toward the rear of the vehicle. The trunk opened and Vince launched himself toward the individual.

The man jerked back, tripped, and fell on his rear. That gave Vince the time to leap from his "prison." He landed on the ground while the guy rolled and lifted his weapon. Pain shot through Vince's wounded calf and he went to his knees—an action that saved his life when the weapon fired and the bullet went over his head.

From his knees, Vince catapulted himself at the man, hooking his arm under the guy's elbow and yanking up. Bone snapped and an agonized scream echoed around him. The gun tumbled from his grasp and Vince slammed a fist into his face.

The guy crumpled to the ground, unconscious.

Panting, wincing at his own pain, wondering if he'd popped a stitch or two, Vince scrambled to his feet and snagged the weapon. He checked it, then shoved it into the back of his jeans and hauled the man to the trunk and searched his pockets. He found the phone, but no wallet. Interesting. He snapped a picture of the unconscious man, then slammed the lid of the trunk. "See how you like it," he muttered.

The pain from the broken arm might wake him up fairly quickly, but frankly, Vince didn't care. For some reason, the guy had expected the drug to last a lot longer than it had. Vince didn't question the why, he was just thankful it had worn off when it did.

He walked to the edge of the mountain and looked down into the drop-off. Probably where "bad guy" had planned to put a bullet in his head and drop him. He returned to the vehicle and searched the glove compartment. A rental. He continued his search. There had to be some clue in it as to where he could find Raina. If they hadn't needed him anymore, it meant they knew where she was.

And they were going after her.

All he could do was pray he could figure it out and find her first.

CHAPTER
TWENTY-FOUR

Raina let out yet another groan of frustration. What was Keith—she was having a hard time calling him that, but whatever—doing? Did he really think he'd be able to get to Michael?

Apparently so.

The clock on the end table said an hour and a half had passed since he'd left the house, and all her attempts to get out the window had failed. The steel was bolted to the side of the house and it wasn't budging.

Trying to get the door open had resulted in the same frustrating failure. Now she examined the bathroom once more, looking for anything that could be used as a weapon.

Before she could find anything, the door opened. "Brianne?"

She pulled in a ragged breath, whispered another prayer, then flushed the toilet and stepped out to find Keith standing in the doorway, a frown on his face. "What are you doing?" he asked.

She raised a brow, doing her best to hide her fear. "Using the bathroom?"

"You can come out of the room now. But if you try anything, I'll have to use this." He held up a taser and she shuddered at the thought of being zapped with it, but at least it didn't shoot bullets.

She nodded and he backed up.

"You came prepared." She waved a hand at the window behind her.

"Of course. Didn't know it was going to be you in there, but glad I was thinking ahead."

"Right. Thinking ahead." With a plan to kidnap a boy and terrorize him, perhaps traumatize him for life. She swallowed her words, but noted Keith never turned his back to her. He was being very careful and she needed him to drop his guard.

Once they reached the end of the hallway, he motioned to her to step past him.

She really didn't want to get that close to him, so kept her back against the wall, not taking her eyes from him.

The front door slammed open and a gunshot sounded. Raina screamed, dropped to the floor, and rolled behind the recliner.

"What are you doing here?" Keith yelled.

"Cleaning up your mess."

Another shot cracked and a hard thud echoed. Raina's ears rang in the sudden quiet.

Raina looked around the edge of the chair and spotted Keith on the floor, empty eyes turned her way. She swallowed a gasp and another scream even as she noted the taser in his outstretched hand. Raina grabbed it.

The gun fired again and the chair's back exploded.

"What are you doing? Why are you shooting at me!"

Another bullet whipped past her face and Raina's heart pounded. She was a sitting duck. And it didn't look like the shooter was interested in talking.

The gun cracked again, and Raina moved, launching herself up from behind the recliner and racing back down the hallway.

Footsteps hurried after her.

She bypassed the room that had been her prison and ran into the master bedroom, slammed the door shut, and locked it. It wouldn't hold long, but maybe long enough to get out the window. With shaking fingers, she unlatched the nearest one and threw herself out. The screen bounced and Raina landed hard on top of it.

Gunshots sounded from within the house. Raina had to get moving, but she needed a second to get her bearings.

Trees, snow, cold. Solitude. A mountain cabin on several acres. No telling which way would take her to safety.

Of course he would pick a place like this to bring his kidnapped son. She headed for the cover of the trees, shivering, but thankful she'd kept her heavy coat on in anticipation of getting out of the room and making a run for it. Thoughts churning, she glanced back at the cabin to see a figure standing at the window, watching. All she could make out was a flannel jacket and a baseball cap. The person disappeared, and Raina figured it was to head to the door to come after her.

She put on a burst of speed and scrambled behind a tree, only to realize she'd left a trail in the snow. Whoever had killed Keith—and obviously planned to kill her—could follow her with no trouble.

Panic tried to set in, but she kept going.

If she couldn't hide, she was going to have to come up with a plan to fight back.

She stepped behind a tree and gripped the taser. She could do this. She'd trained for the time when she'd have to fight for her life. Granted, this wasn't the person she thought she'd be confronting, but the concept was the same.

Raina glanced around the trunk. The shooter came closer, following the path she'd left behind in the snow, just as she figured would happen.

The snow boots crunched their way toward Raina, one step at a time. The gun in the gloved hand was held in a grip that said the attacker knew how to use it. The second bullet from the weapon had certainly nailed Keith without any trouble.

Which meant, she couldn't give the person a target.

Please, God, I know I've had a hard time trusting you, but I still believe and pray you plan to deliver me from this. If not . . . okay. Just make sure Vince knows this isn't his fault because he's going to blame himself.

As she prayed, the attacker advanced. And for the first time, Raina got a good glimpse of the heavily dressed individual. The bulky clothes couldn't hide the slim figure underneath.

She blinked.

The person trying to kill her was *a woman*?

And then there was no more time to process as she stepped through the tree line and Raina fired the taser.

And missed.

The woman swung around and fired the gun. The bullet hit the trunk next to Raina's cheek, blasting her face with particles of wood.

Heart pounding, Raina turned and ran, doing her best to keep herself next to thick trees. The next gunshot echoed, the bullet slamming into the tree in front of her. Raina darted to the right, pushing off the nearest trunk and heading for the big oak just ahead.

She whirled behind it, panting, looking for a weapon. A thick limb about the length of a baseball bat lay five feet away from her and she knelt to grab it.

God, please!

She wouldn't get another chance.

"It's no use, Raina," the woman said, her voice coming from the other side of the huge tree. "You're just prolonging the inevitable."

"Why are you doing this? Who are you? What did I ever do to you?"

"Your very existence is a threat to my future. As was Keith's. I took care of him and now you're the only one left."

Raina whipped her head left, then right. Nowhere to run that wouldn't leave her exposed. She tightened her grip around the limb. "Keith was a killer."

"I know. Trust me. I know. But he enjoyed it. I don't. I didn't want to kill him, but he simply left me no choice."

"And what did I do?"

"He was determined to find that kid of his. And you, I'm sure."

"He *did* find me. Us. How did you find *us*?"

"I tracked his phone. I figured it would come in handy one day, so I took it when he wasn't looking and shared his location with me. Easy enough. Thankfully, he never noticed. Now, come on out and I'll make this as painless as possible."

That would be a hard no. The woman started moving once more, and Raina glanced around the trunk to see the distance. "I'm not coming out. You'll have to come get me."

A sigh sounded from her. "Fine. I'm the one with the gun, remember?"

Oh, she remembered. *Just keep walking. Please keep walking.*

The woman did. And then there was nothing but quiet.

Raina waited for the sound of more footsteps.

Nothing.

She bit her lip. What was she doing?

The snap of a twig to her left spun her around and movement caught her eye. Raina sidestepped around the trunk just as a bullet plowed into the place she'd been standing. Raina kept going. Four steps was all she needed. One, two . . . the woman saw her and the gun swung around . . . three . . . four . . .

. . . swing.

She connected the tree limb with the hand that held the weapon and the gun discharged before it fell to the forest floor.

The bullet missed and the woman screeched her fury. Raina kicked out and connected with her attacker's gut, sending her sprawling.

Still screaming her rage, the woman retched, but managed to scramble to her feet. Raina threw a hard punch to her head, connected at the temple, and the woman went down for the last time.

Raina sucked in a breath, then blew it out on a sob, finally able to release the terror she'd kept in check for the past few hours.

"Raina!"

Panting, knuckles throbbing, tears streaming, Raina jerked her head in the direction of the shout. She knew that voice. "Vince!"

His name was just a whisper on her lips. She wanted to go to him but had to find the gun first.

The woman stirred and groaned.

Panic flared.

Raina felt around the snow-covered forest floor, shoving aside leaves and other debris to no avail. Where was the thing? It had flown from the woman's hand and hit the ground. "Vince!"

Another groan and a grunt reached her. "I'm going to kill you."

This time Raina's scream echoed as her attacker rolled to her feet, the gun held in her right hand.

"Federal agent! Put the weapon down!"

"No!" Her yell pierced Raina's ears even as the woman lifted the weapon to point it at Raina.

Three pops sounded and the woman's eyes went wide, a dark red stain seeping through the holes in her black puffer jacket.

The gun tumbled from her fingers once more and she fell facedown into the snow.

■　■　■

Vince had followed the tracks in the snow and had reached the scene just as the woman had risen to her feet, weapon pointed at Raina. Vince lowered his weapon. Officers hurried toward him while more sirens screamed to a stop in the driveway of the house behind him. Raina knelt next to the woman on the ground and checked her pulse.

Her gaze snapped up to his. "She's still alive!"

Vince rushed to her side. "You okay?"

"Yeah. I'll live. Help me flip her over." He did so and Raina unzipped her attacker's coat and parted it to find the wounds. "That one is the worst." She scooped snow into her bare hands and placed it over the bleeding hole. "Press here. Keep adding snow and make a pack."

He did as instructed, not even questioning the fact that she would work to save the person who'd almost killed her. Raina felt for a pulse once more. "It's pretty strong," she said. "Bullets must not have hit anything too vital."

"Backup is here," Vince said, looking over his shoulder to see more officers and medical personnel heading their way.

Joseph had stopped and was directing the others. He must have noticed they had it under control.

Raina nodded and sniffed. Tears streaked her cheeks, but she simply wiped them on her sleeve and kept working on stemming the flow of blood from the other two wounds.

"Who is she?" he asked.

"No idea. The bullet in her shoulder is a through and through. Saw it when she was on her face."

Vince brushed the hat off her head and strawberry blond hair spilled over the ground. "She looks familiar." Where did he know her from? The picture. "I think that's Leslie Baldridge."

"Who?"

"Keith Baldridge's sister-in-law."

"Wait a minute. The one married to the guy running for governor of California?"

"Yeah."

"Wow."

Paramedics finally arrived as well as more officers. Vince glanced up to find Joseph walking toward them, looking relieved. "Been looking all over for you. Saw you on the security footage walking out with some guy through the back emergency exit. You looked weird, but didn't put up a fight. He have a gun on you?"

"He drugged me. Scopolamine. It's a strange drug. Can turn you into a robot where you'll do just about whatever you're told. You get the guy in the trunk of the sedan parked on the curb?"

"Yep. Got paramedics looking at that arm. How did he break it?"

"I had to stop him from shooting me."

"Makes sense."

Vince handed the weapon to the sheriff. "That's his gun."

Raina had moved to the side and was washing the blood from her hands with sanitizing wipes, but her gaze never left the action.

"You okay now?" Joseph asked Vince. "You need someone to check you out?"

"I'm fine. I don't think he used much of the drug, and it wore off faster than he planned."

"That how you got him in the back of the trunk?"

"Yep."

The sheriff jerked a thumb over his shoulder. "Guy up at the house is dead."

Vince nodded. "Saw him when I got here looking for Raina. I checked on him, but thanks to the bullet in his head, he was probably dead before he hit the floor. Then I heard gunshots and bolted out here."

"The dead guy in the house the one you've been looking for?"

"I think so. Raina will be able to fill us in as soon as they get that woman off to the hospital."

"Who is she?"

"Leslie Baldridge, I think."

"Saw you shoot her."

"She didn't give me a choice."

"Saw that too. You warned her and she very clearly yelled no, and lifted her weapon to kill your friend. It'll go in the statement."

"Thanks." Vince walked over to Raina while the paramedics lifted the injured woman and placed her on the stretcher.

"She's stable," Raina said. She shivered, clasping her hands in front of her. He cupped them with his own larger palms and gasped at the chill.

"They're frozen."

"I . . . I know." And then the shakes set in and more tears dripped from her eyes.

He pulled her against him, wrapped her as tight as he dared without hurting her. For the next few minutes, she trembled and cried. Then gave one final shudder and released a long sigh. "Thank you."

He kissed the top of her head. "I was terrified I was going to lose you."

"I was pretty terrified myself." A pause. "How did you find me?"

He took a deep breath. "Well, it's kind of a long story, but the guy who kidnapped me—"

She jerked back. "What!"

"—and threw me in the pretty spacious trunk of his sedan—"

She gaped.

"—wasn't an idiot by any stretch of the imagination, but he made three mistakes. One, he didn't use enough of the drug to keep me knocked out for very long, and two, he didn't bother to tie me up—"

"And three?"

"He had this address programmed into the rental car's GPS.

Once I knocked him out and dumped him in his own trunk, I finished the drive."

She blinked. Once. Twice. "What?"

"What part do I need to repeat?"

Finally, she snapped her lips closed and shook her head. "Who kidnapped you? *Why* did he kidnap you? And is Michael okay?"

"Michael is fine. I don't know who the guy is, but he's in custody, so hopefully we'll have an ID and he'll start talking soon. But whoever he is, he was working with someone here and it wasn't Kevin."

"Keith," she murmured.

"What?"

"Kevin is Keith Baldridge."

"Oh. Right. Yeah, we figured that part out. Anyway, my kidnapper must have been working with the woman. I overheard them talking, and they'd taken me to lure you to wherever they planned to take me. Only Kevin—Keith—got to you first and they knew it."

"And the woman knew where Keith was because she tracked his phone. She told me that much."

His hand gripped hers. "That phone might just give us some answers as to what's going on."

"Like why my very existence was a threat to her? I mean, I can understand Keith's existence being a threat. After all, if it came out that her governor-wannabe husband's brother was a serial killer, that might just turn the tide of the election. And not the way she would want."

"Exactly."

"Now that I think about it, I guess since I was the only one who could ID Keith as the one who almost killed me, that wouldn't be good for an election either. If I was dead, there wouldn't be any more threats to her husband's bid for governor."

"Good point." He ran a finger down her cheek and pulled her into a tight hug. He might never let her go. "Officers are going over her car. One way or another, we'll have some answers."

"Good. I need answers."

Joseph walked over to them with his hand held out for Raina to shake. Which meant Vince had to release her. He frowned.

"You all right?" the man asked Raina.

"I will be."

"I just got a message that Mr. and Mrs. Harrison want to talk to you."

CHAPTER
TWENTY-FIVE

Raina's breath whooshed from her lungs. "Michael's parents."

"Yes, ma'am."

"All right. Um . . . where? On the phone?"

"No, they've asked if you would be willing to meet them tomorrow if you're going to still be in town. Michael has a full day and then some kind of event party. But they'd like to meet you for a late breakfast in the lodge restaurant."

"I . . . um . . ." She glanced at Vince, who gave her a subtle nod. She was stumbling all over her words, not sure she wanted to say yes, but couldn't bring herself to say no. "Okay. Yes, I . . . we . . . can do that. Thank you."

"I'm guessing you two need a ride back to the lodge?"

"That would be great," Vince said, "thank you."

Vince took Raina's hand and led her to the sheriff's cruiser. She couldn't help noticing Vince's limp. "Did you pull your stitches loose?"

"I haven't looked." He paused. "How do you feel about home-cooked meals?"

"Love them. I often cook at home."

He raised a brow at her. "You do?"

"Yes. Why?"

"My parents want me to come to lunch on Sunday. I wondered if you'd go with me."

Raina thought about it. Meeting his parents? As . . . a friend? Or more? Deciding not to analyze it, she simply said, "Sure, I'd love to."

An hour later, Joseph pulled into the condo parking lot. "I know you said you didn't need to get checked out, but we do have medical staff at the lodge if you'd like to get looked at."

Vince looked at Raina. "You need it?"

She shook her head. "I'm fine, thanks. I just want a shower and to sleep for a while if that's all right."

The men acquiesced, and she soon found herself in the living area of the condo. She really needed to update Penny and the others, but right now, she was out of strength.

Vince joined her after saying goodbye to Joseph. "If you need me to, I can get my own space."

"No. I don't want to be alone. Please stay?"

"Of course." He pointed to her room. "Go. Take a shower, curl up, and go to sleep."

She slipped into his arms and gave him a hug, relishing the feel of him against her. Alive. Warm. Safe. "Thank you for sticking with me through all of this. I wouldn't have made it without you." Like literally, she'd probably be dead, shot by Leslie Baldridge. She pulled back. "What's going to happen to Christopher Baldridge? Do you think he knew about it?"

"I have no idea. I'm hoping to have an update in the morning sometime. I know law enforcement is going gung ho with their investigation in California, so . . . all I can say is we'll wait and hear how it goes."

"Okay."

"Now go. Stop thinking."

She snorted. A low, funny sound that made him smile. "Right," she said. "Stop thinking. As if." She raised on her tiptoes and kissed his cheek. At least she was aiming for his cheek, but he turned his head and met her lips.

And that was just fine with her. He kissed her with tender care, confidence, and tightly leashed passion. When he lifted his head, he studied her, bringing a hand up to stroke her cheek. "Go, Raina. I'll be out here if you need anything."

"Like another kiss?"

A smile ghosted his lips. "Not tonight. It's been a long day for both of us." But his eyes said he really liked the idea of another kiss.

She sighed. "Okay. You're right. I'm procrastinating. I'm . . . jumpy and anxious. That's normal, right?"

"Totally."

"But you're fine?"

He hesitated. "Tell you what, go get your shower, I'll get mine, and let's meet on the couch."

A relieved breath slipped from her. "I like that plan."

Twenty minutes later, dressed in sweats and a long-sleeved T-shirt so thoughtfully provided by Penny, she emerged to find Vince on the couch, socked feet up on the ottoman, television on.

She sat beside him, suddenly nervous for some reason, but also glad he was with her.

"They have a smart TV here, which is awesome," he told her. "I found a movie for us to watch. My favorite. I think you'll like it."

"I might fall asleep in the middle of it." Actually, she'd be surprised if she made it through the opening credits.

"That's the whole point."

"Ah, gotcha." She pulled her feet up under her and got comfortable. "I think I'm going to move to Florida. Key West to be specific."

He paused the movie and turned to her. "I'm sorry, what?"

"I've never been there before, but it's as far south as you can go and still be in the US, so it's got to be warm, right?"

He laughed and wrapped an arm around her shoulder to pull her next to him. "Yes, it's warm there."

It was quite acceptably warm tucked right there next to him. She might not need Florida after all. "You've been?"

"A few times."

After a second's pause, she said, "I'm scared I'm going to have nightmares."

He fell silent, then tugged her a little tighter against him. "I know the feeling."

She lifted her head and caught his gaze. "Really?"

"Guys have nightmares too."

"Yeah," she said, her voice soft. "I'm sorry you got all caught up in this."

"I wouldn't have been anywhere else, Raina. I'm finding comfort in your presence." He took a deep breath and blew it out. "Right after Eden died, I kept replaying her death in my dreams. Even though I didn't see it happen, I could envision it. I didn't sleep through the night without waking up in a sweat for about two years. Finally, with some counseling and the understanding of how the gaslighted person's mind works—and a lot of prayer—I was able to move on. I'm not saying I don't have regrets or wish things had turned out differently, I'm just saying that I don't dream about it anymore . . . much. Every so often something triggers it."

"And you think what we just got through will."

"Yeah."

She leaned her head on his shoulder and closed her eyes. "You're a special man, Vince Covelli."

"As are you, Raina Price. Well, a special woman. You're definitely not a man."

She laughed and he unmuted the television. While *The Fugitive* played and Dr. Richard Kimble ran for his life to find the evidence to clear his name, she breathed in the fresh scent of the man beside her, thinking she was finally right where she belonged.

When she glanced up, he looked down and kissed the tip of her nose, then leaned his head back and closed his eyes.

Hours later when the resort lights filtered through the blinds, Raina stirred. She was stretched out on the couch, head on a soft pillow and a warm blanket wrapped around her.

And Vince was nowhere to be seen.

She sat up, stomach rumbling, reminding her it was still on eastern time and was ready for some food.

Ignoring it, she stood and stretched, noting a difference in her heart this evening. She paused to take stock and finally realized what it was.

She was free.

No more looking over her shoulder, no more running, no more not talking to her parents.

She grabbed her phone and dialed her mother's number.

Halfway through the ring, her mom's beloved greeting caressed her ear. Tears slipped down her cheeks. "Hi, Mom."

■ ■ ■ ■

Simon was asleep in the recliner when they came. The pounding on the door startled him enough that pain shot through his chest. He pressed a hand to it and, when nothing else happened, rose to his feet. He had a bad feeling about what was about to go down but decided to let it play out. He'd know what to do shortly.

"FBI! Simon Baldridge, open the door and keep your hands in sight at all times."

Christopher joined him in the foyer, eyes wide, face pale. "You know what this is about?"

Simon sighed. "Probably something Keith did." He opened the door, holding his hands to shoulder height. Christopher did the same. "Can I help you?"

A man dressed in SWAT gear kept his weapon ready while two plainclothes detectives stepped inside. "Are you Simon Baldridge?"

"I am."

"I'm Detective Frank Garrison and this is my partner Detective Deb Jackson." He handed Simon a folded document. "We have a search warrant."

"For what?"

"That's detailed in there for you to read at your leisure. I need you to head into your den area and have a seat while we conduct the search."

It was futile to protest, so Simon did as instructed and Christopher followed. The female detective followed them, glanced at her screen, then looked at Christopher. "Are you Leslie Baldridge's husband?"

Christopher raised a brow and exchanged a glance with Simon. "Yes. Why?"

The woman's face softened. "I'm sorry to inform you that your wife was shot earlier today. She was transported to a medical facility near Copper Mountain where the shooting occurred, then choppered to Denver so she could get more specialized care. They say she's stable at the moment and should pull through."

Simon gripped his shocked and silent son's arm. Finally Christopher sputtered and shook his head. "I'm sorry, are you sure you have the right woman?"

The detective turned the screen around so both of them could see it.

Simon gasped and Christopher sucked in a harsh breath. "But . . . how? Why? What was she even doing . . ." He bit off his words.

"I hate to be the one to inform you of this," Detective Jackson said, "but she was involved in criminal activities. She was about to shoot a kidnap victim, and that led to your wife being shot by a US Marshal on the scene."

Christopher's jaw dropped and Simon had no idea what to think or say.

Detective Garrison appeared. "Sir, does Keith Baldridge have a room here?"

Simon scratched his head, trying to shift his thoughts from his daughter-in-law to his son. "Um, yes. Up the stairs and turn right. His room is at the end of the hall. But he doesn't live here. Just . . . stays here. Occasionally."

"We've already searched his place. The search warrant covers Leslie Baldridge's belongings and Keith Baldridge's at all residences," Detective Jackson said as her partner headed for the stairs.

"Can someone please tell me what's going on?" Simon did his best to keep the words cordial and not sound like a demand, but he was fast losing patience.

"Yes sir, we're also very sorry to inform you that your son attempted to kidnap a young boy but was interrupted by a woman. He took the woman instead to a remote location on Copper Mountain. She was rescued and is now safe, but reports that Leslie Baldridge shot Keith and then attempted to shoot her."

Simon wilted back onto the sofa cushion, all fight gone from him. "Is Keith dead?"

"I'm also very sorry to say that it's reported he died on the scene. A private investigator—at least that's what he calls himself—by the name of Isaac Martinson was also involved. He's given a formal statement that Mrs. Baldridge hired him to kill a woman by the name of Raina Price. This is the woman who was kidnapped by your son Keith."

Christopher stirred from his stunned silence. "I don't . . . I can't . . . she wouldn't. And Keith's dead?"

"I know this is hard," the detective said, compassion coating her words, "but it's true."

"Deb?" The other detective stood at the entrance to the den holding a spiral notebook. "This goes deeper than we thought." He turned his gaze on Christopher. "Sir, you're going to have to come with us for questioning."

That pulled Simon out of his almost-paralyzed state. He sat up. "What? Why?"

"Because it looks like Mr. Christopher Baldridge has been helping your son Keith hide the fact that he's a serial killer."

Simon swung his gaze to Christopher, who'd gone white. "What is he saying, son?"

"Nothing, Dad. It's not true."

Detective Garrison waved the notebook. "It's all documented right here. Names, dates, everything. And how his brother is always there for him to clean up his messes."

CHAPTER
TWENTY-SIX

FRIDAY MORNING

Vince stood in the suite's kitchen while Raina talked to her parents, making plans to visit. His heart was full for her. Full *of* her. He loved her, he just wasn't sure she was ready to hear it after the crazy past few days. He'd wait and let her get her bearings, find her equilibrium before springing that on her. He glanced at the clock. It would soon be time to head to the lodge to breakfast, but he didn't want to rush her.

She chose that moment to look up and see him watching, then noticed the time and stood. "I've got to go, Mom, but we'll see each other soon. You and Dad are welcome to come my way anytime."

After another round of goodbyes, she hung up and swiped her fingers under her eyes. "I've got to get ready. I don't want to be late."

"They'll wait."

She disappeared into the bathroom and emerged ten minutes later refreshed and looking like a million bucks in spite of everything.

He went to her. "You look amazing. Michael is going to love you. His parents already do."

A shaky smile curved her lips. "You know just what to say, don't you?"

"You ready?"

"Not even close." She swallowed. "So many what-ifs going through my head right now."

"Just take it one step at a time. And hold on to me."

She nodded and gripped his hand. "I can do that."

Together, they walked to the restaurant where they found Michael and his parents waiting just outside the entrance. When Michael saw her, he raced to her and wrapped his arms around her.

■ ■ ■ ■

Raina couldn't move, couldn't think, and didn't know how to even feel really, but holding Michael was a cherished gift she'd never forget as long as she lived. When he stepped back, she let her arms drop to her sides.

"I'm so glad you're okay," he said. "Thank you for what you did. I was so scared for you, but we prayed for you and here you are."

She finally found her voice. "Yes, I'm fine. And I'd do it all over again if I had to." She cleared her throat and introduced Vince.

After handshakes all around, Michael took her hand. "Mom and Dad shared your letter with me."

She froze. "So, you know . . ."

"That you're my birth mother." He nodded. "I'm very happy to meet you."

"Oh my . . . I don't know what to say." She swallowed. "Except that I've dreamed of this moment every day since you were carried out of my life." She glanced at the two individuals looking on with love and a little bit of anxiety in their eyes.

She went to them. "Thank you," she whispered, the lump in her throat so big, she almost choked.

"No," Michael's mother said, gripping Raina's hands, "we thank *you*. You loved him so much you were willing to sacrifice watching him grow up to keep him safe. It's because of that note that we believed what the marshal told us. That we were all in danger because Michael's birth father had seen him on television." She sniffed. "I can't believe a simple interview led to all of this."

Raina smiled. "I can't either, but honestly, I'm glad. Justice has finally been achieved for all of Keith Baldridge's victims and those of us who survived—and our families—are finally free." She looked at Michael and ran her fingers through his hair before she could stop herself. Then clasped her hands in front of her. "Please don't ever think I wanted to give you up or that I thought you weren't worth keeping. I wanted you with every fiber in my young heart, but I also knew I couldn't risk him finding you."

"I understand. Especially now. And I'm very thankful you chose the parents you did for me." He grinned. "You chose the best."

Raina met his parents' eyes. "Yes, I did. But God directed that choice." She shared a smile with his mother, then turned back to Michael. "I look forward to watching you in the Olympics on television when the time comes."

He turned shy all of a sudden. "I hope I'll get to see you again sometime."

She swallowed and kept her gaze on the parents who'd loved him and been there for him when she couldn't. "Well, I suppose we'll just have to play that by—"

"Yes, please," Jan Harrison spoke up. "We want you to be in his life if you want to. We've talked about it and feel like this is something that's important to Michael."

"I'd love that. Thank you." Raina's heart beat faster and

lighter, and she laughed—a breathy, joyous laugh. "I'd really love that."

"Cool," Michael said. "Can we eat now? I'm starving."

The sound of everyone's laughter soothed her soul, and when Vince took her hand, she thought she might explode with joy. Sending up a silent prayer of thanks to the one who'd made this reunion—and the reunion to come with her parents—possible, she walked through the door of the restaurant to have breakfast with her son.

EPILOGUE

Raina had spent the last couple of hours working in her living room, and now she stepped back to take a look at the transformation. Yep. Just about perfect. She had wings, potato wedges, corn on the cob, celery, carrots, dip. The perfect food for her plan.

She'd asked Vince to make sure he had the time off and to be at her house in—she glanced at her phone—thirty minutes. Yikes! She raced to her bathroom and, twenty-three minutes later, exited to take a deep breath and a swig of water.

Nine minutes later—thank goodness he was a little late—her doorbell rang and she wiped sweaty palms on her denim-clad thighs. Second thoughts swirled. Would he hate it? Would it trigger bad memories instead of good? Had she made a horrible mistake?

Too late now.

She walked to the door and opened it. And swallowed hard while her heart picked up speed and her tongue searched for

275

words. Vince held a bouquet of wildflowers in his left hand, his right hand casually tucked into the front pocket of his jeans.

"Hi," she finally managed.

"Hi."

"Come on in." He smiled and she stepped back. "Want to bring those in the kitchen and we'll find a vase for them? They're beautiful."

"They looked like something you might enjoy."

"Absolutely. Thank you." She cleared her throat. "And I did something, but am having second thoughts about it."

He raised a brow. "What'd you do?"

"I think it's best just to show you. Follow me." He'd see on their trek to the kitchen, so she might as well give him a heads-up. "I kind of made a living room fort for us. And I put the TV inside so we could watch cartoons—or a movie or something, but if you hate it—"

"Let me see."

She led the way, and when they came into view of the living area, his jaw dropped slightly, and his eyes reddened while he stopped and stared.

"I'm sorry," Raina rushed to say. "I'll take it down. I just thought it would be a way to—"

"I love it."

His low words snapped her lips shut. He walked the flowers to the kitchen counter, set them down, then returned to her to cup her cheek and cover her lips with his in a not-so-subtle kiss. In fact, the sparks raging between them were enough to make her decide to build a dang den fort every day from now on. She wrapped her arms around his neck and lost herself in the simple joy of being in his arms. And not being afraid to let him know how much she wanted to be there.

He pulled back—much too soon in her opinion—and grinned down at her. "You're amazing and I love you, Raina."

She swallowed. "Oh, Vince . . ."

He pressed a finger to her well-kissed lips. "Hold on, I need to say this, and if you stop me, I might lose my nerve. That night in the condo, when you mentioned moving to Florida, I immediately wondered how long it would take for a transfer to go through." He cleared his throat. "That's when I knew without a doubt that I was head over heels in love with you and wanted my future to include you. My forever to be our forever. And I know your name is Brianne, but you'll always be Raina to me."

With her heart in her throat and unable to speak, she kissed him again. Finally, she found her voice. "It's okay. I like Raina better than I ever liked Brianne." She wasn't talking about the name and he knew it. "I love you too, Vince. More than I ever thought I would love someone. With Kevin I thought I knew what love was." She shook her head. "But this emotion racing through me is more than anything I've ever known. And it's more than just a feeling. It's a decision. I want to love you. I want to be with you. I want everything that comes with a relationship. The ups and downs and working together through the good times and bad."

"Bad times? Downs?"

She wrinkled her nose at him, and he smiled. "Yeah. I want that too."

"To be honest, I never expected to allow myself to love anyone again, but you didn't give me much choice in the matter."

His smug look tugged the laughter from her, then she sobered. "I know I made things very difficult for you in the beginning, but I was scared, unable to trust you or God or anyone else really. But, your faithfulness—and determination—in watching out for me, being there, is really what won me over. That, and the fact that you saved my life." She cleared her throat. "I'm glad Leslie Baldridge isn't going to die. I'm glad she has a chance to repent and make things right in her life before she has to stand before God."

"Her choices have certainly not been good. Let's pray she makes better ones from here on out. I did hear that her husband, Christopher, is divorcing her even though he's been arrested for helping Keith—Kevin—his *brother* cover up the killings."

"His political career is shot for now. You think they'll be able to prove he knew what his wife was doing and add charges for that?"

"I don't know. Watching the media footage of everything, I'm leaning toward he didn't know. She had her own money and paid that guy to do her dirty work. I honestly think he was clueless about that."

"I still can't believe that man killed Trent." She sighed. "I feel so bad about that."

"If only he'd gone to the authorities, it might have ended differently—and a lot sooner."

"He was scared. When we're scared and feel trapped, we can make bad decisions. Which circles us back to Leslie."

"She felt trapped. If it had gotten out about Keith—and it would have—her husband's career would have been toast."

"Which it is. And now her marriage—and life—are too."

"And all of that is good news. I have one more question for you."

"Sure."

"You've never mentioned trying to get custody of Michael back. You've seen him and you were able to walk away." His hand gripped hers. "Are you okay?"

She smiled, her heart still so full of joy with the time she'd spent with Michael and his parents. "I'm so very okay. I would never pull him away from all he's ever known, but the fact that I get to be in his life is a miraculous answer to prayer and I'm so blessed by that. So, yes, I'm fine."

"Good. I thought that's how you felt but wanted to make sure. But now . . ."

"Now?"

He gripped her biceps and pulled her toward the fort. "I want to see inside this masterpiece."

She laughed and followed him in, watching him take in the details. "This is awesome, Raina. Truly awesome." He settled onto the pillows in front of the television and pulled her down next to him. She settled her head on his chest and breathed in his scent. Soap and a woodsy aftershave filled her senses.

He kissed her temple and snuggled her close. "So, I want to forget all about threats and killers and dangerous situations and focus on us."

"Us?"

"Us." He tilted her chin up and lowered his lips to hers.

Until the knock on the door stilled them both. "Who's that?" he whispered, his warm breath tickling her lips. "You expecting company?"

"No."

With regret, she slipped away from him and out of the fort to walk to the door. When she opened it, she gaped. "What are you guys doing here?"

■ ■ ■ ■

Vince heard Raina's exclamation and figured their romantic interlude had just come to a screeching halt. He climbed out of the fort to find Grace, Sam, Julianna, Clay, Penny, and Holt standing at the entrance to the den, mouths open, but smiles spreading.

"Um . . . what's going on here?" Penny asked.

"Just some catching-up time," Vince said. Let them wonder. It wasn't any of their business. And okay, he might be a little perturbed at their arrival.

"Well," Clay said, "we were all at Julianna's, but the power went out and we want to watch the game, so Penny flew us here." He paused and looked at the blank area where Raina's television usually resided. "Uh . . . you get robbed?"

279

Raina rolled her eyes. "It's in the tent." She sighed. "Vince, you want to do the honors?"

"I absolutely do not." He pointed to the door. "Y'all are interrupting a perfectly good proposal. So could you please leave?"

Penny held up a hand. "But we have a surprise—"

"It can wait. I've worked up my nerve for the past twenty-four hours and you're not going to spoil this. So, out." He pointed to the door.

Silence fell. The others looked at one another and left without another word.

Once the door shut behind them, Raina turned to him with wide eyes. "What was that?"

Vince's hands went clammy. "Well, that wasn't exactly how I planned to do this, but why not?" He pulled a small box from his pocket and dropped to one knee. "I had a whole speech planned. A lot of pretty words, all telling you how much you mean to me and how absolutely crazy I am about you. But my brain is kind of short-circuiting at the moment, so, Raina, will you marry me?"

Her jaw was swinging, but she snapped it shut. "Yes. Yes, I will."

"It's not too soon?"

"No. It's definitely not too soon. We've been fighting our feelings for each other for a long time. I think it's time we finally admit that we're supposed to be together come what may."

"Thank God," he whispered. He cupped her face and kissed her. Thoroughly, passionately, and with all the love in his heart. When he finally lifted his head, he smiled at the dazed expression that no doubt mirrored his own. "Should we let them back in?"

"Yes. There's no way they left."

"I didn't hear any car door slams, did you?"

"Nope."

"You think they brought socks?"

"A whole bag full." Throwing socks at the television when there was a bad call was much less damaging than throwing anything else.

"All right then."

Together, hand in hand, they went to the door and opened it. Penny would have fallen inside if Holt hadn't caught her.

"She said yes," Vince said. "Y'all can come back in."

With much whooping and hollering, the gang came inside but paused just inside the doorway. Grace planted her hands on her hips. "Can we share the surprise now?"

"Of course."

Grace opened the door once more. "You can come in now."

Two people Vince had never met before stepped through, and Raina's sharp gasp and subsequent sob was enough to let him know who they were. She flew to her mother and wrapped her arms around the woman. "You came!"

"Nothing was keeping me away a minute longer now that I was assured you were safe."

The man leaned in and wrapped them both in a hug, and Vince might have had to clear his throat and swipe his eyes a time or two. When he glanced at the others, it was clear he wasn't the only one.

Finally, her parents let her go and her father nodded to Penny. "She filled us in on a good private airstrip and we landed an hour ago."

Raina hugged Penny. "Thank you," she whispered. "My heart is so full I almost can't breathe."

"You breathe with your lungs, goofball," Julianna said. "Seems like that would have been a pretty important part of your paramedic training."

Raina laughed at Julianna's uncharacteristic joking. She was usually the more serious one of the group. Clay was a good influence on her.

Raina then introduced Vince to her parents, who hugged and congratulated them. "Sorry about making you wait to see Raina," he said to her mother.

The woman beamed. "Well, after all this time, that would be the only thing worth waiting for. Welcome to the family, son." She hugged him again, and for the next several minutes, Raina, Vince, and her parents caught up. Then Holt went to the fort and slipped in. When he came back out, he held the television. "Everyone ready for a football game slash reunion slash engagement party?"

"Yes," Grace said, glancing at her phone, "but we have one more little surprise and it just got here."

Raina pressed a hand to her heart. "I'm not sure I can take much more."

"You can, trust me." Grace went to the door and opened it. Another gasp slipped from Raina when she saw Michael. He grinned at her. "Mom and Dad want to go out to eat and don't need me tagging along. Is it okay if I watch the game with you?"

"More than okay," Raina whispered. Tears hovered on her lashes and she laughed, waved to his parents who waved back from the car, then ushered him inside. "I'm going to warn you, though, today has been a big day and I'm just a big crybaby right now."

Michael shrugged. "Eh, it's okay. Mom does that too. As long as you don't ask me to throw away the snot rags, we're good."

Another laugh slipped from her. "No snot rags, I promise. That's what I have Vince for."

Vince feigned a cringe. "Hey now . . ."

More laughter all around and Michael went to Raina and hugged her. She gave him a tight squeeze, then sucked in a deep breath. "I have someone I need to introduce you to."

"My other grandparents? Dad said they'd be here."

She nodded and he smiled shyly at the wide-eyed couple standing next to Raina. "Hi. I'm very happy to meet you."

Raina's mom stepped forward. "And we're overjoyed to meet you." Vince watched the touching reunion, recording it on his phone. Raina would want to have all of this for later viewing.

Finally, after wiping away more tears, she clapped her hands. "All right, everyone, let's break down the fort, then grab a seat, the floor, or a bean bag and get the party started."

It didn't take long to clean up the fort. Holt had already put the television back on the wall so everyone could see it.

A sudden surge of emotion caught Vince off guard, and he drew in a shuddering breath. These were his friends, his family, his community. With a silent prayer of gratitude, he settled himself on the sofa while Raina snuggled up next to him. Michael chose the bean bag on the floor in front of her. Her mother sat on the other side of Raina, holding her hand and swiping tears every so often. Her husband wrapped an arm around her while chatting with Holt as the pregame show played.

It was a large group. Some sat on the floor, some at the kitchen table where they could view the screen, but they were all together and that's all that anyone cared about.

Then the game started, and someone passed out the socks, explaining the concept behind them.

Michael laughed and hefted his rolled pair. "This is the best idea ever."

Raina giggled as the others chorused their agreements.

Shortly after the game started and the opposing team was already five yards from the end zone, he looked down to find Raina watching him, love in her eyes.

"You warm enough?"

"Right now, I don't even remember what it felt like to be cold."

Vince brushed a light kiss over her lips, and she grinned, then rested her head against his shoulder, one hand on the head of Michael, sitting on the bean bag in front of her.

And, because all was right in Raina's world, all was right in his.

Dear Reader,

I hope you enjoyed *Countdown* as much as I enjoyed writing it! Raina and Vince stayed with me long after I finished, and their story was a great way to wrap up the Extreme Measures series. While my publisher and I prepare the launch of a brand-new series, coming in January 2024, I wanted to share another writer I think you'll enjoy—Natalie Walters. Natalie, Lynn Blackburn, and I worked together on a terrific novella collection, *Targeted*—if you haven't picked it up yet, please do! In the meantime, here's the first chapter of *Lights Out*, from book 1 in Natalie's SNAP Agency series. Enjoy!

Lynette

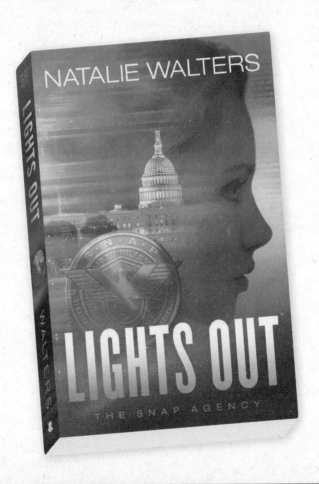

CHAPTER
ONE

Seif El-Deeb watched the noisy trio of American boys cross the street away from Cairo American College. The international school had just let out for the afternoon, and the sound of privileged children laughing about their day mingled with the horns of waiting drivers and taxis trying to navigate the afternoon congestion.

"Seif, you will send your child to this school?"

The old man behind the wooden counter of the koshk laughed at his own question, causing the cigarette at his lips to bounce. Seif ignored the vendor as the man continued chuckling while he straightened the rows of chips and snacks.

Toying with the metal band around his finger, Seif shook his head. Mostly to himself. The vendor already knew the answer, which was why he was laughing. CAC was a private school with a tuition rate only the wealthiest Egyptians could afford. And foreigners. Especially Americans. Or the grandchildren of the former president.

Seif eyed the twelve-foot cement wall surrounding the school. Iron paling embedded at the top gave the impression of a fortress, as did the private security officers positioned at the front and rear entrances to monitor every student, parent, and visitor entering or leaving. Their presence had doubled since the protests against President Talaat began more than a year ago. A promise by both the school and the president that these children would be kept safe at all costs.

A fortress of education and protection Seif's son or daughter would never know.

Lighting his own cigarette, Seif stepped aside as the three American boys walked up to the street kiosk and purchased candy. One of them, a blond, set the Egyptian bill on the worn and splintered counter just as a breeze came through, lifting the money into the air. The boys laughed as the old man scrambled for it, none of them helping as they took their candy and walked away.

Seif hurried, following the money as it floated in the air over the busy intersection. Ignoring the blaring horns and shouts, he stepped into the street and caught the bill before it flew farther away.

"Shukraan." The vendor thanked him before tucking the money into a box. "These kids do not know how fortunate they are. Allah has blessed them, and they forget it can be taken away."

Taking a long drag from his cigarette, Seif continued to watch the boys make their way to a large, white Toyota Sequoia. The heavy *thunk* of the door closing after they crawled in told Seif the vehicle was weighed down with armor.

Allah has blessed them. What about him? Or his wife, Heba? Or his child she was currently carrying? Where was Allah's blessing for them? He'd been good. Memorized the tenets of the

Quran, fasted for Ramadan, never missed a call to prayer, and yet here he was working two jobs just to provide for his family.

A business card burned inside his pocket. Fishing it out, he rolled the curled edges back and studied it.

Mahmoud Farag
+20 010 1251 175

Just a name and a number. The card left on the seat of his work van three weeks ago. Seif assumed it was job related, someone wanting zabbato. A favor. Street deal. As a technician for Nile Telecom, Seif had discovered that while he did not possess the kind of education protected by a fortified wall, he possessed a job that gave him favor. Those zabbatos were what kept Heba happy, safe, and out of the squalor he grew up in.

He dropped the finished cigarette to the ground and smashed it with the toe of his shoe. "Mas salāma."

"En shallah," the old man responded.

God willing. Yes, that was the hope, but the funny thing about hope was that it seemed to be selective—blessing those with the wealth to afford it, the power to control it, or the will to fight for it.

Seif's mobile rang. The number matched that on the card. Did he have the will to fight for it? For himself, he'd grown up suffering. For Heba, she was not his first choice when it came to their arrangement, but he was slowly coming to love her. But for his child, the ever-present ache in his chest pulsed. For his child, he'd do whatever it took.

Spitting the taste of tobacco from his mouth, Seif answered.

"Al salamo aalaykom."

"Wa aalaykom al salam," the male voice responded to the greeting. "White car, to your left. Pink dice in the mirror. Get in and say nothing."

The Arabic came out low and raspy, and Seif had to press his mobile phone to his ear to hear over the din of the growing traffic around him. "White car?"

"White car. On your left. Pink dice. Say nothing."

The clipped response sent a chill across Seif's shoulders despite the rare twenty-one-degree temps keeping the city balmy this early in the year. Searching to his left, Seif panicked. There were nearly a dozen white cars parked or moving in and around the school's barriers. Shading his eyes, he searched for pink dice, but the glare of the sun was too much, forcing him to cross into the chaotic traffic.

A black car screeched to a halt, nearly clipping him, and the driver stuck his head out of the car, cursing. Seif pressed the fingers of his right hand together, a gesture asking for the impatient driver to wait. The irate man inched forward, horn honking until Seif moved far enough over that he could steer around him, leaving a string of curses in his wake.

"You have one minute," the voice said.

"Wait. Please." Seif moved quicker, eyes scanning every car for pink dice. His heart pounded in his chest with each passing second. A ticking time bomb threatening to erase the hope he had allowed to enter his heart.

Seif thought he saw a flicker of something pink. He pushed aside a woman in a burka, no apology on his lips—only a prayer to Allah that this was it. In a near jog, Seif worked his way around a large SUV, ignoring the driver eyeing him with suspicion. He searched every white vehicle around him, until finally—he saw them. Pink dice.

He yanked the back door open and dropped inside, a breath of relief spoiled only by the thick cloud of cigarette smoke filling the vehicle.

"I am here." The words were meant for the man on the phone, but the phone remained silent against his ear. "Hallo? Hallo?"

Seif pulled the phone away to look at the screen just as the driver jerked the car forward and into traffic.

"Say nothing."

Leaning back in his seat, Seif replayed the instructions in his mind. He glanced at the rearview mirror and caught the driver eyeing him. Redirecting his attention out the window, Seif watched as the driver efficiently maneuvered around traffic, taking him out of Ma'adi.

Where was he going?

His mobile vibrated in his hand. Turning it over, he saw Heba's face smiling up at him. He brushed his thumb, fingernail dirty from his last job, across her cheek. He was doing this for her. For their child.

The car hit a pothole, hard, sending Seif bouncing in the back seat. He grabbed the overhead handle and braced himself as he monitored the changing scenery outside the car. They were no longer traveling in the city, crammed with high-rise apartments, shops, and markets. The landscape outside his window had shifted from overcrowded city to arid wilderness.

The wadi. He was being taken to the desert.

Fear sent his heart pounding in an erratic rhythm. He bit down on his lip, holding back the urge to ask questions, find out where he was being taken. The road turned rougher. Large ruts cut into the dirt road sent the car jostling so much that Seif feared he was going to be sick.

Thankfully, the car began to slow as another vehicle approached in a cloud of dirt. When it drew nearer, Seif saw that it was an old pickup truck. The road was narrow, and Seif expected his driver to pull to the side, but he continued going forward much faster than was necessary.

Bracing himself, Seif tightened his grip on the handle when the car lurched to a stop directly in front of the truck. Dust swirled around the vehicles, both drivers remaining where they were, but it was not an impasse.

A man jumped out of the back of the truck and started toward their car. The door at Seif's side was yanked open.

"Come," the man in the cream galabeya commanded. The turban on his head extended over part of his face, exposing only his dark eyes.

Seif got out of the car and wiped his sweaty palms down the back of his jeans. He noticed the man eyeing his choice of clothing with contempt. In the city, Seif blended in, but out here his modern appearance made him stand out. The white car reversed, turning around before barreling back in the direction they had come from.

"Come."

Seif looked around. The wadi stretched out before him, no sign of life or a way to cry for help should he need it. Heba's pregnant form filled his mind, and Seif quieted his nerves. This was for his child.

He followed the man and was directed to climb into the bed of the truck with him. Seif did as told and hung on for his life as the truck sped toward an unknown destination. He quickly realized why the man had his face covered as dirt and rocks flew into the air. Lifting the collar of his shirt over his nose and mouth, Seif prayed once again that he had not misplaced his hope.

Unsure how much time had passed, Seif saw a village dotting the landscape in front of him. The truck slowed to a stop and everyone got out, leaving him to follow. A herd of camels chewed their cud near the small, corrugated metal homes. A trio of stray dogs barked at him while kids played a game of fútbol.

"Seif El-Deeb?"

"Naam." Seif nodded at an older man with a long gray beard and a cane coming toward him. "Farag?"

He shook his head. "Your wife is pregnant? The baby is not well, yes?"

"Yes."

Heba hadn't been feeling well, and her mother took her to the hospital. The doctor did a sonogram and saw the deformity and suggested aborting the child. Heba was inconsolable. Seif promised her he would work harder to pay for the doctors. Whatever his child needed, he would provide . . . except. Except Seif was already working hard to afford the lifestyle Heba was accustomed to. How could he add more work? Her family would look down on him, convinced they had been right about him the entire time.

The man's eyes were cloudy, but the wrinkled skin around them seemed to sag in sadness as he reached into his robe and pulled out an envelope.

"It is good what you are doing for your child. Inshallah, all will be well."

Taking the envelope, Seif nodded. He let the contents fall into his hand, and his knees went wobbly. An Egyptian passport. A mobile phone. And an airline ticket to Washington, DC.

I am going to America?

Seif glanced up, trying to make sense of what was happening—what was being asked of him.

"I don't understand. Heba, my wife, will she not go with me?"

Another shake of the head. "You will travel to America. You will be contacted when you land"—a gnarled finger tapped the cell phone in Seif's hand—"by a man who will give you further instructions."

"La'a." Seif nearly shouted, the act drawing concerned glares from a pair of men standing nearby whom Seif hadn't noticed. Each carried an automatic rifle over his shoulder. "No." In a previous phone call with Mahmoud Farag, he promised he would get Heba the right doctors to help her, to help our child. He looked down at the airline ticket. "She should go to America with me. They have the best doc—"

The man held up a hand, silencing Seif. "Your wife and child will have the best doctors here in Egypt, but first you must do your part."

A car pulled around from the back of the village, exhaust darkening the air behind it.

"You want to help your family, yes?"

"Yes."

"Then go. Inshallah, all will be well."

The idling car's engine rumbled behind Seif like a sinister growl. Dropping the passport and phone back into the envelope, he climbed into the passenger seat. As the village grew smaller with every mile, Seif studied the airline ticket he held in his hand.

Passports, like the education at Cairo American College, were a privilege. Obtaining one took money, connections, and luck. But the ticket to America . . . that was a blessing. Was Allah blessing him? Finally?

Seif's eyes caught the date on the ticket. *Today!* He swiveled in his seat to look over his shoulder at the specks in the distance. In the back seat was a black backpack.

"The bag?"

The driver slid an unfriendly glance his direction. "Yours."

Seif pulled the backpack across the seat and opened it. Inside were a pair of jeans, a T-shirt, a map of Washington, DC, and a roll of American dollars. He zipped the bag and pushed it to the floor between his feet.

Seif had no idea why he was going to America or what his part was, but if this was Allah's blessing, he would accept it— and ignore the feeling he had made a deal with the devil.

ACKNOWLEDGMENTS

As always, there are so many people to thank. I'll start with my friends, FBI Special Agent Wayne Smith (retired) and Supervisory Special Agent Drucilla (Dru) L. Wells (retired), Federal Bureau of Investigations, Behavioral Analysis Unit. You know I couldn't do what I do without you and there will never be enough thank-yous to express my gratitude to you both.

Thank you to Dr. Jan Kneeland, who never fails to give me insightful medical advice like: "You can find that on Google, but . . ." LOL!!! Seriously, I really do appreciate you letting me ask all my weird questions, giving me several treatment options to choose from, and still being my friend.

Thank you to all my brainstorming buddies. I love that I can throw stuff at you and somehow you turn it into great ideas I can use in a story.

Thank you to my family for being my biggest support system. I love you all.

Thank you to Jesus for letting me do something I love that honors him. Anything good that comes from the stories is credited to him.

Thank you to the readers who buy the books. You're the reason I can keep writing! God bless you all!

And finally, I always have to thank my amazing publishing team. You guys are beyond amazing and I REALLY could not do this without you.

Onward to the next one! ☺

Lynette Eason is the *USA Today* bestselling author of *Life Flight*, *Crossfire*, and *Critical Threat*, as well as the Danger Never Sleeps, Blue Justice, Women of Justice, Deadly Reunions, Hidden Identity, and Elite Guardians series. She is the winner of three ACFW Carol Awards, the Selah Award, and the Inspirational Reader's Choice Award, among others. She is a graduate of the University of South Carolina and has a master's degree in education from Converse College. Eason lives in South Carolina with her husband. They have two adult children. Learn more at www.LynetteEason.com.

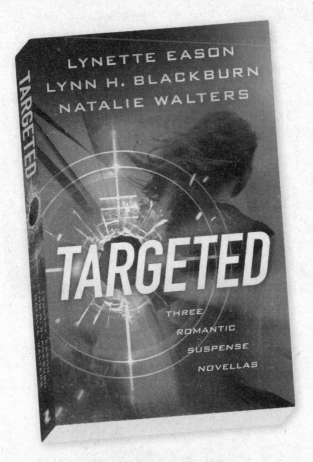

Still can't get enough of the Extreme Measures series?
Check out *Life Flight, Crossfire,* and *Critical Threat!*

"A heart-stopping, breath-stealing masterpiece of romantic suspense!"

—**COLLEEN COBLE,** *USA Today* bestselling author, on *Life Flight*

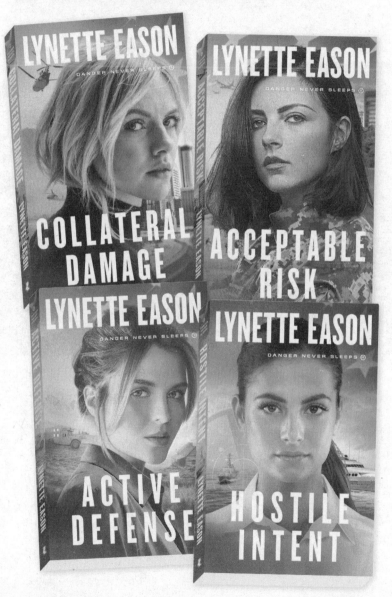